BRICK
BY
BRICK

A SPECTRE THRILLER

C.W. LEMOINE

This book is a work of fiction. Names, characters, places, and incidents are either products of the author's imagination or used fictitiously. Any resemblance to actual events or locales or persons living or dead is entirely coincidental. The views in this book do not represent those of the United States Air Force Reserve or United States Navy Reserve. All units, descriptions, and details related to the military are used solely to enhance the realism and credibility of the story.

Cover artwork by Liz Bemis-Hittinger of Bemis Promotions.
www.postscript-media.com

This book is dedicated to Second Lieutenant David "JINXX" Mitchell, who lost his life in an F-16 eight years ago. Rest in peace, buddy.

"So here's a nickel on the grass to you, my friend, and your spirit, enthusiasm, sacrifice and courage—but most of all to your friendship. Yours is a dying breed and when you are gone, the world will be a lesser place."

—Unknown

THE *SPECTRE* SERIES:

SPECTRE RISING (BOOK 1)

AVOID. NEGOTIATE. KILL. (BOOK 2)

ARCHANGEL FALLEN (BOOK 3)

EXECUTIVE REACTION (BOOK 4)

BRICK BY BRICK (BOOK 5)

SPECTRE: ORIGINS (PREQUEL SHORT STORIES)

Visit www.cwlemoine.com and subscribe to C.W. Lemoine's Newsletter for exclusive offers, updates, and event announcements.

"No war is over until the enemy says it's over. We may think it over, we may declare it over, but in fact, the enemy gets a vote."

— *General James Mattis*

PROLOGUE

Tallahassee Federal Detention Facility
0945 Local Time
One Week Earlier

H e had been here before. The pain and depression of losing loved ones. The first time was when he lost his parents. They had died in a horrific car crash. He was barely a teenager then. It all seemed so distant now.

And then he had lost his fiancée, Chloe Moss. She had dumped him beforehand, but the pain was still immense. He had been told she had crashed in an F-16, but the lack of wreckage and debris caused him to seek answers, eventually leading to the discovery that she had defected to an abandoned airfield in Cuba. She had died in a hospital after the recovery efforts, but the pain remained. It was as if a small piece of him had gone missing. His friends had gotten him through it. Friends like Joe Carpenter and Marcus Anderson, who had been killed by an assassin in South Florida.

Carpenter's death had sent him into a deep depression. He had survivor's guilt. The bomb that had killed Carpenter had been meant for Spectre, he was sure of it.

It was a funny thing – depression. Every major setback seemed to carry with it lower lows and an easier return to the depths of despair pushing him toward the edge. Carpenter's death had done that for him. He had given up, allowing a Cuban thug to capture and torture him without a fight as he tried to drown his sorrows with a bottle of whiskey.

He had gotten through those events, seemingly stronger for it as he climbed out of the valleys and tried to move on. He kept moving forward. He had to, because he still had someone in his life that made him want to live. He had finally found hope in love.

But as Cal "Spectre" Martin lay curled in the corner of the bunk in his prison cell, he realized that the hope was gone. He had reached the deepest valley from which there would be no escape. He had blitzed right through rock bottom and had found himself in a death spiral.

The crumpled newspaper next to him said it all. The headline told of a billionaire's jet crashing off the Atlantic coast, and that search and rescue efforts were underway. Debris had been located, but due to harsh conditions caused by a tropical storm, rescuers were unable to reach the crash site. The article held out a sliver of hope that the people aboard that fateful flight could be found at sea.

But Spectre could read between the lines. He had been in the aviation business long enough to know what that meant. There were no beacons, no mayday calls, and the jet in question had no ejection seats. If a debris field were found, it meant that the plane impacted the water in an attitude that just wasn't survivable. Everyone on that plane was dead. Spectre was sure of it.

Spectre had recognized three of the four names that the newspaper had given. He had worked with Darlene "Jenny" Craig as a fellow pilot with the top-secret special operations group known as Project Archangel. She had a thing for fast Corvettes and Spectre knew she was a great pilot from the many missions he had flown with her. If the plane crashed with Jenny at the controls, Spectre knew she had exhausted every effort to save the aircraft.

Freddie "Kruger" Mack was the second name on the list. Spectre had both respected and feared the bearded ginger. A former elite operator with the famed "Delta" force, Kruger had been an interrogator, sniper, and de facto second-in-command with Project Archangel. He had helped Spectre take down a Chinese intelligence operation in the Gulf of Mexico, and more recently, Spectre had watched Kruger save his new fiancée's life.

He was a ghost, and Spectre knew that if he were listed on the manifest, all hope that the crash was an act of deception was lost. It simply wasn't possible to fabricate Kruger's name like that.

And then there was the last name on the list. *Michelle Decker.* She had become the love of his life, pulling him out of the valley of depression and giving him a reason to live again. She was the most beautiful, intelligent, loyal, and courageous person Spectre had ever met. She made him want to be a better man. She was his hope.

Spectre felt numb. He had loved Chloe, but it was nothing like what he felt for Decker. They were the perfect team, and they had been through so much together. The note wrapped in the newspaper had said it all. YOU WERE WARNED. *God. If only we had just run away together and never looked back.*

As the public address system directed the inmates to prepare for their time in the yard, Spectre rolled off the bottom bunk and slid into his slippers. His cellmate said something, but

Spectre didn't register any of it. He felt like he was underwater, like he was drowning in some sort of lucid dream.

He shuffled out into the blinding sun like a zombie with his shoulders slumped and his head held low. Spectre knew he'd never get out of the prison alive, and he didn't care. He could feel the dozen or so inmates staring at him as he walked across the basketball court toward the bleachers. He thought of spending the rest of his days knowing he would never see Decker again and hoped that one of them would end it for him soon.

Spectre sat down on the bleachers next to his cellmate. A day earlier, he had been alert, watching hands, looking for weapons, reading body language, and gauging general intent in an attempt to survive. Now he found himself staring at the dirt, hearing and seeing nothing as he tuned out the world.

Four inmates approached surrounding Spectre and his cellmate. They exchanged words with his cellmate. Spectre looked up to see one of them holding a switchblade knife. He stood.

Staring straight through the man threatening him, Spectre held his arms out wide with his palms up.

"Do it," he said as he closed his eyes. He had found his release from the pain. Living with the knowledge that Decker was gone forever was just too much to bear. Spectre wasn't a very religious man, but he said a silent prayer, asking to be reunited with her soon. Maybe they would get a second chance in a different life. This one had been less than kind to them.

He heard words and then a scuffle followed by a loud scream. Before he could open his eyes, he felt the tip of the blade as it entered his abdomen. As the blade sliced into his gut, Spectre fell to his knees. The pain was immense, yet muted by his desire to die. He felt the blade withdraw momentarily and then it pierced his chest.

He fell forward and his face crashed into the dirt. Spectre opened his eyes briefly and turned his head, seeing what appeared to be a dozen feet shuffling in the dust. He gasped for air as his vision blurred.

He felt someone grab his shoulders and flip him onto his back as he drifted away into darkness.

He had finally found peace.

CHAPTER ONE

4 Miles North of Mosul, Iraq
0338 Local Time

Freddie "Kruger" Mack pulled down the quad-tube Panoramic Night Vision Goggles (PNVG) over his eyes and then tapped the shoulder of the breacher in front of him. Axe nodded and readied a pair of bolt cutters, waiting for the green light from Guardian 21 over the radio. As they waited, Kruger stretched his trigger finger against the lower receiver of his suppressed H&K 416 chambered in 5.56 NATO and took a deep breath.

"All players, *Leroy Jenkins*," Guardian 21 said over the radio, giving the code for the mission to begin. The dimly lit compound instantly went dark as the power grid was taken off line, leaving only the quarter moon to illuminate the way forward.

Axe sheared the chain and ripped the wooden gate open. Kruger shot through the opening with his rifle up and ready, button hooking to his left as his teammates, Cuda and Beast, followed on his heels. Cuda cleared right as Beast shot straight ahead through the gate. Axe followed, covering their six as the team entered the rear courtyard of the Islamic State training compound.

"Tango down front entrance," Kruger heard Tuna softly announce over the radio. It was the same voice that had given the green light seconds earlier. Kruger's teammates, Tuna and Rage, were perched on the roof of an abandoned house at the edge of the nearby village, providing overwatch with their suppressed sniper rifles.

The rear courtyard of the compound was empty except for various cardboard shooting targets and training obstacles. The team cleared the area without resistance, and they regrouped at the rear door of the mission's objective, a multi-level building near the center of the terrorist camp.

As before, the team stacked up, tapping forward in the line to indicate they were ready to move. Axe checked the door, quietly verifying that it was unlocked.

"Front courtyard is clear," Tuna announced over the tactical frequency.

Axe pulled the door open and Kruger bolted in. Cuda and Beast stepped into the narrow hallway. As before, Axe raised his rifle and entered behind them. The team moved quickly down the hallway toward the front of the three-story building.

"Door left," Kruger announced.

As they approached the door, Beast and Axe peeled off and entered while Kruger and Cuda continued forward and covered the front and rear of the hallway. Kruger could hear the muffled pops of suppressed gunfire as Beast and Axe dispatched the ISIL fighters in the room.

"Door right," Cuda said as Beast and Axe reemerged behind them. Kruger followed as Cuda opened the door and moved in, clearing left as he entered. Kruger cleared right and found two fighters sleeping with rifles propped against their beds. He aimed the holographic sight of his EOTech and fired two rounds into each man, killing them both in their sleep before Cuda whispered, "Clear."

Flipping up his PNVGs, Kruger quickly checked the faces of the dead fighters against the picture he had of the man they were looking for. Satisfied they hadn't found him, Kruger gave a thumbs down to Cuda and flipped his PNVGs back down over his face.

With the room clear, Kruger and Cuda reentered the hallway where Beast and Axe were still covering. The team reformed and headed up the nearby stairway toward the second floor. They moved quickly and quietly up the dark stairway, sweeping for threats as they entered the second floor hallway.

They cleared the second floor as they did the first, splitting off into two-man teams to clear each room and take out the sleeping fighters. Kruger grew increasingly frustrated as they continued to have no luck in finding the man they were looking for.

Kruger led the way up the next flight of stairs toward the third floor. He slowed as he neared the top, seeing a man exit into the hallway while shining a flashlight toward the nearby rooms. Kruger lowered his rifle and swung it around on its single point sling against his body armor before unsheathing his double-edge HRT tactical knife from his vest.

As the others covered the hallway, Kruger silently approached the man from behind. As he came to within a few feet, he surged, covering the man's mouth with his left hand as he jabbed the knife into the man's throat with his right. He twisted the knife and pulled it away, slicing the man's jugular as he struggled against Kruger's grip. As the man's body fell limp, Kruger dragged it out of the way and briefly raised his goggles to check the man's identity. *Still not him.*

The team searched two more rooms with similar results. Kruger followed Axe to the last door in the narrow hallway. Axe kicked the door open with the heel of his boot and carried his momentum into the room.

"Fuck!" Kruger hissed as he realized their search had come to a dead end. They had entered a makeshift office with laptops and file cabinets. "He's not here!"

"Clear," Axe said, ignoring Kruger as he stuck to protocol in clearing the room.

Kruger flipped up his goggles and pulled out a flashlight, shining it around the room. They had found a gold mine of intelligence in the form of hard drives and files that would eventually be useful, but the man responsible for the brutal public execution of four American aid workers captured in Baghdad was gone.

"Tuna, SITREP," Kruger said over the secure radio.

"No movement outside," Tuna replied from his rooftop overwatch position. "Still quiet."

"Ok, let's get what we can from this shithole and get out of here," Kruger said as he slung his weapon and took off his backpack. "Cuda, you and Beast go through this roach motel one more time. Make sure we didn't miss this son of a bitch."

"Copy," Cuda said as he raised his weapon and continued down the hall with Beast.

"I can't believe this fucker got away from us," Kruger said, shaking his head in disgust as he ripped a hard drive from the nearby desktop and stuffed it in his bag.

Axe froze as he reached a table in the corner of the room. Shining his light on the desk, he found several booklets and maps. "Uhh, Kruger, you might want to look at this," he said as he thumbed through the documents.

"What is it?"

"My Russian isn't so good, but I'm pretty sure this is a picture of an SA-24 MANPAD," Axe said, shining his light on the picture of a man holding a man portable surface to air missile launcher.

"No shit?" Kruger asked as he turned to inspect Axe's discovery with his flashlight. "This part is English, look. Grinch 9K338 Igla-S portable air defense missile system. Son of a bitch!"

"SA-24," Axe said. "How the hell did they get their hands on those? I thought these dudes were pretty limited in their surface to air capes?"

"Libya," Kruger said as he shuffled through the papers on the desk. "Shit, look at this."

Kruger held up a map. It showed the U.S.-Mexico border and had Ciudad Juárez in the Mexican state of Chihuahua circled with a red marker. There were three arrows showing routes across the border into Acala, Texas; Santa Teresa, New Mexico; and Fort Hancock, Texas.

"Do you think they're trying to smuggle these into the U.S.?" Axe asked as he studied the map.

Kruger stuffed the manuals and maps into his backpack and zipped it as he flipped his goggles back down. "All players, *Millertime*," he directed over the tactical frequency.

"That's why this place was so lightly manned," Kruger said as he started toward the doorway with his rifle up. "Our intel was bad; he's been gone for a while."

"Dude, if he's planning to shoot down an airliner—"

"We have to get to him in Mexico before he crosses the border," Kruger said, cutting Axe off. "I just hope we're not too late."

* * *

Anapra, Ciudad Juarez, Mexico
0125 Local Time

"Jefe, it's time," a deep voice said in the darkness.

Tariq Qafir slowly rolled over on his cot in the dusty hut. As sleeping conditions went, he had experienced worse. While fighting in Syria and Iraq, he had slept everywhere - from the beds of pickup trucks to dug-in bunkers - while the Americans bombed the buildings around him. A cot with a fan wasn't quite like Saddam's palaces they had captured from the Iraqis, but it also wasn't a war zone either.

Sitting up, Qafir put on his boots as the man closed the makeshift door behind him and waited outside. He was alone in the shack, a gesture of respect for Qafir's position as an Islamic State commander. He picked up the Quran from the egg crate serving as his bedside table and gently placed it in his bag before standing and stretching. He had a long journey ahead of him.

Qafir stepped out into the warm night air to find Alejandro waiting just outside. Like Qafir, his face was marked with the scars of war, although Alejandro's war had been much different. As a coyote for the Juarez Cartel, he had fought rival cartels, Mexican soldiers, and Americans while smuggling people, weapons, and drugs into America and bringing back U.S. dollars on his return.

The Islamic State of Iraq and Levant (ISIL)'s relationship with the Juarez Cartel was purely a business arrangement. The Cartel gave ISIL a safe haven to muster its forces in Anapra, away from the Mexican Army and Federal law enforcement officials, and helped ISIL fighters get into and out of America. In exchange, ISIL funneled millions in profits from the Iraqi and Syrian oil fields it had captured to pay the Cartel. Experienced in mountain warfare, ISIL also provided spotters in the East

Potrillo Mountains of New Mexico to help the "coyotes" of the Cartel smuggle people into and out of America.

"Right this way," Alejandro said in heavily accented English as he motioned for Qafir to follow. The camp was quiet, lit only by a few gas lamps hanging near the larger shacks where dozens of Qafir's fellow holy warriors slept.

Qafir followed Alejandro past guards posted at the edge of the camp. They were a mix of Mexican and ISIL fighters, carrying American M4 and Russian AK-47 rifles. The Cartel guards ignored him, but the ISIL fighters recognized Qafir, quietly whispering, "Assalamu alaikum," as he passed. *Peace be unto you.*

Alejandro led Qafir to an older model pickup truck. "Please," he said, gesturing to the front passenger seat. As Qafir entered, he noticed four other men packed tightly into the back seat. They were a mix of Hispanic and Muslim men, but Qafir did not recognize any of his Muslim brothers. He assumed they were also on a path to bring Jihad to the Americans. He greeted them and settled into his seat for the remaining journey ahead.

It had been ten days since he had left the camp in northern Mosul. With the help of his most trusted lieutenant, it had taken two days to drive to Damascus, where he used his Saudi credentials to fly into Dubai International in the United Arab Emirates.

After a short layover, Qafir took an Emirates flight into São Paulo–Guarulhos International Airport in Brazil, where he connected to El Dorado International Airport in Bogotá, Colombia. Changing passports and identities in Colombia, Qafir caught the next flight from Bogotá to Mexico City, where a member of the Juarez Cartel waited to take him the final twelve hundred miles to Ciudad Juarez. He was jet lagged and weary from nearly two weeks of travel, but Qafir was dedicated to his mission.

Qafir stroked his dark beard as he watched Alejandro direct three more men with rifles into the bed of the truck and then take his place in the driver's seat. The armed men used the truck's roof mounted off road lights for support as they waited for the truck to move. It reminded Qafir of the convoys he had been a part of in Iraq as they rolled over the Iraqi Security Forces and took control of Iraq's major cities.

Alejandro started the truck and then pulled a rifle out from under the bench seat. He chambered a round and then placed it back under the seat before putting the truck in drive and waving for the guards to open the gate.

"Do you have a weapon for me?" Qafir asked, eyeing the handgun holstered on Alejandro's right hip.

Alejandro smiled, revealing a row of gold upper teeth. "No, Jefe," he said. "Where we are going, that won't be necessary. We have plenty of protection." He motioned to another truck off to the right full of Cartel fighters. As he drove through the camp's chain link gates, the second truck pulled out of the camp close behind them.

Satisfied, Qafir nodded and watched the road as the small convoy headed west out of Anapra. Alejandro turned up the radio, blasting Mexican techno music through the truck's meager sound system as they sped through the residential areas. To his right, Qafir could see the glow of El Paso and the lights reflecting off the Rio Grande. The infidel Americans were likely sleeping soundly, oblivious of the Holy War raging across the globe. *That would soon change.* The thought made him smile with anticipation.

Annoyed by the music, Qafir reached up and spun the volume knob, killing the music as they continued toward the edge of the city. Alejandro was far too casual, given the risks of the mission. It was simply unacceptable.

"Qué!" Alejandro yelped as he threw his hand up in protest.

Qafir gave him a menacing glare. "We cannot afford failure," he said. "No distractions."

"Relax, Jefe," Alejandro said, flashing his gold teeth again with a knowing smile as he reached up and flicked the radio back on louder than before.

As Qafir glared at Alejandro, the smile suddenly vanished from Alejandro's face. "Remember, you are our guest here, Jefe," Alejandro warned. "Do not test my hospitality."

The warning enraged Qafir, but he didn't show it. Alejandro was an infidel no different from the Americans. If he weren't a necessary tool in the global Jihad, he would have dispatched the insubordinate fool without hesitation. In Iraq, he would have quickly made an example of the man.

But they weren't in Iraq, and Alejandro wasn't one of his fighters. He bit his tongue as Alejandro continued tapping the steering wheel as he sang along with the noise blaring from the radio.

Clearing the edge of town, Alejandro led the convoy down an isolated desert highway. In the distance, Qafir could see flashing red lights in the roadway. *A checkpoint.* Qafir's body tensed.

Alejandro continued merrily singing along with the radio as the convoy closed on the flashing lights. He seemed completely unfazed by the potential danger ahead. With his right hand, Qafir slowly reached down for his boot knife. If he had to, he planned to kill the imbecile next to him and use the weapon beneath the seat to fight his way out. He had no intentions of going to a Mexican prison and failing his mission.

Reaching up and turning the radio off, Alejandro gave another knowing smile to Qafir as they approached the checkpoint. The highway was empty except for the two Mexican police vehicles blocking the road. Qafir unsheathed his knife and held it low against his calf.

"Relax, Jefe," Alejandro said as he saw the concern in Qafir's dark eyes. "It is taken care of."

Qafir hesitated. The truck pulled to a stop as a Mexican official approached the driver's side. Before Alejandro could lower his window, the officer motioned for his comrade to remove the barricade. He smiled as he waved them through.

Alejandro laughed as he maneuvered the truck around the roadblock. "See? No worries!"

Qafir slowly replaced his boot knife. His adrenaline was surging. He did not like such surprises. He much preferred to be in command and aware of every aspect of the plan.

"Will there be any further surprises?" he asked angrily.

"That was not a surprise," Alejandro said as he cranked the volume knob on the radio.

Qafir clenched his jaw. He had only interacted with Alejandro briefly at the ISIL camp, enough to discuss the basic plan into America. At no point had Alejandro mentioned dealing with authorities. Alejandro seemed to be enjoying Qafir's stress.

They drove down the highway for several more minutes before Alejandro veered onto a dark, dirt road. The two vehicles drove north until reaching a small farmhouse isolated in the middle of the vast desert. As they approached, Alejandro killed the lights and slowed the truck to a crawl a few hundred feet from the barn.

As the truck rolled to a stop, Alejandro put it in park and jumped out. The men crammed into the backseat exited as Qafir slowly stepped out. The farmhouse seemed abandoned; all was quiet except for the buzz of cicadas and the howl of a coyote off in the distance.

"We're here," Alejandro said as he motioned for Qafir to follow.

The armed men that had accompanied them took up defensive positions outside the barn as Alejandro led the rest of the men inside. After pushing aside a pair of hay bales,

Alejandro went to work clearing away a thin layer of dirt and hay revealing a wooden panel. Qafir watched as Alejandro pulled out a claw hammer and pried the panel up. With the cover out of the way, Alejandro pulled out a flashlight, illuminating a tunnel underneath the barn.

"Right this way," he said as he descended into the tunnel.

Qafir followed, making the four-foot jump into the small tunnel. It was hot and musty, barely enough room to crouch as Alejandro used his light to guide the way. The other four men followed closely behind.

They walked for what seemed like hours. Qafir could hear cars above them at several points as dirt and dust shook loose from the ceiling and into his face. At many points, he was sure the cramped passageway would cave in around him. He silently chanted, "Allahu Akbar" to himself as they made their way through the tunnel.

Reaching the end, Alejandro pushed aside another makeshift cover. Qafir followed him out, climbing out into the warm desert air. Qafir took a deep breath as Alejandro helped the others out of the tunnel. He had never been so relieved to see a clear desert sky, but it looked like they had gone nowhere.

"Welcome to America," Alejandro said, flashing his gold teeth.

Alejandro pulled his flashlight out of his pocket and held it up, flashing it twice out into the darkness. Moments later, a pair of headlights flashed three times in reply. "They will take you the rest of the way. Go."

"Gracias," Qafir said as Alejandro turned toward the tunnel. He lagged behind as the others headed toward the waiting vehicle.

"Your Spanish is terrible, amigo," Alejandro said with a hearty laugh. Qafir had reached the limit of his patience with this man. He had made up his mind.

Qafir had pulled his knife out of his boot as he exited the tunnel. He lunged toward Alejandro, grabbing him and driving the blade into the man's sternum. Alejandro tried to scream, but Qafir covered the man's mouth as he twisted the blade and wrenched it upward until Alejandro stopped struggling.

"Infidel," Qafir said with disgust as he withdrew the blade and wiped the blood off on Alejandro's clothes. He pushed Alejandro's lifeless body back into the hole, burying him like the rat he was. He replaced the cover before turning back to the others. Dusting himself off, he walked calmly through the desert. He would not be deterred from striking a blow to the American war machine and defeating the infidels.

Strive hard against the unbelievers and the hypocrites and be unyielding to them; and their abode is hell, and evil is the destination.

Qafir smiled.

CHAPTER TWO

Arlington, VA
0635 Local Time

"**M**ichelle," he whimpered as he stared at himself in the mirror. "Help!"

"What's wrong, Cal?" she asked as she walked out of the bathroom. Cal "Spectre" Martin dropped the ends of his blue tie and turned to her. She was still in her underwear, her golden blonde hair up in a ponytail with a stray strand dangling over her sky blue eyes. He caught himself gawking as she approached with a look of motherly concern over his struggle to tie his tie.

"You can fly multi-million-dollar fighter jets, but you're befuddled by *a tie?*" his fiancée asked with a chuckle as she went to work on a Windsor knot.

"Flight suits have zippers, not fancy knots," Spectre protested. "Besides, you remember what happened the last time I wore a tie? It's bad luck!"

Michelle Decker frowned. "Cal, you're going to have to get used to it," she said. "I don't think Senator Wilson would appreciate you showing up in your pilot pajamas, and it's not bad luck."

"Flight suit," Spectre corrected her as he leaned in for a kiss. Decker tiptoed to kiss him as she adjusted the tie against his dress white shirt. "I could just wear a clip on."

"That's tacky!" Decker yelped.

"Tacky?" Spectre asked. "Or tactical? When's the last time someone was choked out with their own clip on?"

"I need to go get dressed," she said, rolling her eyes as she turned to walk away. "And don't think you're getting out of wearing a real bow tie for our wedding. No clip-ons!"

"Yes, ma'am," Spectre submitted as he watched her walk away. She was stunningly beautiful, a woman who prided herself on staying in top physical condition. But she was also extremely intelligent and capable - something Spectre loved most about her. He had seen her overcome situations that would make most people crumble, approaching life with vigor and a strong sense of the greater good. For her, no odds were too great when it came to doing the right thing.

And although he didn't always agree with Decker's passion for the greater good, he admired her for it. He had seen her risk everything on numerous occasions – once to save the President of the United States, and before that, his own life.

In truth, Decker was his second chance. She had seen the good in him when others cast him as the villain. She had supported him when others called him a fool. She had even saved his life, first by giving him a reason to fight and live, and then by pulling him out of harm's way. He owed his life to her.

But more importantly to Spectre, Michelle Decker was his second chance at love. After his ex-fiancée had abandoned him and defected to Cuba with a stolen F-16, Spectre didn't think it was possible to love again. Even after first meeting Michelle, her advances were met with aloof disinterest. Spectre just didn't think love was possible again after such a betrayal. Over time, however, those feelings changed.

His love for Decker had become his guiding light. In times of crisis and despair, his number one priority had become their survival as a couple. The rest of the world could fend for themselves. Unfortunately, though, Decker's overarching moral compass was much too strong and she was simply too hardheaded to go along with that. And so, instead of running off to a deserted island far, far away, he found himself returning to the fight time and again. Decker wasn't one to run.

Spectre combed his light brown hair in the mirror and then grabbed his coat while Decker continued to get ready. He headed downstairs to the first floor of their suburban townhome and grabbed a protein bar for breakfast. He poured a cup of dog food into Zeus's bowl and then leaned against the stove as he watched the retired military working dog eat.

Hearing Decker descend the stairs a few minutes behind him, Spectre poured coffee into her thermos and set it out on the marble countertop for her. Zeus finished and exited through the doggy door into their tiny yard as Decker appeared from the staircase rolling a lint roller against her navy blue pantsuit.

"I'm pretty sure I could build a new dog with all this hair," she said as Spectre offered her the thermos of coffee.

"You're going to hurt his feelings," Spectre said as Decker graciously accepted the thermos.

"He's not even in here," she said, looking around.

"He knew you were mad at him," Spectre replied.

"I'm not mad at him!" Decker shot back with a grin. "I love him, but I just don't want to bring him with me on the first day of a new assignment, that's all."

"Well, you look great," Spectre said with a boyish grin. "With or without Zeus's help."

"And you look handsome," Decker replied. She clipped her FBI Special Agent badge to her belt and walked over to the coat closet underneath the staircase. Opening the safe inside, she pulled out her issued Glock 17 and secured it in the paddle holster on her right hip. "Are you excited about your first day with Senator Wilson?" she asked.

"As a political advisor?" he asked, rolling his eyes as he made air quotes with his hands. "Maybe. But I don't get a cool badge and gun like you, though."

"I know you'd rather use bombs and bullets, but we both know this is the right way to take that son of a bitch Johnson down," Decker said as she locked the safe and closed the closet. "It's a political war now."

"Funny, I don't remember much of a political process when his Cuban buddies strung me up in a barn and interrogated me," Spectre replied. "Or when he blew up my best friends. I don't remember a whole lot of democracy there either."

"We're going to be late," Decker said, changing the subject as she picked up her keys. "Just promise me you'll keep an open mind."

Spectre sighed. "Fine," he said finally. "But I'm still going to kill him."

Decker grimaced. "I thought you said you were done with killing," she said as she led the way out the door.

"I am," Spectre said, arming the alarm as he followed her out. "But for him? I'll make an exception."

They took Decker's FBI-issued Ford Focus. Traffic was exactly as Spectre had expected for a Monday morning commute into the nation's capital, turning what should have been a twenty-minute drive into an hour-long ordeal.

Ordinarily, the traffic would've caused Spectre to arrive at his new job ready to snap the neck of the first bureaucrat that crossed him, but Decker was a soothing presence. She had a way of keeping him calm and happy. They chatted about current events, sports, and their upcoming wedding. She kept him very centered, something he appreciated most about her.

They parked in the secure lot a block from the Russell Senate Office Building and made their way to Senator Wilson's office. Although Decker was officially assigned to the D.C. field office, she had been detailed to the Senate Select Committee on Intelligence through the FBI Office of Congressional Affairs. It had been a backdoor deal with FBI Director Schultz. Wilson had managed to arrange for Spectre and Decker to work together for him.

Wilson had approached them in Hawaii as they recovered from the attack on Air Force One on Midway Island. As the Chairman of the Intelligence Committee, Wilson was intimately familiar with Spectre's resume, including his involvement with the unacknowledged Special Operations organization known as Project Archangel.

A former Presidential contender, Wilson approached Spectre and Decker with a proposition – help him take down a common enemy – Kerry Johnson. To Spectre's surprise, Wilson had been able to piece together the reason he and Decker had been on Air Force One when it was diverted to Midway Island. He also believed that Vice President Kerry Johnson had a traitorous alliance with the Chinese, but had no way of proving it. His suspicions were based on circumstantial evidence found during his campaign. It was sketchy at best.

The attack on Air Force One and thwarted assassination attempt by Chinese mercenaries cemented Wilson's beliefs. After reading Spectre's after action report of the Midway incident, he believed Spectre and Decker could be the key to unlocking the conspiracy, so he approached them. His proposal was simple – find the truth and bury Johnson with it.

At first, Spectre was reluctant. He had nearly lost Decker in the battle on Midway Island. He never even wanted to be there in the first place, content to stay hiding and enjoy their love together. But she had talked him into doing the right thing – taking the evidence they had found on a thumb drive in Tampa directly to the President of the United States. And that decision had nearly cost them both their lives.

In the aftermath, Spectre was content to count their blessings and let it go. The thumb drive had been lost and Johnson wasn't worth risking the loss of what he treasured most. Senator Wilson's offer had been intriguing, but it didn't seem worth it. That was until Spectre came face to face with Vice President Johnson at an awards ceremony at the White House.

Shaking hands with the man that had nearly cost him everything, Spectre felt a rage he had never felt before. He looked into the man's dark, dead eyes. The man was pure evil, a demon that had killed Spectre's friends in cold blood. Spectre's resolve was suddenly solidified.

Three months had passed since that bone-chilling encounter, but Spectre still couldn't shake the rage he felt. As he walked into the waiting area, he hoped Senator Wilson could deliver on the promises he had made.

"Cal Martin and Michelle Decker to see Senator Wilson," Spectre said to the young staffer sitting behind a desk in the waiting area. He checked his watch. "We have a 9 AM appointment."

"One minute," the girl said as she picked up the phone. Moments later, a gray haired man appeared wearing a dark three-piece suit.

"Mr. Martin, Miss Decker, welcome," Senator Wilson said with a smile. "I trust you had no problems finding my office."

"None at all," Decker said.

Wilson ushered them into his spacious office and offered them seats in the plush leather chairs across from his mahogany desk. As they took their seats, he moved to the high-back leather chair across from them and sat.

"Let's get to business, then," he said as he leaned back in his chair. "Don't worry; I have this office swept for bugs every morning. You may speak freely."

"Well, sir, when we spoke on the phone, you weren't really clear on what exactly you wanted us to do," Spectre began. "So how about we start there?"

"Fair enough," Wilson said. "Let's start with your meeting with the President. When we spoke in Hawaii, you said you had more than just circumstantial evidence to give to President Clifton. What was it?"

Spectre shifted in his seat as he looked at Decker for reassurance. He still wasn't sure how much he trusted the politician seated across from him. *Was it a trap to find out what he knew?*

"I'd rather not," Spectre said flatly. "Not yet anyway."

"You don't trust me," Wilson replied.

"We barely know each other," Spectre said with a nervous laugh.

"Ok, how about I start then?"

Spectre nodded.

"Last year, you were working for a group called Project Archangel run by Charles Steele," Wilson said. "Correct?"

Spectre sat still, refusing to acknowledge the existence of the covert program.

Wilson continued, "You were flying a Super Tucano while supporting a mission to secure chemical weapons in Eastern Syria. The official story is that you were shot down due to your own failure to assess the Syrian Air Force threat. You were subsequently captured in Syria and rescued. Does that sound right?"

"Bullshit," Spectre hissed.

Wilson smiled knowingly. "But that's not what really happened, Cal. Not even close."

Spectre raised an eyebrow before looking at Decker. "Go on," he said.

"Every intel report in theater at the time stated that the Syrian IADS was down in the eastern half of the country and the alert fighters had all been moved west of Damascus due to an Israeli threat. Getting warmer?" Wilson asked.

"That's what we were told, yes," Spectre acknowledged.

"What if I told you the intel was dead on?"

"I'm listening."

"Those Syrian MiG-21s you shot down weren't alert fighters at all. They were launched on an intercept mission knowing full well that your aircraft would be there. Now, why do you suppose that is?"

"Someone tipped them off," Spectre said angrily. The peace he had felt on the drive over had suddenly vanished as he remembered nearly getting his head chopped off in the Syrian desert.

"Exactly!" Wilson said. "And who tipped them off?"

"Johnson," Spectre growled.

"Not quite," Wilson replied, wagging his finger. "If that were the case, he'd be in jail right now. No, it's much more complicated than that."

"Ok, who?" Spectre snapped.

"The Syrian Air Defense Force received a warning of an unauthorized Iraqi Air Force flight two hours before your takeoff. They launched the flight of MiG-21s from Damascus knowing the exact strength and composition of the airborne package. They received that message through a secure transmission from the Chinese Embassy in Syria," Wilson explained.

"Which came from their Embassy in Tripoli," Spectre added.

"So you're aware?" Wilson asked.

Spectre nodded. "The thumb drive we had was a testimony by Charles Steele saying that Johnson or his staff had sent the flight schedule to Tripoli and that he was working with Chinese Intelligence. But if you know that already, why haven't you acted?"

"We don't have any traces of how they got the information, Cal," Wilson said. "The trail went cold there."

"So why do you think that Johnson was involved?"

"Call it a hunch, but very few people knew about your mission, Cal," Wilson replied.

"Apparently you did too. How do I know you didn't tip off the Chinese?"

Wilson smiled. "I only found out about your missions in the After Action Reports. Steele reported directly to the Secretary of Defense, who authorized missions on behalf of the President. They were the only three who knew about the missions beforehand. And only one of those three had known associations with the Chinese."

"Circumstantial," Decker said, speaking up for the first time after remaining quiet while Wilson and Spectre went back and forth.

"Exactly!" Wilson said. "Everything I have to date on this man has been circumstantial at best. Nothing will stick to him. That's why I need the two of you."

"Why don't you do it?" Spectre asked suspiciously.

"Because I'm the candidate that lost to his boss last year," Wilson said, shaking his head. "Anything I do directly will get crushed by the politics of the Beltway."

"But aren't we technically working for you?" Decker asked. "How does that make it better?"

"You're not," Wilson replied. "But Mr. Martin is."

"What exactly am I here to do?" Spectre asked.

"Officially, you will be my Veterans Affairs liaison," Wilson said with a grin. "As a combat veteran and having won the

Presidential Medal of Freedom, you're in a perfect position to reach out on veterans' issues."

"And unofficially?" Spectre asked cautiously.

"I can't tell you what to do with your own time, Mr. Martin, but if you decide to do some digging, I wouldn't fault you," Wilson replied.

Wilson stood to usher them out. As he opened the door, the young staffer from the lobby appeared.

"Diane will show you to your new office," Wilson said. "Please let me know if you need anything."

CHAPTER THREE

The office Senator Wilson's staffer had taken them to seemed to be little more than a janitor's closet in the basement of the Russell Building. In fact, Spectre wasn't so sure it hadn't been the week prior. It was barely big enough for the desk that nearly took up the entire width of the room, with just enough space to squeeze by and get to the secretary's chair behind it. On it, sat a laptop and phone, their wires dangling loosely off the edge toward another leather back chair across from the desk. It was spartan at best.

Spectre took off his coat and draped it over the back of the wooden visitor's chair, taking his seat as Decker squeezed by to sit behind the desk. After asking if they needed anything else, the staffer excused herself and closed the door behind her.

"So do we trust him?" Spectre asked as he leaned back and crossed his leg over his thigh.

"As much as I trust anyone in this city," Decker replied. "But you work for him, so you tell me."

"He was surprisingly well-versed in my former life, including the mission to Cuba that no one outside this room should still know about," Spectre said, pausing as he remembered his friends that had died since he had risked everything to save his ex-fiancée, and a stolen F-16 from a Chinese espionage operation based in Cuba.

"Access to information doesn't necessarily mean he's on our side, Cal," Decker responded, breaking the moment of silence.

"Well, at the very least we know that he's not a fan of Johnson because of the election. So for now, the enemy of our enemy is our friend, right?" Spectre asked.

"For now," Decker said with a frown.

Seeing how uncomfortable Decker was, Spectre leaned forward and held her hand in his. "You ok? We've both been through a lot. I have no problems with leaving this city and disappearing like we should've done a year ago."

Putting her free hand on top of his, Decker said, "Maybe we should." She looked deeply into Spectre's blue eyes. "Last time I pushed you into doing the right thing, we nearly lost it all. I can't ask you to do that again. We should've stayed in hiding."

"No," Spectre said, shaking his head. "You were right. If we hadn't been on that airplane when it diverted to Midway, the President would've been killed and that dickhead would be in charge right now. You saved the President's life. You made the right call."

"Cal, we couldn't have known that."

"It doesn't matter," Spectre said. "I've been thinking about this a lot over the past few months. Believe me, I desperately wanted for us to just go away and never have to deal with this again. But the more I thought about it, the more I realized that would never be possible – not until Johnson is dead at least."

"Cal, lower your voice," Decker whispered, withdrawing her hand as she looked around, worried that someone would hear him. "You can't kill the Vice President. You know that."

"Either way, that son of a bitch won't just leave us alone," Spectre said. "We're loose ends that he will eventually try to tie up. If not now, then when he runs for President down the road, and by then it really will be too late to do anything about him. If we don't get to him before he gets to us, we'll never have peace."

"So it's just self-preservation?" Decker asked. "No other reason?"

"Revenge is not a valid motive," Spectre said. "Killing him will never bring back Marcus or Joe or Baxter or the countless other people that have died as a result of his actions."

"Or Chloe," Decker interjected, naming Spectre's ex-fiancée that had died after the mission to rescue her in Cuba.

"Chloe died because of Chloe," Spectre replied flatly. "I can't blame him for what she freely did."

"I'm sorry for bringing her up," Decker said, putting her hand back on Spectre's.

"Don't be," Spectre replied. "It's in the past. I love you now and my future is with you, and the only way I see that future being safe is by standing down this threat."

"I love you too," Decker said with a warm smile. "So let's get to it then."

"The sooner, the better," Spectre said, leaning forward in his chair. "Where do we start?"

"Well, while you were talking to the Senator, I had an idea. I know we lost the thumb drive, but remember Steele said he had his computer guy do the traces? Maybe we could find the computer guy and recreate that data? Surely he has to know something?"

"Coolio," Spectre said with a chuckle.

"Who?" Decker gave a confused look.

"Julio Meeks," Spectre replied. "We called him 'Coolio.' He's a really smart computer guy that worked as an analyst for us. I'd be willing to bet he was either the person who did the tracing or knew of it. That kid was really good at hacking stuff. He was very helpful when we took down that oil rig in New Orleans."

"Well, he's obviously not working for that group anymore," Decker said. "How do we find him?"

Spectre considered the question for a moment. Project Archangel had been disbanded shortly after Johnson left his position as Secretary of Defense to join President Clifton's campaign. Since then, all of the members of the top-secret organization had seemingly scattered to the four winds. Some of the pilots had given up the fast life to work more steady jobs in the airline industry, while the operators had worked everything from private security consulting to car sales.

But in the wake of the Midway Island incident, Spectre had talked to the group's most recent leader. Freddie "Kruger" Mack had somehow gone from working at a small Sheriff's Department in Florida to working with another paramilitary organization. Spectre had talked to Kruger briefly while recovering in Hawaii. Kruger didn't say much, but Spectre got the feeling that Kruger was somehow back in the game. And when the lifeless body of the man behind the Midway Island attack showed up at 1600 Pennsylvania Avenue a few days after the dust settled, Spectre was almost sure Kruger was involved.

One of the things Kruger did mention in their short talks, however, was that Meeks had found employment working for the State Department as a cyber-analyst. He had mentioned it after confessing to Spectre that Meeks had been the one to notify Kruger of the attack on Midway.

"If I remember correctly, he works at the State Department," Spectre replied. "Don't you have a contact there?"

Decker opened the laptop and logged in. "One," Decker said as she logged into her email.

A few seconds later, she picked up the phone and dialed.

"Hey, it's Michelle Decker," she said as Spectre watched.

"I'm great. How've you been?" Decker asked.

"No, we still haven't set an exact date yet," she said, shooting a glare at Spectre who retreated into his seat.

"Listen, I need a favor," she continued. "Can you get me contact info on someone?"

"Julio Meeks," Decker said after a pause. "Should be a cyber analyst, not sure where but that's not a real common name."

There was another pause as Decker waited for the person on the other end to look him up.

"You're sure?" Decker asked with a frown as she shook her head at Spectre.

"No record at all?"

"Do you know when? Three months?"

"Ok, dear. Thanks for your help. Yes, you will receive an invitation as soon as we set a date. Bye," Decker said as she hung up.

"That doesn't sound like winning comm.," Spectre said.

"He turned in his resignation shortly after the Midway Island incident. No one has seen or heard from him since," Decker said. "Any other ideas?"

CHAPTER FOUR

Falls Church, Virginia
1320 Local Time

It was late summer in Virginia, but Julio Meeks was freezing his ass off. The server room in the basement of the secure facility was kept at a chilly sixty degrees to prevent damage to the racks of computer equipment lining the walls. Despite the two sweaters and jacket he wore every day since taking the job at Odin, Meeks had never quite gotten used to working in the "Dungeon" as he called it. He much preferred his office upstairs.

But when the teams were on an operation, he needed the enhanced security and processing power that the Dungeon provided. Its sophistication rivaled the most advanced NSA SCIF. Meeks's employers had spared no expense. And as Meeks waited for his search to complete, he was glad to have the processing power despite his chattering teeth.

The computer chimed just as Meeks finished his last Rip-It energy drink and crushed the can. Adjusting his glasses, the MIT graduate analyzed the results. His search had scoured every military and law enforcement database trying to find the man. Databases like Thinkstream, NGI, NCIC, MIDB, and ALPRS were all at his fingertips through one interface. If the man they were looking for was in the United States, Meeks intended to find him.

"Got you!" Meeks said as the results displayed on the middle of his three 21" LCD monitors. Using facial recognition software, he had tracked Tariq Qafir as he made his way from the Middle East to South America and eventually Mexico. As the trail had seemingly run cold, Meeks focused his search on known ISIL locations near the border.

Meeks studied the results. The facial recognition software had picked up Qafir outside a Wal-Mart in El Paso. Using the hacked security camera feeds, Meeks isolated the late model SUV Qafir was driving and plugged its plate into the Automated License Plate Reader System database from the Texas Department of Public Safety.

"Slayer Six-One, this is Oracle," Meeks said as he keyed the secure radio.

"Send it, Oracle," Kruger responded after a brief pause.

"Boylover is headed east on I-10, last hit at Exit 28," Meeks replied. He still couldn't get over the code word for Qafir. Kruger always tended to give the "High Value Targets" demeaning callsigns, a testament to his detest for the savages they hunted.

"What's the vehicle description?" Kruger asked.

"2011 Chevrolet Suburban, red in color, registered to Khaleed al-Awaki," Meeks said reading from the Texas DPS database. "Texas tag Victor Alpha Juliet Six Seven Five, how copy?"

"We'll take the Loop and cut them off. Can you disable an '11?" Kruger asked.

"I think so, let me get to work," Meeks replied as he pulled up the hacked interface into the On Star network.

"Slayer copies, we're en route," Kruger said.

*　*　*

El Paso, TX

Kruger flipped the lights and siren on in the unmarked black Tahoe as he pushed the gas pedal down to the floor. As a former Sheriff's Deputy, Kruger was the closest thing to law enforcement in the vehicle, but each of the four was carrying forged Department of Homeland Security badges and credentials. It wasn't foolproof, but enough to get them past run-ins with local law enforcement.

As cars veered out of the way, Kruger maneuvered the Tahoe through traffic using the travel lanes, the paved median, and the shoulder as they raced along their intercept course. Axe, Tuna, and Rage readied their FNH SCAR PDW short-barreled rifles chambered in 5.56 and checked their plate carriers a final time. They fully expected Qafir to be armed and ready to fight to the death and were ready to arrange his meeting with Allah if necessary.

"I've got a good handshake with On Star," Meeks reported over their tactical frequency. They were each wearing earbud transmitters connected to a secure satellite radio mounted on their plate carrier. "He's passing Exit 32 now."

Kruger could see the exit to merge onto I-10E up ahead. "When he hits Exit 34, do it," Kruger directed.

"It's not that easy," Meeks protested. "I'm using ALPR cameras; the next one isn't until—"

"Do it now then, Coolio!" Kruger barked.

"Copy that, it'll take a minute for the signal to go through," Meeks replied.

Kruger killed the lights and siren as he hit the exit ramp. He slowed the Tahoe to pace merging traffic as he searched for the red Suburban. "Shit, are we in front of him?"

"I've sent the kill signal to the vehicle, should be disabled shortly," Meeks reported. Using the system's anti-theft feature, Meeks sent a signal through the Suburban's On Star system to kill the ignition and disable the vehicle.

Kruger slowed as he merged onto I-10E. "Where are they Coolio?" he asked frantically. "Did we fucking pass them?"

"The next set of cameras isn't until Exit 50," Meeks said. "I don't know, boss."

"Fuck!" Kruger said as he pulled to the shoulder.

"Look!" Axe shouted from the front seat. "There's a vehicle on the side of the road up there!"

Kruger floored it, cutting off a semi as he merged into traffic. "Get ready," he advised his teammates. "Oracle, Slayer is about to make contact with Boylover, start working on an exfil plan and monitor local law enforcement traffic."

"Copy that," Meeks replied.

"Contact right," Kruger said. He saw a red SUV on the side of the road with its hazard lights on and the hood up. "Standby."

Kruger stopped a few car lengths short of the Suburban on the shoulder and threw the vehicle into park. In unison, all four doors of the Tahoe were flung open and the operators had boots on the ground with rifles up, moving rapidly toward the Suburban.

Kruger and Rage approached the driver's side while Axe and Tuna approached from the passenger side. As they neared the Suburban, one of the men stepped to the passenger side from the engine bay and saw them. As the man reached for his waistband, Tuna fired three rounds and dropped him; the register of his weapon was muffled by the sound of cars buzzing by on the interstate next to them.

After dropping the first hostile, Tuna and Axe gave the vehicle a wide berth as they continued toward the front. Stopping at the left rear driver's side door, Kruger opened it as Rage quickly cleared it. As they were clearing the vehicle, a second man rushed to the first man's body.

"Show me your hands!" Axe ordered. "Down on your knees, do it now!"

The man froze near the passenger side headlight. Axe maintained contact as Tuna continued forward to flank the man.

"Hands on your head!" Axe repeated as loudly as he could over the sound of passing cars.

With the vehicle clear, Kruger continued around the driver's side toward the man. Axe continued yelling loud verbal commands as the man finally put his hands on top of his head. Slinging his weapon around his back, Kruger approached the man as Axe nodded to acknowledge Kruger.

Kruger closed the distance quickly, grabbing the man's interlaced hands and pulling him backward as he drove his boot into the man's left knee. The man buckled and fell to his knees. Kruger Flexcuffed the man's hands behind him and dragged him back to his feet.

"One KIA, not our guy," Rage reported as Kruger dragged the man toward their Tahoe.

"Copy, he's not here," Kruger replied. "Oracle, status?"

"DPS just got a call from a passing motorist, you've got three minutes," Meeks replied.

"What's our exfil?" he asked as he reached the cargo area of the Tahoe. He opened the rear door and shoved the man in before securing the man's feet and throwing a hood over his face.

"Got it!" Meeks shouted. "Next exit is an airport. Take Pellicano Drive. I'm working on access codes for a hangar for you. Give me two minutes."

"Copy that," Kruger said as the team loaded back up. "We're rolling."

CHAPTER FIVE

The metal Quonset hangar Meeks had found for them was tucked away on the northern side of the abandoned airfield. According to Meeks, the Horizon Airport on the east side of El Paso had been closed since undergoing runway repairs in 2014. Although the runway was fully repaved, for whatever reason the powers that be decided not to reopen it after construction was complete.

The hangar Meeks chose was owned by an estate that had gone unsettled for years. Based on his quick research, Meeks was absolutely convinced that the hangar would be unoccupied as the team attempted to gather intel from the man he had identified as Khaleed al-Awaki.

After breaking the door's padlock and clearing the small hangar, Kruger and Rage went to work setting their suspect up for interrogation, while Axe and Tuna set up a defensive perimeter outside. As Meeks had suggested, the hangar was empty except for some personal items and airplane parts that likely belonged to the deceased owner. The electricity in the small hangar was still connected, allowing Rage to turn on the large overhead lights.

Kruger grabbed a chair from the corner and sat al-Awaki down before ripping the bag from his head. The man attempted to spit at Kruger, causing Kruger to smash the man's nose with his fist as he avoided the disgusting volley of saliva.

"Not a good way to start this, bub," Kruger said as the man groaned. Blood flowed from the man's nose as he looked up angrily at the red-bearded man standing over him.

"Fuck you!" al-Awaki yelled defiantly. "You cannot do this! I want a lawyer."

Kruger smiled, causing al-Awaki to shift uncomfortably in his chair as his demands seemed to fall on deaf ears. "This is brutality! I have rights! I want a lawyer!" he repeated.

The smile suddenly vanished as Kruger lunged toward the man, grabbing the man's hair and pulling his head back as he closed to within inches of the man's face. "Let's get one thing straight," he growled, "you have no rights here. I am the judge, jury, and executioner. Got it?"

The man nodded nervously as Kruger stepped back and folded his arms. He had spent most of his career interrogating terrorists. He had intimidated terrorists into thinking he had absolute authority many times before, but for the most part, they were empty threats. He'd always had a chain of command to answer to, whether in Delta or the top-secret group known as Project Archangel. But since moving to Odin, his whole paradigm had changed.

As a group, Odin answered to no one. Financed by a group of billionaires with nearly a century's worth of history and wealth, the group simply did not exist. They were completely autonomous, able to go places and do things no other organization could even dream of. Comprised of operators from countries around the world, they were the most elite group of soldiers Kruger had ever served with – and they were well compensated for it.

Although the lack of rules held the risk of abuse of power, Kruger had yet to see it. The group had been nothing but the pinnacle of professionalism. They killed when it was necessary. They could be absolutely ruthless against those that deserved it, but they weren't indiscriminate. They lived and operated in a very gray area, but Kruger was constantly impressed by the amount of control these men exhibited.

"What is your name?" Kruger asked the man as he walked behind him.

"Muhammad," the man said.

Standing behind the man, Kruger drove his thumb into the mandibular angle pressure point near al-Awaki's jaw. The man tensed and grunted under the intense pain as Kruger calmly applied pressure.

"Please!" al-Awaki screamed. Kruger eased the pressure and nodded at Rage. Rage disappeared in search of supplies for the next phase of the interrogation.

"Stop lying to me and the pain stops," Kruger said.

"Khaleed al-Awaki!" the man yelped.

Kruger walked around to the front of the man and squatted down across from him. "I'm going to be honest with you, Khaleed, I don't have a lot of time," he said calmly as he looked the man in the eyes.

"You should know that everyone breaks," Kruger said in a soft voice. "Some more quickly than others, but in the end, no one can hold out forever. You may think you're winning, but you're only prolonging the inevitable."

"I have nothing to tell you," al-Awaki said. "I drive a taxi in El Paso."

Kruger nodded. "I'm sure, but I'm not worried about you right now. You're nothing to me," he said as he shook his head.

"Then why am I here?" al-Awaki asked. "Release me!"

Kruger looked back to see Rage return with a bucket filled with water in one hand and a towel in the other. He looked back at al-Awaki to see a pair of wide eyes staring at the former Filipino Special Forces operator walking toward him.

"No! Please!" al-Awaki pleaded.

"You're quite perceptive for just a cab driver," Kruger said as al-Awaki intently watched Rage approach.

"Anyway, as I was saying, everyone breaks eventually. Some more quickly than others. The only question you have to answer for yourself is how much pain you're willing to endure before you do," Kruger said.

"I don't know anything. What do you want from me?" al-Awaki asked nervously.

"Tariq Qafir," Kruger said as he watched the recognition in al-Awaki's face.

"Who?" al-Awaki said as he tried to avoid eye contact.

Kruger kicked al-Awaki's chair back and motioned to Rage. Kruger was instantly on top of al-Awaki as he struggled against his restraints and pleaded for Kruger to stop. Rage handed Kruger one of the towels and brought the water-filled bucket up to al-Awaki's face.

"I warned you," Kruger said as he held the towel tightly over al-Awaki's face. Rage poured the water over the towel; it was the closest feeling to drowning a man could get without actually drowning. Kruger didn't enjoy doing it, but he needed answers and didn't have time to play games with the defiant taxi driver from El Paso. American lives were at stake.

As Rage stopped the flow of water, Kruger removed the towel from al-Awaki's face. Al-Awaki coughed and gasped for air. Kruger squatted over him, waiting for him to recover.

"It's only going to get worse from here," Kruger warned. "Where is Tariq Qafir?"

"He was in another car!" al-Awaki said still gasping for air.

"What kind of car?" Kruger demanded.

"Honda Civic," al-Awaki replied nervously. "I swear."

"Where was he going?" Kruger asked.

"I don't know!"

"Wrong answer," Kruger said as he pushed the towel back down over al-Awaki's nose and mouth and Rage started pouring water again.

"Try again!" Kruger barked as he removed the towel once again.

"He went to the airport. He's going to Florida, but I don't know where. I swear!" al-Awaki said between gasps of air.

"What airline?"

Al-Awaki shook his head vigorously. "Not an airline. A small plane. We were taking him to the airport when we broke down. Abdul was following him and took him."

"What is his plan?" Kruger asked.

"I don't—"

Kruger stopped him mid-sentence as he held the towel ominously above the man's face.

"Okay!" al-Awaki stopped as he tried to turn his face away. "He's got missiles and he's going to shoot down an airplane."

"What kind of missiles?"

"Russian shoulder-fired missiles!"

"What is his target?" Kruger asked. "Last chance."

"He didn't tell us. We just smuggled the missiles in from Mexico and arranged to fly him out."

"Not good enough," Kruger said, wrapping the towel back around al-Awaki's face as Rage poured the remainder of the water.

"I swear!" al-Awaki said as Kruger once again removed the wet towel. "He didn't tell us, but the damage to the infidels will be great. I hope he kills hundreds."

"Copy that," Kruger said as he stood and nodded at Rage.

"Oracle, it's Slayer, we're looking for a Honda Civic that was near the Suburban. It headed to the El Paso airport," Kruger said into his secure radio. "Took a light civil to Florida, destination unknown."

As Kruger relayed the information to Meeks, Rage screwed the suppressor onto his Glock 21SF and casually walked over to where al-Awaki was still on the floor. "Night, night," he said as he dispatched al-Awaki with a suppressed .45ACP round to the forehead.

"Boss, that's a needle in a haystack," Meeks argued. "Without a registration number or a flight plan, that could be any one of hundreds of airplanes."

"Start working, Coolio," Kruger said. "What's the status of our bird?"

"Landing at your location in twenty mikes," Meeks replied.

"Copy that," Kruger said as he motioned to Rage. "We'll get this cleaned up and stand by for extract. You can do this buddy; I have faith in you. Find that piece of shit before he kills more innocent people."

"I'll do my best, boss," Meeks replied.

CHAPTER SIX

Springfield, VA
0940 Local Time

The moderately sized colonial home still looked like a crime scene. Bright yellow barricade tape was scattered about the overgrown grass. Some of the windows had been boarded shut. Spectre thought it could've easily doubled as the setting for a low budget horror movie.

They pulled to a stop behind an unmarked Chevy Tahoe parked across the street. After reaching a dead end trying to track down the source of Steele's information, Decker had reverted to old-fashioned police work. They had spent the evening going through the case files that Decker could get her hands on from the incident at Midway. They decided to work backwards until they found a lead that could point them in the right direction.

Most of the investigation into the President's taking by Chinese mercenaries had been sealed or turned over to various intelligence agencies for action. The Secret Service had taken the lead in investigating the circumstances under which Air Force One was taken. That investigation had primarily centered on Air Force Lieutenant Colonel Jason Waxburn.

In sworn affidavits, the pilot of Air Force One, Colonel Carl Sullivan had told investigators that he had left the cockpit of Air Force One to use the restroom while cruising under escort to Hickam Air Force Base in Honolulu, Hawaii. Per Air Force Instructions and Federal Aviation Regulations, Lt Col Waxburn had donned an oxygen mask as the lone pilot since they were above twenty-five thousand feet.

But when Col Sullivan returned the cockpit, he discovered the door had been secured shut and the access keypad disabled. Col Sullivan reported feeling hypoxic during this time, and further stated that he lost consciousness after unsuccessfully attempting reentry.

Sullivan told investigators that he regained consciousness as the President's 747 made its approach to land at Henderson Airfield, and with the help of the Secret Service detail aboard, continued the effort to force entry into the cockpit even as the airplane rolled to a stop on the runway.

They quickly discovered that the aircraft was under siege by unknown hostiles on the runway at Midway Island. After the ensuing battle, Sullivan was taken hostage by the combatants that had entered through the cockpit. Sullivan had noted that Waxburn had been killed during the siege.

During the hostage standoff, Waxburn's house had been raided by Secret Service investigators and local law enforcement. According to the report, they had found the bodies of Waxburn's wife and son in a freezer in the basement. They had also found a Quran with several key passages highlighted regarding the killing of the nonbelievers.

Despite later findings that Chinese intelligence agents were at least partly behind the assassination attempt, the investigation into Waxburn's involvement seemed to end there. Secret Service Agents investigating Waxburn seemed to accept that Waxburn had been radicalized and acted alone. Whether they truly believed it or had been ordered to discontinue their search for answers was up for debate, but the investigation had been deemed officially closed by the senior field agents leading it.

This didn't sit well with Decker or Spectre. The proverbial smoke seemed to be leading them to another cover up, making Waxburn's involvement worth investigating further. It was nothing more than a hunch, but they agreed that it was a good starting point, so they called the deputy responsible for the crime scene to set up a visit to Waxburn's house.

As Decker put her unmarked Ford into park, a female detective exited the Tahoe. She was wearing a black polo shirt with a gold badge embroidered on the chest and khaki tactical pants. Spectre and Decker exited and approached the large black woman.

"Special Agent Decker?" she asked as she extended her hand with a smile. She had a slight southern accent.

Decker shook the woman's hand and held up her credentials with her left hand. "Yes, ma'am, and this is Cal Martin."

"Oh honey that's quite the ring," she said, admiring Decker's hand before turning to Spectre. "Is this the lucky man?"

Spectre smiled sheepishly as he shook the woman's hand. "The luckiest," he replied. "Cal Martin, nice to meet you."

"Detective Laura Jackson," the detective said. "I must say I was surprised when I heard the FBI was interested in this place again. It has sat empty for months now."

"But you can get us in?" Spectre asked.

"That's why I'm here, honey," she said with a sly smile. "But don't be too disappointed when you see inside."

Detective Jackson led the couple up the steps of the deteriorating house. Spectre noticed several broken windows not covered by the boards as Jackson fished out her key and unlocked the door.

"Jesus!" Decker cried as the smell hit her. It smelled like a mix of dead bodies, feces, and mildew. She held back a dry heave as she pinched her nose.

"What," Spectre began as he followed behind before stopping dead in his tracks and covering his mouth. "Fuck me! What is that smell?"

"About a month ago we found an elderly homeless man dead in the living room," Jackson explained, unfazed by the smell. "He had been dead for several weeks, which, as you know, involves severe decomposition, especially in a house with no electricity in the record high heat we've been having."

"How does this not bother you?" Spectre asked in a nasal tone as he pinched his nose like a five-year old.

"I started my career in Atlanta," Jackson explained. "I've seen much worse. Even in this house. I was here when they served the warrant."

"I thought I recognized the accent, I went to UGA," Decker said still holding her nose.

"Wait. Where's all the furniture? Why is the house empty?" Spectre interrupted.

"Gone," Jackson said, shaking her head. "The family has been trying to sell the house since it happened, but they couldn't get the smell out of it. It was buried in the fiber of everything. So they sold what they could and the house has been empty ever since. I'm not really sure what they plan on doing with it."

"Burn it to the ground," Spectre suggested, as he pushed past Decker and Jackson toward the door and into fresh air.

Jackson and Decker rejoined Spectre as he dry heaved in the yard, bending down with one hand on his knees and the other holding his tie to his chest. "You ok, sweetie?" Decker asked as she approached.

"I have to ask, what are you guys hoping to find here, ma'am?" Jackson asked while Decker tended to Spectre.

"We were hoping to learn more about Waxburn's involvement," Decker said as Spectre recovered.

"You mean in killing his own family?" Jackson asked.

"You said you were here the night they raided this place, what did you see?" Spectre asked as he slowly stood and walked back to Jackson who was still standing on the front porch.

"Like any other federal operation, it was signal seven," Jackson said, rolling her eyes. "No offense."

"Signal seven?" Spectre asked.

"A train wreck," Jackson replied. "AFU."

"Got it, go on," Decker said.

"Well, we helped execute the warrant, but obviously, the Fed boys wanted the lead, so we secured the perimeter and couldn't go in until it was code four," Jackson said.

"All clear and safe for the crime scene investigators to enter," Jackson added as she saw Spectre mouth 'Code four?' to Decker.

"Anyway," she continued, "we helped process the crime scene and tag the evidence. It was pretty nasty. That guy had chopped up the bodies and put them in garbage bags in the freezer. You think this smelled bad? It was way worse.

"So we helped canvass the neighborhood. Talked to neighbors. You know, standard crime scene investigation," Jackson said, shrugging her broad shoulders.

"Anything seem out of the ordinary to you?" Decker asked.

"Well, again, no offense, but everything you Feds do seems out of the ordinary to me," Jackson said. "But did the hair stand up on the back of my neck? Absolutely."

"What do you mean?" Spectre asked. "A threat?"

"No, let's call it intuition," Jackson said. "The scene was way too clean. I've been to some gruesome crime scenes created by very crazy individuals, and this matched nothing I'd seen."

"How so?" Decker asked.

"I can't explain it exactly," Jackson said, "but it almost seemed like someone *wanted* us to find the killer."

"Well, sometimes the psychopaths do," Decker offered.

"Honey, I know psychopaths," Jackson said, shaking her head. "This didn't feel crazy, it felt *professional*. Like something out of Crime Scene Investigator classes."

"Staged?" Spectre asked.

"I'm not saying that," Jackson said. "But it's possible. Especially the way the Quran was left out and the blood trail to the freezer. The guy had taken so much care to hide the bodies, but got sloppy at the end? And more importantly, what was his motive? From every neighbor I talked to, this guy was gone a lot, but a model father when he was home."

"What did the neighbors say?" Decker asked.

"Same old song and dance," Jackson replied. "He seemed like such a nice man. No one could believe it. The only thing we did find was that he had received some kind of bad news a few days earlier."

"How?" Decker asked.

Jackson pointed across the street. "That neighbor right there. She's an old widower who said she heard him come home one night and go out to the mailbox. She's a bit of a nosy neighbor as you can imagine. Anyway, she heard him cry out and she looked outside to see him at his mailbox holding a letter. She thought the missus had left him and taken the kid while he had been gone because she hadn't seen either of them in a couple days."

"And no one thought to follow up on that?" Spectre asked.

"They did more than follow up," Jackson said. "She even had security cameras. The Feds took those hard drives."

"That wasn't in the report," Decker said with a frown.

"I'm not surprised," Jackson said with a derisive look. "There were so many different agencies here, each with their own little empire to protect. It was a circus and the chain of evidence was very muddled."

"What are the odds we could go talk to her?" Spectre asked.

"I'd say pretty good since she's looking out her window at us right now," Jackson said, pointing at the small woman peering through the blinds.

CHAPTER SEVEN

"Y'all can't go stealing my stuff again!" the old woman yelled as she opened the front door. "I still haven't been reimbursed for the hard drive you people stole."

Spectre sidestepped behind Decker as the angry woman emerged onto the front porch. She adjusted her glasses for a better look as Jackson held out her Sheriff's star. "Ma'am, we just want to talk."

"I've already said all I'm going to say," the old woman replied. "All you people are doing now is bringing down the neighborhood, leaving that poor homeless man to die in there. That's just not right!"

"Yes, ma'am," Jackson responded. "We'd just like to talk to you for a few minutes, and then we'll be on our way."

"He's cute," the old woman said. "I'll talk to him."

Spectre flashed a boyish grin, still hiding behind Decker to avoid the wrath of the angry old woman. "I'm not a cop if that makes you feel any better," Spectre offered. "But I'll vouch for these two anyway. My name is Cal Martin."

"Oh, you're the man the media tried to blame the President's disappearance on. And then they gave you a medal instead!" the woman said.

"I hadn't heard that," Spectre said.

"Oh yes. Your face was all over the news. They said you had a criminal history and were on the plane with the President. People were all speculating that you helped take her hostage, but I knew better!"

"You did?" Spectre asked.

"Cute boy like you? You ain't no criminal," the woman said with a flirty smile. "And then when they showed you on TV getting that medal, I knew they made all that stuff up."

"Well, thank you," Spectre replied graciously. "I'm actually here about that incident, ma'am."

"Ethel Watson," the woman said, extending her hand. "But you can call me Ethel."

Spectre shook the woman's hand and gave Decker a confused look as she tried to hold back a laugh. "Thanks, Ethel," he said as the old woman held his hand a little too long for comfort.

"Please, come in," Ethel said with a warm smile. "Would you like something to drink, Cal?"

"No, ma'am, thank you," Spectre said as he followed the old woman into her modest home. Jackson and Decker exchanged a look and laughed as they followed behind the unlikely couple.

"I told you to call me Ethel," the woman said as she offered them a seat in the living room.

"So what can I do for you?" Ethel asked as she stroked her salt and pepper hair.

"What did you know about Lieutenant Colonel Waxburn, Ethel?" Spectre asked nervously, still confused by the woman's advances.

Ethel's face puckered as if she had just been forced to eat a lemon. "Shame what happened to that family. They were good people. He was gone a lot, but he was always outside playing with his son when the weather was nice. They used to wait outside on the front porch rocking chairs waiting for him to come home every evening. Nicest family," Ethel said, shaking her head.

"Did he ever talk about Islam?" Spectre asked.

"You mean, was he a terrorist?" Ethel asked.

"Do you think he converted to radical Islam?" Decker interjected.

Ethel ignored Decker as she tried to make eye contact with Spectre who was distracted by the various figurines carefully positioned around the house.

"Jason wasn't a terrorist, Cal," she said, ignoring Decker. "He was a good man like you."

"When did you see him last?" Decker asked.

"Are you sure I can't get you anything?" Ethel asked, not hiding the fact that she wanted nothing to do with either of the two women accompanying the subject of her interest.

"No, ma'am, we're good," Spectre said. "But you know Michelle here actually saved the President's life. I was just there. She deserves all the credit."

"That's nice, dear," Ethel said without even acknowledging Decker. "What else would you like to know, Cal?"

Spectre looked at Decker and shrugged. She nodded for him to keep the lead in questioning the old lady.

"Can you tell me about the last time you saw the colonel or his family?" Spectre asked.

Ethel smiled. "Sure," she said. "It was a couple of days before Valentine's Day. Jason was gone on one of his trips. Clare used to always tell me when he was leaving and sometimes I'd watch their little boy, John. Anyway, I heard him come home and then a few minutes later he was screaming and throwing up in the yard.

"I put my robe on and went over to check on him. He was acting really strange. He was shaking and holding an envelope. Said it was nothing and didn't want to talk about it," Ethel said shaking her head. "I thought Clare had left him, because I hadn't seen them home in a couple of days, which didn't make sense."

"Why didn't it make sense?" Spectre asked.

"They never just left without asking me to watch the place," Ethel replied. "They were always asking me to check in on the place while they were gone. They were very good about that."

"So you thought she left him?" Spectre asked.

"Well, a few days earlier Clare had visitors in the evening, so I thought maybe that's when she left," Ethel said as she fixed her glasses.

"Visitors?"

"Yeah, there was a big white Suburban that stayed for a while," Ethel said. "I just thought it was one of the other wives. They all drive big gas guzzling SUVs. I figured she might have stayed with them."

"Did you tell this to investigators?" Spectre asked.

Ethel nodded. "Yup, and that's when they asked about my cameras and took the hard drive out of the machine. They said they were going to mail me a new one, but, of course, they never did. If it weren't for the internet these cameras would be useless right now."

"Do you remember who you talked to?" Spectre asked.

"They said they were Homeland Security or some such. They had badges, but I didn't pay much attention, honey. They didn't look like the other people that were there, though," Ethel said.

"What do you mean?"

"They weren't nice like you, dear," she replied. "Very uptight. Military haircuts. They sat up straight like they were in boot camp. Didn't talk much."

"You said the cameras were on the internet?" Decker asked, hoping the woman would finally acknowledge her.

Ethel smiled. "My grandson is a very smart boy. Good with computers. He set all that up so I can watch it from my phone here," she said, picking up her smart phone.

"Does it save video to the internet?" Decker asked.

"It puts everything on the sky or cloud or whatever it's called," Ethel replied. "You'd have to ask my grandson."

"Would you mind if we talked to him, Ethel?" Spectre asked.

"Anything for you, sweetie. Here, let me get you his number," she said as she took off for the kitchen.

"I knew nothing about this," Jackson whispered. "Nothing about visitors a few days prior made any of our reports."

"It didn't make the Secret Service's report either. Do you know who it could've been?" Decker asked.

"There were so many agencies here," Jackson said, shaking her head. "Like I said, it was a circus. I think I can find out from our crime scene log though, if you want."

"Please do," Decker whispered as Ethel returned with a yellow sticky note.

"This is his number and address," Ethel said as she handed the paper to Spectre. "He lives in Arlington. Works in the city for a computer company."

"Thank you, Ethel," Spectre said as he took the note and stood. "You've been a great help today. We should get going."

"Are you sure you have to leave?" Ethel protested as the trio stood.

"You've been great, but I'd like to talk to your grandson if that's ok," Spectre said as he headed for the door.

"Ok, Cal, but you can come back any time," Ethel said with a wink.

Ethel ushered them out the door, staring at Spectre as he walked out behind Decker and Jackson. They stopped at the front of Decker's car as Ethel finally went back into her house and closed the door after lingering for a few seconds.

"Should I be worried?" Decker asked playfully.

"I feel so violated," Spectre said with an exaggerated shudder. "That was weird."

"Detective Jackson, thank you so much for your help," Decker said as she laughed and turned to Jackson.

"I will try to get you a copy of the crime scene log and find out who was on scene and talked to Mrs. Watson," Jackson said. "Or is it Mrs. Martin now?"

"Very funny," Spectre said.

Decker handed Jackson her card. "Call my cell when you find out, please. I'm going to get my fiancé out of here before it's too late. Thanks again," she said with a chuckle.

CHAPTER EIGHT

Choctawhatchee Bay, Destin, FL
2115 Local Time

"We are here," Tariq Qafir said as he looked at his handheld GPS. "Kill the engine."

Ahmad Abraham shut the 200 horsepower outboard engine off on the twenty-four-foot bay boat as they coasted to a stop on the calm bay waters. He walked forward from the operator's console and picked up the anchor. "Here?" he asked as he held it up.

Tariq nodded as he walked to the back of the boat. He stopped at the six-foot crate and opened it, revealing a five-foot tube and targeting components. He looked at his watch before pulling out the components. He had less than fifteen minutes before their target would be overhead.

As Tariq went to work assembling the cigar box-shaped targeting system to the long tube, he looked back over at Ahmad. The success of the operation had rested on the shoulders of the man currently smoking a cigarette and staring aimlessly out into the bay. Ahmad had been the leader of the cell responsible for gathering intelligence and confirming that the target would be in the right place at the right time. He had also been responsible for knowing the patrol patterns of local law enforcement in the bay. Tariq's ability to carry out the mission hinged upon the man's competence.

But given the extraordinary lengths to which Tariq had gone to get to this point, there was simply no other way. After he had narrowly avoided capture in El Paso as he made off in a small aircraft, he had driven from Alabama to Florida before meeting up with the cell in Pensacola. Every minute Tariq was in public, he risked a bloody fight to the death with American law enforcement.

The mission, he had determined, was more than worth it. In just a few minutes, Tariq was sure he would deal a blow to the Americans that would send ripples throughout the world. In his mind, it was a brilliant plan.

Tariq heard the sound of aircraft in the distance as he stood the Igla-S man portable surface to air missile on its tail. He powered it on, verifying the seeker was cooled and capable of tracking as the jet noise grew closer.

"They are coming," Tariq whispered to Ahmad.

Ahmad flicked his cigarette into the water and grabbed a pair of binoculars from the captain's console. He scanned the shores to their north and south, verifying that no boats were in the area before turning his attention to the incoming aircraft.

"Clear," Ahmad said in a low voice.

Tariq could see the flashing strobes of two aircraft approaching low over the horizon. As the specs on the horizon grew closer, the first aircraft lowered its landing gear, illuminating the bright landing light on the nose gear.

Tariq picked up the Igla-S and mounted it on his shoulder. He targeted the first aircraft, searching for a sweet spot as the guidance system transmitted a high-pitched aural tone. Through the viewfinder, he targeted the rear of the aircraft first. The seeker tone was suitable, but not ideal. He adjusted his aim on the aircraft as it grew closer, settling on the landing light as the seeker screamed its tone indicating it was locked on.

Tariq exhaled slowly, saying, "Allahu Akbar," as he braced himself and pulled the trigger. *Nothing.*

Tariq squeezed the trigger again as the aircraft neared. *Nothing.* His heart raced. Had he come all the way and gone through so much just to fail? Had Allah cursed him? He cursed loudly as the fighter jet flew over them, its single engine screaming as the pilot focused on landing at the nearby airfield.

"Flashlight! Now!" Tariq barked as he pulled the MANPAD off his shoulder and examined it. Ahmad raced to shine the flashlight on the trigger assembly. Tariq could hear a second aircraft approaching in the distance. He had one final chance before the mission would be a complete failure.

Tariq tried to calm himself as he desperately searched for the problem. Finally, it hit him. He had failed to connect the firing mechanism to the missile, a holdover of training with just the seeker hundreds of times before. He connected it and cursed himself as he threw the fifty-pound launcher back over his shoulder and took aim.

The second jet was just a few miles away when the seeker locked on. Tariq excitedly pulled the trigger, nearly being thrown overboard by the blast as the missile was sent screaming toward the approaching aircraft.

Seconds later, the missile impacted the cockpit of the fighter jet, erupting into a fireball. Tariq tossed the launcher tube to the side as he regained his bearing in the rocking boat.

"Allahu Akbar!" Ahmad yelled, pumping his fist as the fireball descended into the bay away from them.

Tariq smiled as he watched the jet plummet into the water. There was no ejection attempt. The quarter-billion-dollar aircraft and its pilot were lost. His mission had been accomplished.

"We must go!" Tariq ordered as Ahmad stood speechless watching the jet crash.

Ahmad pulled the anchor from the water and rushed to start the engine. Seconds later, they were speeding away toward Destin where they would exit the bay and head out into the Gulf of Mexico away from the Americans that would soon be descending upon the crash site.

As the salty sea air hit Tariq's face, he couldn't stop smiling. He had just shown the Americans that their arrogance and dependence on excess could never keep them safe from the will of Allah. He had taken out the symbol of American waste by shooting down the F-35. It was a great day for the Islamic State and its Holy Warriors.

But Tariq knew his mission was far from over. While this attack struck a blow to the Great Satan's bloated war machine, his next attack would show the American infidels that the war had come to them. No longer could they sleep peacefully in their beds while sending their cowardly murderers to kill innocent Muslims. They too would bear the price of the war they had started. A war, Tariq was sure, the Americans would soon lose their will to fight.

CHAPTER NINE

Washington, D.C.
0745 Local Time

Spectre and Decker had spent the previous afternoon trying to find a connection to the men Ethel had told them about. They searched through the crime scene logs of the Secret Service raids on various houses of the Air Force One passengers, hoping to find a person or agency that didn't seem to belong.

They had come up short, but late in the evening, Ethel's grandson Jake Watson had finally returned their phone call and agreed to meet with Spectre and Decker at his office the next morning. They had only told him that they were following up on an investigation that his grandmother had been involved with and wished to speak with him about her surveillance setup.

Located just outside the downtown district, the small IT firm had its offices on the fourth floor of the newly renovated office building. The couple reached the glass doors labeled EMPIRE TECHNICAL SOLUTIONS to see a large man with thick glasses and comb over chatting with the average-looking receptionist. Spectre opened the door for Decker as the man turned and smiled at Decker, revealing his coffee stained teeth.

"You must be Agent Decker," he said as he turned to greet her.

"Special Agent Decker and Cal Martin," she said, holding up her credentials. "We spoke on the phone earlier."

"Oh, I definitely remember," Watson said with a cheesy grin. "But I didn't expect someone so beautiful, though."

"Is there some place we could talk privately?" Decker asked.

"My place," Watson replied. "I'll make you my famous lasagna and you can ask me anything you want."

Decker smiled politely as Spectre chuckled at the man before him. Watson was, at least, two inches taller and outweighed the 6'1", 190 pound Krav Maga black belt by two hundred or more pounds, but Spectre was completely confident in his ability to neutralize the threat should the need arise. Although he knew he would never need to. Decker was more than capable of handling herself if things got out of hand.

For the time being, however, Spectre was taking great pleasure in the fact that the tables had turned – and with a member of the same family no less.

"I think a private place here would be just fine," Decker said as she casually brushed her neck with her left hand, revealing the diamond engagement ring Spectre had given her.

"Suit yourself," Watson said with a shrug. "Follow me."

"Goodbye, Meredith," he said with a wink as he waved at the receptionist and led them to his office. Decker and Spectre exchanged a look. Spectre was doing everything in his power not to burst out laughing at the "smooth operator" making a play on Decker as they followed the man down the hallway.

"Please have a seat," he said as he took his seat at his desk in the tiny office. Decker took the only seat as Spectre stood behind her. "Now what about Gammy's surveillance system did you want to talk about? I'm fairly busy."

"You set up your grandmother's surveillance system for her, correct?" Decker asked.

"Correct," Watson replied as he turned his attention to his e-mail.

"Did you set up a backup?" Spectre asked.

"Did I set up a backup?" Watson asked mockingly as he rolled his eyes. "I don't know, did I?"

Decker grabbed Spectre's hand. She sensed him tense up behind her, considering his options among the fifty ways he could choke out the overweight IT specialist in front of them.

"The hard drive from your grandmother's surveillance system was removed," Decker replied calmly. "Your grandmother mentioned that you had set up a cloud storage for the system. We know it's been a few months, but we were wondering if you still had that setup."

"Everything is uploaded to a two terabyte server, backed up daily," Watson said smugly. "Of course I still have it."

"Would it be possible for you to give us access to it?" Decker asked.

"Yes, it would," Watson said as he smiled.

As he considered expediting their Q&A session using a more hands-on approach, Spectre felt his phone vibrating in his pocket. He looked at the caller ID to find that Senator Wilson's office was calling. He rejected the call and put the phone back in his pocket before returning his attention to Watson.

"How do we get access to the surveillance footage?" Spectre asked impatiently.

"I would be more than happy to give you the footage," Watson said smugly. "But…"

"But, what?" Spectre snapped. "But you think this is a game? But you want to sit here and interfere with a federal investigation? But you think federal prison is a joke?"

"But it's on a hard drive at my house," Watson said, retreating into his leather chair. "It's only stored on the server until it's automatically backed up on my hard drive weekly."

"What time are you going home today?" Spectre asked menacingly as he stepped forward.

"I get off at five," Watson said sheepishly.

"Great, we'll meet you there at six," Spectre said.

"But—"

"Your cooperation in this investigation is appreciated, Mr. Watson," Decker added.

"Hurry home," Spectre said with a wink and a smile as Decker stood to leave. "We'll be there."

Spectre held the door open as Decker exited into the hall. "Don't be late!" he added before following Decker out.

"That was a little harsh, Cal," Decker said as they entered the elevator.

"We don't have time to play games," Spectre replied as he pulled out his phone. "The Senator's office just called and left a text message saying to call back as soon as possible. Something's up."

"Well, call them," Decker said as she looked at Spectre's phone.

"No reception in the elevator," Spectre said as he held the phone up. "I'll do it outside."

They exited the elevator and walked through the lobby. Spectre held up the phone, hoping to get a signal as they left the building onto the busy side street.

As Spectre started to hit SEND, a vehicle across the street caught his eye. "Hold on a second," he said.

"What?"

"Don't look now, but have you seen that white Jeep Cherokee across the street before?" Spectre asked as he turned his back to the vehicle.

Decker glanced quickly at the Jeep before turning back to Spectre. "Grandma Watson's house?"

"Let's walk," Spectre said as he turned Decker and started toward the parking lot behind Watson's building. "It passed as we were talking to the detective when we first got there. I'm sure of it."

"You think we're being followed?"

"You don't?" Spectre asked as they ducked into the side street.

"Fair point," Decker said as she glanced over her shoulder.

As they reached Decker's car, Spectre pulled out his phone and dialed the Senator's office as Decker kept watch. A few minutes later, Spectre hung up.

"What is it?" Decker asked as she saw the concerned look on Spectre's face.

"It was Wilson's chief of staff," Spectre said. "He wants us to head straight to his office. Something big has happened."

"Like what?"

"He wouldn't say," Spectre said, shaking his head.

* * *

After executing a series of surveillance detection routes to ensure the white Cherokee was no longer following them, Spectre and Decker had finally made it to the Russell Building. Decker wasn't sure that the Cherokee had been anything more than a coincidence or just two very similar vehicles, but the hair on the back of Spectre's neck was standing up. He had just been through too much to believe in coincidences anymore. It made him very uneasy.

Chet Marks was waiting for Spectre and Decker as they walked into the waiting area of Senator Wilson's D.C. office. The Senator's Chief of Staff was young. In his late thirties, he was just a few years older than Spectre, but the gray specks peppering his jet-black hair made him look much older.

He was a rising star in the Beltway, having taken over as the head of Wilson's staff after the failed Presidential campaign a little over a year earlier. He had spent his entire career in politics, starting first as a college student volunteering for various campaigns until moving on as a staffer for a junior senator named Madeline Clifton.

Marks had done what few people in Washington did – switched parties during a close Presidential race. He had done so after Clifton made quite controversial remarks during a debate over Taiwan's push for sovereignty. In what many thought to be a gaffe, Clifton had put her foot down on the issue, stating that she would back any country's peaceful opposition to aggressive overreach by world superpowers. Many had thought it would be the end of Clifton's historic campaign, including Marks. He resigned a week later along with several of his colleagues hoping to abandon the sinking ship.

Like every other chameleon in Washington, Marks completely changed his ideology and took a spot on Wilson's campaign. But unfortunately for Marks, Clifton and her running mate Kerry Johnson had managed to right the ship, and surged ahead in the polls. The hard-line stance while stressing peaceful opposition and continued talks were enough to win over moderates who were on the fence on the issue and the rest was history.

Marks had picked the wrong horse, and as Wilson cleaned house in the wake of their losing battle, Marks found himself to be the last man standing. A few weeks after President Clifton was sworn in as the first female president, Marks accepted a position as Wilson's Chief of Staff.

Spectre and Decker had only met him briefly in Hawaii, but from what Spectre had seen, he was just like everyone else in Washington. Everything about the man seemed fake to Spectre, from his tanning bed tan, to his ultra-white teeth, to his cheesy smile and limp handshake. It didn't surprise Spectre at all that Marks would bounce around Washington.

As they walked into the waiting area, Spectre was surprised to see Marks frowning as he leaned against the receptionist's desk. He couldn't help but wonder if it were an act or something genuinely was wrong, but the man seemed very distraught as Spectre and Decker approached.

"Thanks for coming in so quickly," Marks said softly. "It's been a rough night."

"What's up?" Spectre asked. As he got closer, he could see bags under the man's eyes. He looked tired and beleaguered.

"I'm sure you heard about the F-35 crash in Florida last night," he said, shaking his head as he stared at the floor.

"Yeah, I saw it on the news this morning," Spectre said. "Wasn't that supposed to be the last night flight before it goes IOC Friday?"

Spectre hadn't really been keeping up with the F-35 program, but knew that it had been plagued with delays and cost issues since its inception. It was part of the reason his old squadron in Homestead had upgraded its F-16s to have AESA radars and conformal fuel tanks – to bridge the gap as the F-35 kept getting pushed farther and farther to the right.

The only thing Spectre had seen in the news was that the Air Force's first F-35 squadron at Eglin Air Force Base was to have a ceremony declaring Initial Operational Capability on Friday after its last series of night test flights.

Spectre guessed that the reason Marks was so distraught was that Wilson somehow had a political interest in the F-35 going IOC on time and that the crash would cause some political backlash or more delays. The news report he had heard that morning hadn't said much except that the aircraft was making its landing approach when it went down in the bay near the base. The condition of the pilot was unknown, which usually meant that the pilot had died and they were waiting for next of kin notifications to release his name.

Marks nodded. "Senator Wilson is down there right now and requested that you two meet him there as soon as possible," he said.

Spectre frowned and shook his head. "We've got some fairly decent leads here," Spectre replied. "I don't think we would be much help. We need to be here."

Decker squeezed Spectre's hand and asked, "What would the Senator like us to do?"

"He would like you to assist with the investigation," Marks said. "It's very important to him."

"A Safety Investigation Board will be convened," Spectre said. "I don't think there's much we could do besides get in the way. I've never been to Safety School."

"Is foul play suspected?" Decker asked as she squeezed Spectre's hand again.

"You don't know, do you?" Marks asked as he looked up at them.

"Know what?" Spectre asked impatiently. "What is the Senator's interest in this?"

"The pilot was Major Kenny Long," Marks said.

"Doesn't ring any bells," Spectre said.

Marks sighed. "Senator Wilson's first wife was Janice Long. She was pregnant when they divorced and changed her name. Kenneth Long is Senator Wilson's son."

CHAPTER TEN

Number One Observatory Circle
United States Naval Observatory
Washington, D.C.
0915 Local Time

Marvin Bradley was thumbing through the classified report in the library of the large Victorian home of the Vice President when Johnson walked in. He stood to greet the elder statesman as he set the report aside. The Vice President was still wearing his tracksuit from his morning jog as an entourage of aides and Secret Service agents followed in behind him.

"Did you have a good run, sir?" Bradley asked as he nodded to the staffers and agents to leave them alone in the room.

Johnson scowled as he wiped his wrinkled face with the towel wrapped around his neck. "Does it look like I had fun?" Johnson asked, his chest still heaving. "I'm only doing this because you made me."

"For your own good, sir," Bradley replied. "The media caught wind of your last physical. If you're going to be President, we can't have them questioning whether you'll survive the stresses."

"I survived Midway," Johnson shot back.

"And you were only President for twenty-four hours," Bradley replied. "We have to think about the long game now."

Shortly after their election, President Clifton had gone to Taiwan to promote her Free Taiwan stance. During her speech, a series of terror attacks across the Pacific had forced the Secret Service to evacuate her to Hawaii on Air Force One, but a coerced Air Force One pilot had landed the aircraft on Midway Island instead. A group of commandos was waiting and took the President hostage, allowing the Vice President and the President's Cabinet to invoke the Twenty-Fifth Amendment.

Johnson had been sure that the President was dead after a nuclear device was detonated during their rescue attempt, but the President had managed to escape thanks to a thorn in Johnson's side that just wouldn't go away – Cal Martin.

In the aftermath of the attack, the President seemed none the wiser that Johnson and Bradley had been behind the assassination attempt, but that didn't stop Johnson's end game to become the most powerful man in the free world. It had just forced him to bide his time and do it the old-fashioned way.

"What are you doing here?" Johnson asked. "I thought you were supposed to be working on the energy proposal on the Hill until ten?"

Bradley picked up the report and handed it to Johnson. "We've got a problem," he said.

Johnson held the report between his long, slender fingers as he pulled his eyeglasses out of their case and propped them on his crooked nose. Bradley watched in silence as Johnson frowned as he read the report.

"Have you asked our contact about this?" Johnson asked in a hushed tone as he sat down.

Bradley sat on the chair next to him and leaned in. "I did. They had nothing to do with this. This is 100% an act of terrorism," Bradley whispered.

"What is the media saying?" Johnson asked.

"Nothing on it yet," Bradley said. "ISIS claims responsibility for every crash as part of their propaganda campaign. The problem is, this time we believe they really did it."

"This can't get out," Johnson said, shaking his head. "We finally put the Midway incident to bed."

The attack had been orchestrated by Chinese commandos posing as fighters for the Islamic State of Uyghur. It had been part of Johnson's plan to create a tangible enemy in the wake of what he hoped would be the President's assassination and his rise to power. But when she survived, the Administration had to save face.

Unable to publicly out the Chinese government's supposed involvement in the plot for fear of kicking off a World War, the Administration quietly allowed the media's narrative to survive. Islamic terrorists from the Chinese province of Uyghur had carried out the attack, and in cooperation with the Chinese government, had been dealt with. A new bombing campaign had also been kicked off in Syria and Iraq – a show of force to appease the American public with very little risk or actual reward.

But Johnson knew that a terror attack on U.S. soil, shooting down America's brand new quarter-billion dollar apiece fighter, would crush their already-struggling poll numbers. Clifton had very quietly announced that she only intended to serve one term as she struggled with the Post-Traumatic Stress effects of watching some of her cabinet members beheaded in front of her. The election was Johnson's to take – as long as he could keep the current presidency afloat.

"It gets worse," Bradley said as Johnson closed the file.

"How?"

"The pilot was Senator Wilson's son," Bradley said.

"You're not serious?" Johnson asked as he pulled off his reading glasses and tossed them aside.

Bradley nodded. "Different names due to a divorce, but Wilson is down there right now."

"If he finds out that this was a terror attack…"

"That may be the least of our worries," Bradley said. "There's something else."

"What is it, Marvin?"

Bradley leaned in closer as he looked around the room to ensure no one was within earshot. "Remember how I told you I found out Cal Martin and his girlfriend were in town?"

"Don't tell me," Johnson said as he leaned back in the plush chair and closed his eyes.

"I think they're working for Wilson," Bradley whispered. "My guys have been watching him and he's been at the Senator's office. Yesterday he was at Waxburn's residence poking around."

"Waxburn? Refresh my memory."

"The Air Force One pilot we leveraged," Bradley whispered.

"Fuck!" Johnson barked. Seconds later, a Secret Service agent walked in to investigate his outburst.

"Everything ok, sir?" the female agent asked.

"It's fine," Bradley said with a forced smile as Johnson fumed, staring at the ground. "He just read the report about the mishap last night. Very tragic."

The agent shook her head as if to agree that the loss was very sad. "I heard he had a young daughter and a child on the way. Very sad," she said empathetically.

"Yes, very," Bradley said. "Can you give us a few more minutes?"

"Yes, sir," she said as she retreated from view.

"If he's working for Wilson, he'll be down there with him. They could both ruin us," Johnson said with a look of disgust.

"Don't worry, sir," Bradley whispered. "I have a plan."

"Really?" Johnson asked facetiously. "Because every plan we've ever had that involves that pest usually ends in failure. And like any pest, the only way he'll go away is extermination."

Bradley smiled. "If he goes down to Florida with the Senator, we will be able to kill two birds with one stone," Bradley said with a chuckle. "Figuratively speaking, of course."

Johnson leaned forward, putting both elbows on his knees as he rubbed his temple. "I'm tired of hearing about Cal Martin," Johnson said.

"Don't worry," Bradley said. "The next time you hear his name, you'll smile. Trust me."

CHAPTER ELEVEN

Jackson, MS
1017 Local Time

They had been on the road for nearly twelve hours when they made the final turn onto the narrow gravel drive. The mosque was on a large plot of land in an isolated suburban neighborhood. There was only one road in with large, mossy oak trees surrounding it. There was no good way to do surveillance except from the air, making it an ideal location to regroup.

Trees provided ample shade for the quarter-mile winding driveway. It made for a perfect ambush location, in the event that the infidels decided to attack. Tariq knew that his men had set up sensors and wireless cameras, to give them ample warning and time to prepare for a final battle should the need arise.

Ahmad drove right up to the front of the mosque and parked his truck next to a silver BMW. Tariq could hear his fellow warriors in morning prayer as he got out and walked up to the door. The building appeared to be a two-story structure that had been recently renovated. It looked more like a small apartment complex than a house of prayer, but it was better than anything Tariq had seen in Iraq and Syria.

Ahmad collected Tariq's bags and joined him at the front door. Tariq knocked three times as he peered cautiously around each side of the building, ensuring no Americans were lying in wait. Seconds after he knocked, the door opened. Tariq recognized the man immediately.

"Imam Farah," he said to the portly man standing in front of him. "As-salaamu 'alaykum!"

"Wa 'alaykum assalaam," Farah replied as he embraced his old friend.

"It is good to see you," Tariq said as he stepped back from Farah. "It has been many years."

"Too many," Farah said. "Please, come in and rest. You have traveled far."

Farah ushered them in. Young, fit-looking warriors were just finishing their prayers. Tariq stopped to observe them. Like a field general assessing his troops, Tariq looked each of the eight holy warriors over. They were lean. Some had scars from fighting in Iraq and Syria. Others were fresh faces. They all had very serious looks about them. Tariq smiled.

"Your room is right this way," Farah said as he gestured for Tariq to follow. Tariq nodded and continued on their tour as Ahmad carried his bags. After the victory the night prior, Tariq was very pleased with the way the operation was proceeding. Allah had given them a great victory.

Ahmad stopped at the room and opened the door. It was very spacious with a large bed and nightstand and a private bathroom. It rivaled the amenities he had found while staying in Saddam's palaces in Iraq.

"I hope these arrangements will meet your satisfaction," Farah said with a smile.

"Do you have the supplies I asked for?" Tariq asked.

"Indeed, I do," Farah said. "In the basement, you will find everything you requested."

"Show me," Tariq ordered.

Farah nodded submissively and led Tariq down a narrow hallway. He turned left and guided them to a doorway. Pulling out a set of keys, he unlocked the door and flipped a light switch, illuminating a narrow stairway.

Tariq and Ahmad followed Farah down into the basement. Farah turned the lights on, revealing several large crates with U.S. military labels.

"Everything you asked for, plus additional items," Farah said.

Tariq walked over to one of the crates and flipped it open, revealing several AK-74U rifles. He pulled one out, cleared it with the charging handle, and then pulled the trigger as it gave a satisfying *CLICK*.

"Additional items?" Tariq asked with a raised eyebrow as he put the rifle back in the crate.

Farah walked over to a crate in the corner and opened it. "Claymore mines!" he said excitedly.

"Where did you get this?" Tariq asked angrily as he approached Farah.

"Kaleed got them," Farah said as he cowered. "He said that you would want them."

"I asked for a very specific list of items," Tariq growled. "Kaleed has never been in battle. This will only alert the Americans."

Farah held up his hands and said, "Brother, I understand, but we were very discreet in how we acquired these. The Americans will never know."

"You were foolish," Tariq said, shaking his head. "And so was Kaleed."

"Kaleed has made all of this possible," Farah said. "You would not have been so successful last night without him. Remember that."

"He is naïve," Tariq said dismissively. Kaleed Adid was nothing more than a spoiled child to Tariq. The son of a Saudi prince, Kaleed Adid was the Chair of the Southeastern Division of the Coalition of Islamic-American Cooperation, an organization with great financial reach and influence within the American government. Although Kaleed claimed to be a believer, Tariq knew he was like all of the other Saudis that had come to America – corrupted by Western ways. His involvement was merely a means to an end and nothing more.

Farah frowned. "He is very powerful, Tariq," he said in a hushed tone. "He is not one to be crossed."

Tariq laughed. "You have changed, old friend. Too many years living among the infidels, I think."

"Perhaps," Farah said. "Or perhaps you have been fighting them for far too long."

The smile vanished from Tariq's face. "And who will fight them instead? You? Kaleed? You have no idea what the Americans are capable of!"

"But brother, you struck a great blow to the Americans last night. Their most expensive fighter jet, taken down so easily. They will know that they will never be safe, for we are fierce warriors with a righteous cause!" Farah said as he put his hand on Tariq's shoulder.

"It is not enough," Tariq said. "They must know that no one is innocent in this war. They must know what it is like to lose children as we have. They must know the cost of the wars they wage."

"Allahu Akbar!" Farah shouted.

"Enough of this," Tariq said, waving his hand dismissively. "Let me meet the men. I wish to see what I am working with."

"Very well," Farah said.

He led them back up the stairs and locked the door. They followed him into the main dining area. The men had just sat down to eat, but as Tariq entered, they all stood.

Farah stepped aside as Tariq approached the man closest to him. He looked the man over and then said, "You. What is your name?"

"Muhammed al-Iraqi," the man replied as he stood at attention.

"These scars, where are they from?" Tariq asked, examining the scars and burn marks on the man's face and hands.

"Fallujah," Muhammed said. "Fighting the Americans and last year fighting the Iraqis."

Satisfied, Tariq stepped to the next man. He was very tall compared to the other men. "And you? What is your name?" Tariq asked.

"Siddiqui Ghalib, sir," the man barked.

"And you have fought, yes?"

"I have served Allah," Ghalib replied.

"And you have killed?"

"When it is called for in battle," Ghalib said stoically.

"Is it called for here?" Tariq queried. "Can you kill here?"

Ghalib smiled. "I have been in America for many months now. No one is innocent here. They are all infidels in the eyes of Allah."

Satisfied, Tariq felt inspired to talk to the men about the mission ahead. As he began, however, one of the younger warriors caught his eye. Unlike the others, he was staring at the floor with his hands crossed in front of him. He refused to look at Tariq.

Tariq walked up to the man, but the young warrior refused to acknowledge Tariq's presence. "Your name?"

"Ad... Adam... Faris," the young man said nervously.

"Adam Faris?" Tariq asked mockingly. "That is your name?"

Faris nodded, still staring at the floor.

"Where are you from, *Adam*?"

"New Orleans," Faris said.

Tariq laughed. "An American," he said.

"I am a Muslim," Faris replied.

"I see," Tariq said as he began to pace in front of Faris. "And are you a warrior?"

"Yes, sir," Faris replied.

"Ready to die a martyr?"

"Yes, sir."

"And kill?"

Faris hesitated. "Yes."

Tariq stopped his pacing and lunged to within a foot of Faris. The sudden movement caused the nervous teenager to jump.

"Even women and children?"

Faris was silent. For the first time, he looked up at Tariq.

"I am—"

Before he could finish, Tariq drove his fist into Faris's gut, causing him to double over. As he did, he followed with an uppercut that drove Faris back into the table behind him. Instantly, Tariq was on top of him, his knife drawn and held against Faris's throat.

"Please!" Faris yelled.

"Weakness will not be tolerated," he said as he looked at the men standing around the table. The battle-hardened veterans were all staring straight ahead while the remaining men that had been recruited locally watched Tariq with wide eyes.

Tariq removed the knife from the teenager's throat as he stepped back. Faris grabbed his neck and withdrew his hand, staring at the blood the sharp blade had drawn before collapsing to the ground.

"Know this in your hearts," Tariq warned. "No one is innocent. Allah wills our success. Weakness will not be tolerated."

CHAPTER TWELVE

Eglin Air Force Base, FL
1508 Local Time

The white Air Force C-21 pulled up to the Base Operations building as a Lieutenant Colonel in a green flight suit stood just outside the door waiting. He covered his ears as the military Lear Jet was marshaled into its parking spot and shut down its engines. The door opened and the pilot, dressed in Air Force blues, emerged escorting two men and a very attractive blonde out of the small business jet.

As the Safety Officer for the 90th Test and Evaluation Squadron, Lieutenant Colonel Neal Sharper was coordinating the investigation on the F-35A mishap. He had not stopped working since the crash and was running on caffeine and sheer willpower. From securing the scene, to notifying the family, to coordinating the arrival of the investigation team, Sharper felt like he had been awake for three days straight.

He forced a smile as the trio from the latest dog and pony show approached. The F-35A was already a high profile aircraft, one that had been lucky enough to have zero fatal mishaps as it went through testing. To have a mishap just a few days from being declared IOC was a huge hit to the program, but the fact that it was Senator Wilson's son that had been flying it made it worse.

Sharper believed that Major Ken "NotSo" Long had been a good fighter pilot. He had taken after his dad, a man who had flown F-4 Phantoms in intense combat in Vietnam and lived to tell about it. Although people often poked fun at him for being the son of a Presidential candidate, NotSo was always humble and approachable. He was the true embodiment of a United States Fighter Weapons School graduate and Operational Test pilot.

But what was a tragic loss for a tight-knit squadron was made worse by the attention his father's presence brought to the investigation. It made a relatively high profile investigation turn into a full-blown media spectacle, and Sharper felt like he kept getting thrust into the middle of it, taken away to escort dignitary after dignitary to the squadron. It was exhausting.

"Mr. Marks?" Sharper asked, directing his attention to the most senior-looking man who appeared to lead the way.

"Chet Marks," the man said, extending his hand. "You must be Colonel Sharp."

"Lieutenant Colonel Neal Sharper," Sharper said. "I'm the Chief of Safety for the 90th and will be escorting you to the squadron."

"Sorry, Lieutenant Colonel, this is Cal Martin and Michelle Decker," Marks said, nodding toward the attractive blonde and the man with her. "They will be assisting on the investigation."

Well aware of their purpose for being there, Sharper did his best not to show his distaste. Safety privilege existed, so that the people involved in the mishap could speak freely in a confidential setting without fear of reprisal or sensitive information going public. Introducing unqualified outsiders compromised that principle and the integrity of the investigation process. It also introduced yet another distraction that no one involved needed at the moment.

"Welcome to Eglin Air Force Base," Sharper replied. "You can leave your bags here and they will be waiting for you at your rooms. Senator Wilson is expecting you at the squadron."

"We shouldn't keep him waiting," Marks said.

Sharper led them through the Base Operations building and into the parking lot where a Chevy Suburban was waiting. He hopped into the front seat as Decker, Spectre, and Marks crammed into the back.

The young female airman drove them across the flight line to the brand new multi-million-dollar squadron operations building. Spectre couldn't help but stare at the F-35s sitting under the sun shelters on the nearby flight line. Despite its shortcomings, it was still an impressive fighter.

They followed Sharper into the squadron. It had been two years since Spectre had set foot in an Air Force fighter squadron and even longer since he had done so as a fighter pilot. The last time was in the aftermath of his ex-fiancée disappearing during a routine training mission. That squadron had been equally hectic, but there were at least twice as many people here.

As they passed the operations desk with LED screens and radios, Spectre couldn't help but be nostalgic about his flying days. He missed suiting up and getting the step brief, focusing on the mission. The smell of jet fuel. The sounds of jet engines firing up on the flight line. It was something he knew he'd never experience again. His career had been cut short far too soon.

"Senator Wilson is in the Group Commander's conference room," Sharper said as he led them through the sea of fighter pilots and other personnel. "He asked that you be brought directly to him for the latest briefing."

Sharper led them down the hallway past the large vault door that led into the squadron's vault. Spectre watched as pilots entered and exited, swiping their badges as the secure keypad beeped and turned green. It was where everything happened in a squadron, and Spectre knew a jet like the F-35 was probably much worse when it came to security protocols. Everything about the jet was classified, even down to its maintenance. Spectre wondered just how detailed their brief would be since it was happening outside of the vault and then hoped Wilson could figure out a way to get him cleared in. He was just curious what a two hundred-million-dollar fighter was capable of these days.

Senator Wilson was sitting at the head of the oak conference table talking to a colonel when Sharper knocked and ushered them in. His eyes were bloodshot, but he tried to appear stoic as he saw Spectre and Decker enter. He stood and walked around to greet them as they entered.

"Thank you for coming," he said softly.

"I am so sorry for your loss," Decker said as she hugged him.

Spectre shook Wilson's hand as Decker stepped aside. It was a much weaker grip than the first time they had met. He was weak and probably exhausted. Spectre had been there. Losing someone close was never easy.

"You remind me a lot of Kenny," Wilson said as he looked at Spectre with glassy eyes. "You two would have gotten along well."

"I am sorry I didn't meet him," Spectre replied. "But I am here to help where I can."

"Thank you," Wilson said as he put his shaking hand on Spectre's shoulder. "Please, sit down. I've asked Colonel Ellis to give you full access to the investigation."

Spectre and Decker introduced themselves to the colonel as they sat down. He was also wearing a green flight suit and appeared to be in his late fifties. Ellis stood after the introductions were over and walked to the front of the conference room.

"Good afternoon," he said as he cleared his throat and opened the laptop at the podium. The projector came alive, showing a blue opening slide with the squadron and wing patches bracketing his name. "I'm Colonel Fred Ellis from the Air Force Safety Center. I am the chief investigator on this mishap which will be chaired by Brigadier General Maxwell."

Ellis clicked the mouse, advancing the slide to a timeline of events.

"At approximately twenty-hundred hours local last night, a flight of two F-35A jets departed on a night intercept mission. The flight, callsign Blitz One-One, was led by Major Julie Ward with Major Ken Long as dash-two. They departed normally under Visual Meteorological Conditions to work in Warning Area Whiskey One Fifty-One to complete the last of the F-35A's night validation flights," Ellis said.

Spectre saw the pain in Wilson's eyes as he heard his son's name. He wasn't sure how close they were, given the difference in last names, but he could tell Wilson was not taking it very well. He felt bad for the man. Losing parents and close friends had been difficult for Spectre, but he couldn't imagine losing his only son.

"The mission proceeded uneventfully in the Warning Area, and at approximately Twenty-One Fifteen, Major Ward called Knock It Off and brought the flight home. Major Long followed Major Ward home in a two-mile radar trail formation for the precision approach to Runway Three-Zero," Ellis continued. He advanced the slide, showing the ILS approach to Runway 30 at Eglin Air Force Base.

"At approximately twenty-one twenty-eight hours, Blitz One-One called glide slope intercept at SHYPP, which is five point four miles from the field. According to radar, Blitz One-

Two was established two and a half miles in trail," Ellis said, advancing the slide to show an animation of an aircraft passing over the bay toward the runway with a second aircraft in trail.

"At twenty-one thirty hours, Blitz One-Two keyed up the radio at the same fix, but tower reported only hearing the mic click. At twenty-one thirty and forty seconds, Blitz One-Two disappeared from approach radar," Ellis said as he paused and clicked the slide forward. The slide animation transitioned to the first aircraft landing and the second aircraft disappearing at the final approach fix.

"After several attempts to raise Blitz One-Two, search and rescue assets were scrambled at approximately twenty-one thirty-one hours. The debris field was subsequently located four miles off the coast of Choctawhatchee Bay," Ellis said as he paused to take a drink from a water bottle he had under the podium.

A tear rolled down Wilson's face. Spectre felt for the man and vowed to find answers for him. Spectre knew how hard it could be, not knowing what really happened to someone he loved. It was no way to live.

"Major Long's body was found within the debris field," Ellis continued. "Preliminary indications are that no ejection attempt was made, and based on his communications with approach control, tower, and Major Ward, there is no indication that he had been experiencing an aircraft malfunction at the time of the mishap."

Ellis advanced to the next slide, showing a map of Choctawhatchee Bay with red and yellow shaded areas near where the aircraft went down. "The small red area indicates the debris field," Ellis explained. "And the yellow area is the current search cordon. We have divers currently in the water searching the wreckage and will be removing what we can to a hangar here for processing hopefully by tonight or tomorrow morning at the latest."

"How does this happen, Colonel?" Wilson asked before putting his head in his hands.

Ellis hesitated. Spectre knew speculation was not something a mishap investigator would want to do. Their job was not to speculate, but to gather all of the facts and come up with a valid explanation for the mishap and how to learn from it. But Wilson's status as a Senator was pressure for the colonel to give answers.

"Sir, I can't say for sure at this point," Ellis replied after Wilson looked back up at him.

"Have you ever seen anything like this?" Wilson asked.

"No, sir," Ellis answered.

"I'm pleading with you as a father, not as a Senator or former fighter pilot," Wilson said. "Please find out what happened to my son."

"We will, sir," Ellis said with a thoughtful nod.

"Thank you," Wilson said before turning to Spectre. "This is Cal Martin. He is a former F-16 pilot who has experience with things like this. I want him to have full access to this investigation."

"Sir, we have a lot of experience on this team," Ellis protested.

"I understand, Cal will be present on a not-to-interfere basis," Wilson said, waving his hand dismissively. "But he will have full access. Is that clear?"

"Yes, sir," Ellis replied submissively. "Are there any further questions?"

Wilson looked at Spectre who was busy taking notes from the presentation. "Got anything, Cal?"

Spectre finished writing his notes and shook his head. "No, sir. But obviously Michelle will get full access too, right?"

"Colonel?" Wilson asked.

"We will accommodate whomever you send, sir," Ellis said.

"Good," Wilson replied.

"If there's nothing else, sir, I will have Sharper escort these two into the staging hangar," Ellis said.

Spectre and Decker stood as Wilson nodded. Spectre felt honored that Wilson thought so highly of him to include him in the investigation, but deep down he wondered if he were out of his league. He had never been to Air Force Safety School or conducted a real mishap investigation. He had only barely stumbled upon the truth behind his ex-fiancée's disappearance. And more importantly, every second he wasted away from his real investigation was another that Vice President Johnson had to continue his cover up.

Spectre pulled Decker aside as they exited the conference room. He asked the colonel to give them a moment as they moved out of earshot.

"Do we really want to be spending time down here?" Spectre asked in a whisper.

Decker shrugged. "This is your area of expertise, sweetie, not mine. I will be here to support you with whatever you decide," Decker whispered.

"I just think we should be focusing on what's important. I don't see how I won't just be in the way here," Spectre replied.

"You have plenty to add," Decker said. "You figured out what happened to Chloe. The Senator knows it and that's why he asked you here."

"Maybe so," Spectre said.

"Just observe and see if anything stands out," Decker offered. "If there's nothing suspicious, we'll get back to D.C."

"Fair enough," Spectre said as he leaned in to kiss her. "You're always the wise one."

CHAPTER THIRTEEN

After signing a Non-Disclosure Agreement and being read-in on the classified nature of the F-35A, they were escorted by Lt Col Sharper to the staging hangar where the investigation team had begun its work. There were contractors, pilots, and other investigators busy setting up the investigation area and coordinating the recovery efforts. It looked like nothing but chaos, but Spectre knew everyone there was working as quickly and methodically as possible to find a reason for the mishap.

"Any theories so far?" Spectre asked as he watched a truck full of parts back into the hangar. Crews quickly moved them to the reconstruction area, where pieces of the aircraft had already begun to collect.

"Catastrophic fire? Incapacitation of the pilot? Shot down by a MANPAD? There are a lot of theories floating around, but it's too early to tell," Sharper replied.

"MANPAD? Really?" Spectre asked.

"The tower controller reported seeing the aircraft fall from the sky in a bright ball of fire shortly after NotSo keyed up to report his position," Sharper said. "There aren't a whole lot of things that can cause that."

"I heard something about Daesh claiming responsibility for shooting it down," Spectre said. "Do you think they really did?"

Sharper shrugged. "You know how it is. Anytime any military jet goes down, those lunatics are celebrating saying that they caused it. It's really hard to take them seriously when it comes to this sort of thing."

"But you haven't ruled it out?" Decker asked.

"It's been brought up," Sharper replied. "But that theory was crushed pretty quickly."

"Why?" Spectre asked.

Sharper looked around before pulling Spectre and Decker away from the chaotic scene. When he was sure no one was within earshot, he said, "I don't know if you've been following this program, but it's extremely high visibility right now. A mishap a few days before IOC is bad, but being shot down is infinitely worse."

"That doesn't make sense," Spectre said. "Wouldn't it be worse if the jet crashed due to a malfunction?"

Sharper shook his head. "Not for the latest fifth generation fighter. We've pushed it as the replacement for a lot of platforms. To admit that it could be shot down so easily would be a huge black eye."

"But this jet was on final and landing in Destin, Florida, not Baghdad. You know as well as I do that if it was a MANPAD, there's no jet in the world that could've defended against this. It has nothing to do with the jet. No one could be ready for this at home station," Spectre shot back.

Sharper laughed cynically. "You must not be following this program very well. *Anything* bad that happens to this jet, regardless of its relevance to the program, is considered a program failure. Even flights where we just went out to get test data were considered failures. This is more than just a jet, it's a political monster."

"So, if that really did happen, the Defense Department would rather admit that there's a jet malfunction than consider the possibility of a shoot down?" Spectre asked skeptically.

"I don't know what your background is, but you live in a pretty black and white world, Mr. Martin. Unfortunately, there are gray areas here. It's not that simple," Sharper replied.

"Ok, now I have to ask, what is that supposed to mean?" Decker interjected. "Gray area?"

"He means that they're going to blame it on Major Long if they can," Spectre replied.

"The investigation is still ongoing," Sharper reiterated. "A Safety Investigation Board will look at it very thoroughly, as will the Accident Investigation Board that releases its findings to the public."

"Total bullshit," Spectre said as he looked at Decker. "Same dog and pony show we dealt with when Chloe disappeared."

"Do you fly, Mr. Martin?" Sharper asked.

"Used to," Spectre replied. "F-16s."

"Then you know what I'm talking about. It's the nature of the beast," Sharper said.

"Well, if you don't mind, I'll make my own judgments," Spectre replied.

"Fair enough, Mr. Martin. But I will remind you of the Safety Privilege and Non-Disclosure Agreement you signed. Whatever you learn through interviews or evidence examination must be kept confidential," Sharper said.

"Got it," Spectre said.

Sharper excused himself as his phone rang. Spectre and Decker casually walked around the hangar, taking note of the various stations and people cataloging pieces of debris, taking witness statements, and making notes.

As they stood at the roped-off area where the aircraft was being reconstructed, Spectre noticed a female fighter pilot watching the investigators sort through the debris. She was about Decker's height with light brown hair. Her arms were folded and she appeared to be crying softly.

Spectre and Decker walked over to her. As she turned, Spectre saw her name tag and realized she was Julie Ward, the mishap flight lead.

"I'm sorry for your loss," Spectre said softly.

"Thanks," she said, wiping her eyes. "NotSo was a good guy. He's going to be missed."

"I'm Cal Martin and this is Michelle Decker," Spectre said.

"Major Julie Ward, but I go by 'Psycho.'"

"I'm Spectre."

"What do you fly?" Psycho asked.

"I used to fly Vipers, but I've been out of the cockpit for a while now," Spectre replied.

"And you?" Psycho asked, sizing Decker up.

"No flying for me," Decker replied. "I'm happy to stay on the ground."

"There are so many people here. Are you part of the investigating team?" Psycho asked.

"Unofficially," Spectre replied. "We're just here to take a look around."

"Another one of those," Psycho said, rolling her eyes.

"Another?" Spectre asked.

"There were some suits here earlier. Didn't say who they were working for. Asked a lot of questions. I think they were from the Pentagon," Psycho replied.

Decker and Spectre exchanged a look as they waited for Psycho to continue. He could tell she was thinking it too. Intervention from the Pentagon was a very bad sign. It reeked of Johnson.

"What did they tell you?" Decker asked.

"They asked for another statement from me for the flight, and then they wanted to know if I had seen anything while on final," Psycho replied.

"Did you?" Spectre asked.

"No," Psycho replied. "I saw his jet drop off the datalink, but I didn't think anything of it until I heard the SOF calling for him."

"SOF?" Decker asked.

"Supervisor of Flying," Spectre explained. "Does your SOF sit in the tower?"

Psycho nodded. "He saw the whole thing happen."

"I'd like to speak to him," Spectre said. "Who was the SOF?"

"Blade," Psycho said as she stared off into the distance.

"What's his real name?" Decker asked.

"Lieutenant Colonel Sharper," Psycho replied.

Spectre's eyes widened as he began searching the hangar for Sharper. He had not mentioned it. *Something was definitely going on.*

CHAPTER FOURTEEN

C olonel Ellis had found Spectre and Decker as they searched the hangar for Sharper. He had been instructed by Senator Wilson to retrieve them to accompany Wilson as they took a Coast Guard boat out to the crash site. Spectre asked Ellis if he had seen Sharper, but Ellis could only remember seeing Sharper at the squadron. Spectre didn't like it.

Spectre and Decker piled into the back of a Chevy Suburban as Ellis took shotgun. Another pilot from the mishap board that introduced himself as "Bull" hopped into the driver's seat to take them to the boat launch.

"You ok?" Decker whispered, squeezing his hand as she watched Spectre staring out the window in deep thought.

Snapping out of it, Spectre leaned forward toward Ellis. "Sir, have you interviewed Lieutenant Colonel Sharper yet?"

Ellis turned in his seat to face Spectre. "I haven't, personally, no, but he was the SOF, so he should be on the list, why?"

"I'm supposed to talk to him after I drop you off," Bull chimed in.

"But you've talked to Psycho already?" Spectre asked.

Ellis nodded. "It has been less than twenty-four hours, so we have only had a chance to interview the Mishap Flight Lead since the search and rescue effort became a recovery mission."

"So no one has interviewed Sharper yet?" Spectre asked.

"Not to my knowledge," Ellis replied. "What are you getting at, Mr. Martin?"

"Have you heard any theories about the aircraft being shot down?" Spectre asked.

Ellis chuckled as he exchanged a look with Bull. "Every time a military aircraft goes down, some terrorist group tries to claim responsibility. Of course, it's always a possibility, but for now we're going to focus on what we can piece together."

"Psycho said she was interviewed by a group of suits, any idea who those might have been?" Spectre asked. "She mentioned they might be from the Pentagon."

"Mr. Martin, as you can imagine, this mishap is pretty high profile. As much as I would like a sealed investigation with no outside influence, including political observers like yourself, the reality is that there are going to be many outsiders trying to ask questions," Ellis replied dismissively. "Could be anyone, really."

"But the read-in on this aircraft and the Safety Privilege training was pretty extensive," Decker pointed out. "Surely these people have all been vetted and went through the same process we did, didn't they?"

"Of course," Ellis replied as Bull turned toward the boat launch where several dozen police, federal, and military vehicles were parked. "But that still leaves quite a few people – contractors, civilians, political appointees, AFOSI, you name it."

"AFOSI? They're here?" Spectre asked. AFOSI was the acronym for the Air Force Office of Special Investigations, the criminal investigations division of the Air Force. He had worked closely with an AFOSI agent that had been assigned to the Miami Joint Terrorism Task Force when his ex-fiancée had gone missing in Homestead.

"They send a representative on most investigations," Ellis explained. "It doesn't necessarily mean there's criminal activity, but if there is, they're here to start their investigation concurrently."

Spectre saw Senator Wilson standing next to Chet Marks as Bull found a spot and parked near them. The two were talking to a one-star general and several pilots in flight suits, as well as other men in business suits. Spectre noticed a security detail, keeping watch a few yards away.

"Any other questions, Mr. Martin?" Ellis asked.

"I'd like to attend the interview with Lieutenant Colonel Sharper, if that's ok," Spectre said.

"Very well," Ellis said with a nod to Bull before exiting the Suburban.

Spectre and Decker exited and headed toward Wilson and his entourage. Ellis and Bull saluted the general as they approached the group. Out in the bay, Spectre could see a small barge returning with what looked to be wreckage from the downed F-35. He watched Wilson also notice it and then quickly turn away as one of the pilots continued to talk to him.

As Spectre approached, Wilson turned away from the pilot talking to him and walked over to meet Spectre. "What have you learned?" he asked anxiously.

"It's still very early, sir," Spectre replied. "But I have some leads I would like to follow up on later today."

"Have you been given full access? Everything you need?" Wilson asked.

"So far," Spectre said. "Can I talk to you in private for a second?"

"Sure," Wilson said.

Spectre pulled Wilson aside and looked to make sure no one else was within earshot. "Do you know what other agencies are here, sir?"

"What do you mean?" Wilson asked. "It's a circus here."

"I get that, but what about federal agencies," Spectre said. "Suits."

"I haven't seen any," Wilson replied. "But that doesn't mean they're not here. What are you thinking, Cal?"

"It may be nothing, sir, but I talked to the flight lead of the mission and she said that she had been debriefed twice. The second time was by a group of suits that she thought might be from the puzzle palace."

Wilson shook his head. "No, the Pentagon knows better than to interfere with this investigation."

"Exactly, and from what I remember, usually the Safety Board does the interviews for the safety privilege. She wouldn't have been interviewed twice in a row like that," Spectre whispered.

Wilson frowned. "I'll have Chet look into it. If the DOD is sticking their noses where they don't belong, I'll have their asses."

"Maybe hold off on that for now, sir," Spectre said. "I have my suspicions, but it's early and I don't want to tip our hand. Give me some time to flesh this out. I am going to sit in on an interview later today that may answer a lot of questions for us."

"Ok, Cal," Wilson said. "Thank you for doing this for me. I really appreciate it."

"I'm honored you asked me to," Spectre replied as he put his hand on the elder statesman's shoulder. "I'm sorry for your loss, sir."

"Thank you," Wilson said, looking away. "Listen, I want you and Michelle to join me for dinner tonight. Can you swing by my room at eight?"

"Where are you staying?" Spectre asked.

"Distinguished Visitors Suite, Room 4E," Wilson said.

"We'll be there," Spectre replied before turning back to join Decker as their boat arrived.

CHAPTER FIFTEEN

S pectre checked his watch as Lt Col Sharper strolled into the small briefing room. It was almost 6 PM. Depending on how long the interview took, he and Decker probably would have to go straight from the squadron to meet up with Senator Wilson for dinner.

The crash scene had been sobering. The local law enforcement agencies and Coast Guard had done a good job of cordoning off the debris field, but there still seemed to be aircraft pieces floating everywhere. Despite the sunny skies and a slight breeze that would have made it a perfect day to be out on the water, everyone involved seemed to fully understand the gravity of the situation. They were all working diligently to recover what they could.

From an investigation standpoint, there wasn't much Spectre gained from the trip. He had little experience in actual crash investigations. The debris field didn't tell him much about how the aircraft crashed. It was what he expected for an aircraft flying approach speeds at low altitude.

The theory that the aircraft had been shot down had lingered the entire time they were anchored. It was certainly feasible that a MANPAD had been shot from a small boat in the general area of the wreckage. The shoulder-launched missiles used passive infrared seekers, meaning the pilot would have had no indication that he was being targeted, and at low altitude, there was little he could do to react anyway. Spectre doubted the aircraft even had its missile warning software turned on. There was very little the pilot could've done without changing his flight profile and actively looking for a threat.

They had made it back to the dock just in time for Spectre and Decker to accompany Bull to the squadron for Sharper's interview. Wilson remained stoic, but Spectre knew that it was killing the man inside. Losing his only son had to be gut-wrenching. It motivated Spectre even further to give the man closure.

"You've met Mr. Martin and Ms. Decker, I presume," Bull said as he shook Sharper's hand.

"I have," Sharper said with a smile. "Sorry I had to run off at the hangar earlier, but Colonel Ellis said he found you guys."

"Where did you have to go?" Spectre asked.

Sharper looked away and then at the water bottle in front of him. "Is this mine?" he asked as he picked it up. Bull nodded and Sharper opened the cap before taking a long swig.

"It's hot out there, sorry," Sharper said as he put the cap back on the bottle. "Anyway, I had to run back to the office for a moment. As you can imagine, it's been pretty hectic coordinating all the agencies."

"Of course," Bull said, taking over the interview. Bull placed a digital recorder on the table between them and hit record. "This is Interview Number Four of SIB Sixteen Oh Five. Let's start with your full name, rank, and position for the record."

"Lieutenant Colonel Neal Sharper, Chief of Safety, Ninetieth Test and Evaluation Squadron."

"Lieutenant Colonel Sharper, your testimony is considered confidential and therefore protected by safety privilege. Nothing you say here will go outside of official safety channels and cannot be used for any prosecution or disciplinary actions. All statements are voluntary, do you understand, sir?"

"I do," Sharper replied.

"Ok, sir, what was your involvement on the night of the mishap?" Bull asked, checking off the first item on his hand written checklist he had made on a yellow legal pad.

"I was sitting SOF in the Tower."

"What is that?" Decker asked. "Sorry, not a pilot."

"It's no problem," Sharper said, flashing a smile and a wink. "SOF stands for Supervisor of Flying. I'm the Operations Group Commander's direct representative. I help make flying operational decisions on his behalf and assist in the event of an emergency. I also serve as a liaison between the squadron and the air traffic controllers by sitting in the tower to ensure the airfield remains suitable."

"And this is part of your job as Chief of Safety?" Decker asked as she scribbled notes.

"No, ma'am," Sharper replied. "It's an additional duty for pilots in the squadron. We're qualified in the jet, so when a pilot has an emergency, we can help read checklists, coordinate emergency equipment, and make recommendations. During normal flight ops, we also send the jet status back to maintenance so they know whether the jets are broken or ready to be flown again. Does that answer your question?"

"It does," Decker said as she nodded to Bull to continue.

"In your own words, please tell us what happened," Bull said.

"Where would you like me to start?" Sharper asked.

"Anything relevant from the beginning of the flight to the conclusion of your involvement," Bull replied.

Sharper took another sip of water as he nodded.

"I started at around 19:00 yesterday evening. I did an airfield inspection with the SOF truck as we do every day. Bird status was low, meaning low risk for bird strike. The active runways were clear and free of obvious damage. I made it up to the tower around 19:30. There was only one flight scheduled for the evening – a night intercept flight to complete the required night certification for the jet.

"Psycho – sorry, Major Ward – in Blitz One-One called for words at a few minutes before 20:00. At that time, I passed that the field was green and had no words. The weather was sky clear with unrestricted visibility. Blitz One-One flight took off at 20:00 en route to the area.

"As far as I know, everything went as planned. I don't know the exact time, but at around 21:20, Major Long in Blitz One-Two called in and said both jets were Code One, meaning they were both coming back without any maintenance issues and said they would be landing in ten minutes.

"Sometime between then and 21:30, I heard Blitz One-One call glide slope intercept and the tower controller cleared her to land. They were in a trail recovery, which is standard practice for night operations here. A few minutes later, we heard the radio key up. The controller thought maybe NotSo clipped his call and cleared him to land anyway, but never heard a reply.

"I looked up when I heard the controller say 'Oh my God.' At that time, I saw a glowing fire in the distance. The controller attempted contact on tower, approach, and uniform guard frequencies. I also tried on our ops frequency," Sharper paused and rubbed his eyes as he stared down at the table.

"I knew it was bad. I started the crash response in accordance with our wing instruction. The tower supervisor alerted the Coast Guard for search and rescue as well as local law enforcement, and I contacted Colonel Taylor, the Operations Group Commander, as well as the Squadron Commander and Director of Operations," Sharper continued. "From there I left the tower and continued the crash response protocols as the Safety Officer."

There was a brief pause as Sharper looked at Bull to see if he needed any more of a narrative. Before Bull could finish his notes, Spectre chimed in.

"So the tower controller saw the crash?" Spectre asked.

Sharper took another sip of water and shook his head. "No, not until it was on fire in the water," he said.

"Didn't you tell us the tower controller saw it erupt into a fireball and fall from the sky?" Spectre asked.

Bull stopped the recorder on the table. "Mr. Martin, during the official interview, anything discussed previously is not admissible. The intent here is to gather privileged information, not start an inquiry into the veracity of statements."

"Am I mistaken?" Spectre asked with a raised eyebrow.

"Unfortunately, you are, Mr. Martin," Sharper said. "I may have said that the controller saw a fireball, but it was well after it crashed."

"What's your theory on what happened?" Decker asked.

Bull raised his hand sternly. "You two are interfering now," he said angrily. "Speculation has no business in this."

"Answer the question," Spectre growled.

Sharper took another sip of water and smiled. "It's fine," he said calmly. "It's off the record and we wouldn't want to piss off the senator."

"Well?" Spectre asked.

"Obviously, we won't know until the investigation is complete, but if I had to guess," Sharper said with another dramatic pause. "I'd say it's likely that it was pilot error caused by spatial disorientation. NotSo's helmet and displays probably failed while he was heads down in the cockpit. He didn't have enough altitude to recover and crashed into the bay."

"Are you fucking serious?" Spectre barked as he stood, knocking his chair over. The sudden movement startled Sharper and caused him to lean back in his seat. "What about your MANPAD theory?"

Sharper laughed nervously. "I'm afraid you're mistaken, Mr. Martin."

"He's not," Decker said as she touched Spectre's arm in an attempt to get him to calm down. "I remember it very plainly."

"Ma'am, I've been up since yesterday morning. I have not slept for almost thirty hours. I'm exhausted. I've lost a good friend. If I said something like that, I'm sorry. I'm just very tired and maybe it would be better if we picked this up after I have had a chance to go home and get some sleep," Sharper said softly, rubbing his forehead.

"Bullshit!" Spectre said. "What are you hiding?"

"I'm very sorry," Sharper said, avoiding eye contact with Spectre.

"Have you done any other interviews?" Decker asked calmly as she scribbled notes on her notepad.

"What do you mean?" Sharper asked as he looked up at Decker.

"Have you told anyone else what happened last night? Officially?" Decker asked.

"No," Sharper said flatly as he folded his arms.

"No one from any other agencies?" Decker asked.

"Not at all," Sharper replied.

"What about Major Ward?" Decker asked while nodding her head.

"What about her?"

"Do you know if she talked to anyone else?" Decker asked.

"No," Sharper said.

"'No' as in you don't know or 'No' as in she didn't talk to anyone?"

"She didn't talk to anyone," Sharper answered.

"You're sure?"

"Well, it wasn't my turn to watch her, but yeah, as far as I know she has only talked to the SIB, right?" Sharper looked at Bull who nodded.

"I think we should continue this interview tomorrow," Bull said. "I didn't realize you had been running so hard, Blade."

"Don't worry," Sharper replied. "I'll sleep tonight."

"I think we've heard enough," Spectre said as he turned to walk out. "Thank you for your time."

"By the way, what did you say the controller's name was?" Decker asked as she stood to follow.

"Which one?" Sharper asked.

"The one who saw the fireball."

"Max Simpson."

"Thank you," Decker said as she jotted the name down in her notes.

Decker followed Spectre, closing the door behind her as they left Bull and Sharper in the briefing room.

"Well, that went well," Decker said.

"He's lying," Spectre said as he started toward the door.

"We need to talk to Mr. Simpson," Decker said as she glanced at her notes.

Spectre frowned. "If they haven't gotten to him already. We also need to figure out who has Sharper so spooked."

Decker looked at her watch. "It's almost 7:30," she said. "It'll have to wait until tomorrow."

"What do we tell Senator Wilson?" Spectre asked.

"The truth," Decker replied. "He deserves that much."

CHAPTER SIXTEEN

"We don't have time to go back to the room," Spectre said checking his watch. "Senator Wilson is expecting us in fifteen and it looks like we're on foot."

"It's a nice night for a walk," Decker said as she hooked Spectre's arm. "Do you know where his room is?"

"Shouldn't be far," Spectre said. "It's been a few years since I've been here, but I think lodging is only about a half mile from here."

They walked arm in arm, enjoying the sunset together as they made their way to the Senator's room. The flight line was quiet. All of the jets had been grounded since the mishap. Spectre had learned that the IOC ceremony had been postponed until next week, pending the results of the initial investigation. Although Spectre knew investigators from the Mishap Board were still busily working, the base seemed dead.

"What are you thinking?" Decker asked as she ran her fingers through his hair.

"Someone is busy changing the narrative," Spectre replied.

"Johnson?" Decker whispered.

Spectre shrugged. "Maybe, but I'm not sure why he would care. I don't think he has any ties to this program."

"Conspiracy theories aside, do you think it's possible the jet just crashed?"

"Sure," Spectre said. "Anything is possible. Do I think it's likely? Not really. That debris field was pretty spread out. I think that jet came apart in flight, which supports the idea that it was shot down, especially with no ejection attempt or any hint of a problem beforehand."

"So let's say someone did shoot it down. Why?"

"Well, for starters, they killed Senator Wilson's son and shot down our newest fighter, so that seems like motive-enough for me," Spectre said. "Could be terrorism. Could be someone who wanted to see the program get another black eye before IOC. It looks pretty bad to have the latest fifth generation fighter shot down so easily."

"Then why cover it up? Why go to all that trouble to silence the witnesses?" Decker asked.

"Your guess is as good as mine. This jet is hyper-political. Maybe it looks worse to admit that it was shot down than to call it 'pilot error.'" Spectre held up his hands to make air quotes.

"Well, I agree that Sharper is definitely hiding something. The nervous water drinking, looking away, indirect answers – they were all tells. He's lying and scared," Decker said.

"Well, hopefully no one has gotten to the tower controller yet. We can figure it out tomorr—"

The ground shook as they heard a loud explosion. Spectre stopped in his tracks, they were just a few hundred yards from lodging. Spectre could see smoke start to billow out from the ground floor.

"Jesus, let's go!" Spectre said as he took off in a sprint toward the building. Decker kept pace as they ran toward the fire. As they neared the building, Spectre could see the door and windows blown out from one of the rooms as smoke and fire engulfed the first floor suites. Fire alarms sounded as people began to evacuate nearby rooms. In the distance, Spectre could hear approaching sirens.

They stopped in the parking lot in front of the suites. A group of evacuees had assembled, watching the flames engulf the first floor suite. Spectre counted rooms. His heart sank as he realized the blast had come from 4E – Senator Wilson's room. He turned his attention to the crowd, searching frantically for Wilson or his chief of staff.

"That's the Senator's room!" Spectre yelled to Decker. "Fuck!"

"Look! There's Marks!" Decker shouted, pointing to a disheveled man stumbling toward them. Decker rushed to Marks's aid with Spectre in tow, pulling Marks away from the burning fire as first responders began to arrive.

"Chet, what happened?" Spectre asked Marks as they guided him to safety.

"Bomb... Someone planted a bomb," Marks said, still disoriented.

"Where's the Senator?" Spectre shouted over the sound of sirens and people yelling. "Was he in the room?"

Marks nodded. His hand was shaking as he tried to wipe the blood off his forehead. "We were in his room waiting for you and having a drink. I walked out to get some more ice and when I came back, a bomb went off. It's awful! He's gone!"

"It's going to be ok," Decker said as she walked him to a nearby paramedic.

"Who did this?" Spectre asked. Marks ignored him as a medic took his vitals. Spectre asked once more to no avail. Marks was too dazed to be of any further help.

"What do we do now?" Spectre asked Decker.

"We need to get our bags and get off this base," Decker replied. "I have a bad feeling about this."

Spectre nodded and started jogging toward their building. It was a few buildings over from Senator Wilson's suite, across the courtyard. Spectre heard more sirens as Decker followed. He slowed to a walk as he neared the breezeway at the rear of their building. Rounding the corner, Spectre froze.

In the parking lot in front of their room were a half dozen marked and unmarked police vehicles with their emergency lights flashing. Spectre peered around the corner, seeing military police and men wearing FEDERAL AGENT jackets carrying their bags out of the room.

"Shit," Spectre hissed as he pushed Decker back and took cover behind the wall.

"What is it?" Decker whispered.

"They're raiding our room," Spectre said. "We have to get out of here."

"What?" Decker asked. "Why?"

"Why else? We're being set up," Spectre replied. His face felt flush as the anger grew.

"No way," Decker said with disbelief.

"Yes," Spectre said. "I guess that answers who's behind all of this."

"Where do we go now?" Decker asked. "This base is on lockdown. There's no way we get out."

Hearing agents approaching, Spectre's adrenaline surged. *Fight or flight.* He had run so many times, but never with Decker. They had come so far, but they couldn't run. There was nowhere to run, and they would both be arrested or be killed in the process. He couldn't risk it.

"Ok, let's go this way," Spectre whispered, pointing back to the courtyard behind them.

As Decker turned to walk away, Spectre grabbed her, putting his left arm around her neck as he drew her Glock from its holster. "I love you," he said as he pulled her close to him. "Forgive me."

"Cal!" Decker shrieked. "What are you doing?"

Spectre pulled her around the corner, startling the agents who drew down on him. "Put down your weapons!" Spectre ordered.

The agents stood with guns raised as Spectre inched toward them, ensuring his back was to the brick wall behind them.

"I said put down your weapons or I'll kill her!" Spectre yelled as he held the Glock against her head.

"Cal!" Decker yelped.

"Shut up!" Spectre shouted. The group of military police and other agents all had their rifles pointed at him.

"Drop your guns or she dies!" Spectre yelled.

"Take it easy," one of the agents said. "No one has to die here. Let's talk it out."

"There's nothing to talk about!" Spectre yelled. "Put down your weapons and step away or she dies!"

The agents backed away, keeping their weapons trained on Spectre as he stopped in front of them.

"Let's just calm down," the agent said. "No one has to get hurt. Tell us what you want."

"I want safe passage out of here!"

"That's not going to happen," the agent said. "You killed a senator. Let her go and turn yourself in. No one else needs to die here today."

"I didn't kill anyone!" Spectre yelled.

"Cal, what are you doing?" Decker whispered frantically.

"That's ok," the agent said. "We can talk about that, but first you need to let her go and put your gun down. There's no reason any more innocent people need to die today."

Spectre had heard everything he needed to hear. Pushing Decker forward, Spectre tossed the Glock aside and dropped to his knees, holding his hands out with his fingers spread.

"On your belly, do it now!" the agents barked. Spectre saw one of them grab Decker and pull her away as the others rushed Spectre. He closed his eyes as he felt a knee on his neck and his arms wrestled behind him.

He gave no resistance as they cuffed him and dragged him to his feet. Two men rushed him toward one of the police cars as they read him his rights per Miranda. He looked over his shoulder and saw them tending to Decker. She was crying as a medic looked her over.

Spectre breathed a sigh of relief.

CHAPTER SEVENTEEN

Situation Room
White House
0658 Local Time

"**P**lease, take your seats," President Madeline Clifton said as she entered the room. Her Chief of Staff, Todd Plonski, handed her a folder marked TOP SECRET as she took her seat at the head of the conference table in the Situation Room.

Clifton thumbed through the summary as the Cabinet Members took their seats. Plonski took his place to her left. Attending the meeting were FBI Director Dave Schultz, Secret Service Director Debbie Tucker, Secretary of Defense Chaz Hunt, and Director of Central Intelligence David Chapman. They waited patiently for President Clifton to speak as she finished reviewing the briefing summary.

Closing the folder, Clifton sat back and rubbed her temples. Her Presidency had been one of turmoil, having been held hostage on Midway Island just weeks after her inauguration. Although she had barely escaped, the long-term effects had been devastating. She suffered from Post-Traumatic Stress Disorder and the nightmares of watching her cabinet members brutally executed still haunted her. She had briefly considered resigning the Presidency, but decided it would be best to see her first term through before calling it quits.

But as she stared at the folder, she questioned her decision to stick it out. The negatives of the job seemed to far outweigh the positives. A sitting Senator had been murdered. And although he had run against her for the Presidency, she still considered him a good man and friend on the Hill.

"Where is Kerry?" Clifton asked her chief of staff.

"He's on his way, ma'am," Plonski replied as he leaned in close. "I talked to Marvin Bradley and he said they would be a few minutes late."

"He can be briefed later then," Clifton said. "Director Schultz, what do we know?"

Schultz cleared his throat as he stood. "Well, ma'am, the investigation is still ongoing, but as the briefing indicates, a small explosive device was detonated in Senator Wilson's room shortly before 8 PM local time last night. We have one suspect in custody at this time."

"Pretend I didn't read the briefing, Director. Tell me how a sitting U.S. Senator is killed by a bomb on a military installation," Clifton said impatiently.

"Yes, ma'am," Schultz replied as he reviewed the notes he had written on his legal pad.

"What we know so far is that Senator Wilson was at Eglin Air Force Base in response to the death of his son in the F-35 crash the night before last," Schultz said.

"Hold on," Clifton interrupted as she looked to her Secretary of Defense. "Chaz, do we think these events are related? Didn't I hear something about a terrorist group claiming responsibility for that?"

"No, ma'am," Secretary of Defense Hunt replied flatly. "There is currently no evidence in the investigation to indicate that the reports of terrorist activity are founded. These groups always try to take credit, regardless of whether it's even plausible. The investigation is currently pointing to controlled flight into terrain – pilot error."

"It's not out of the realm of possibility," Director Chapman chimed in.

"Excuse me?" Hunt snapped as he looked to his right at the nation's top spy.

"We have intelligence to suggest that Daesh has been planning an attack against high value military targets as well as soft civilian targets," Chapman said, ignoring the look of disdain from the Secretary of Defense.

"Just as you had intelligence on the attack at Midway, right?" Hunt shot back.

"Enough!" Clifton shouted before Chapman could reply. "Sidebar it for later. Director Chapman, do you have any direct evidence of terrorist involvement at this time?"

"No, ma'am," Chapman submitted.

"Then we will put that theory to bed for now," Clifton said, shaking her head. "Director Schultz, please continue."

Before Schultz could continue, the magnetic lock on the secure door clicked open. Vice President Johnson and his top aide, Marvin Bradley, entered and took their seats next to the President.

"Sorry I'm late, Madeline," Johnson said. "I wanted to verify some information I received before we met."

"What information?" Clifton asked.

"Has the suspect been identified already?" Johnson asked.

"I was just getting to that," Director Schultz said.

"Dave, go ahead," Clifton replied. "You can add your information when he's done, Kerry."

"As I was saying," Schultz continued. "Senator Wilson arrived on station shortly after midnight, a few hours after the crash. The next morning, according to his top aide, he asked for Cal Martin and Special Agent Michelle Decker to join him and sent an Air Force C-21 to pick them up at Andrews."

"Hold on, Cal Martin? As in *the* Cal Martin?" Clifton asked.

"The same, ma'am," Schultz said.

"Why him?" Clifton asked. "I didn't know he had a relationship with Wilson."

"I have that information, ma'am," Johnson interjected with a crooked smile.

"Ok, finish what you were saying, Director," Clifton said.

"Martin and Decker arrived early afternoon with Chet Marks," Schultz said. "According to Marks, they met with Senator Wilson privately and then set out to observe the investigation. They separated for a little over an hour before they joined Wilson and Marks to view the crash site in the bay at which time Wilson invited them to meet him for dinner at 8 PM."

"The time of the explosion?" Clifton asked.

"Yes, ma'am," Schultz replied. "Marks said he did not see or hear from them again until after the explosion when he found them watching from a nearby parking lot and Special Agent Decker helped him seek medical attention."

Schultz paused as he flipped to the second page of his notepad. "Shortly after the explosion, Air Force Security Forces and Office of Special Investigations agents received an anonymous call that there was another explosive device in room 131 of Building 92, a nearby lodging facility. EOD secured the scene and discovered the presence of remote detonators, blasting caps, and C4 residue in one of the bags found in the room.

"While securing the room, agents reported that a white male approached with a female hostage at gunpoint. After a brief standoff with agents and law enforcement personnel, the suspect surrendered and was taken into custody. He was later identified as Cal Martin," Schultz said with a frown.

"What?" Clifton yelped. "How? Why?"

"Motive is not clear at this time, ma'am," Schultz said. "But the room belonged to Mr. Martin and Special Agent Decker. Special Agent Decker said that they had not been in the room since landing at Eglin. Their bags had been delivered by someone else because they went straight to the squadron building after landing. She has been very cooperative and has not been charged yet," Schultz said.

"Why not?" President Clifton asked. "If you believe that Martin was behind this, why not both?"

"Because Martin confessed that he was behind it and Decker had no involvement," Schultz said. "Based on that and the hostage situation, we have no reason to charge her at this time. We found nothing in her bags as well."

"This makes no sense," Clifton said. "Are you telling me that this man went from national hero to murderer in just a few months?"

"Not quite," Johnson interjected. "I have some information that you may be interested in as well."

"What's that?"

"Director Schultz, I hope you don't mind, but once I heard about Mr. Martin's involvement, I called in a request to the ATF. You should be receiving the report soon, but the explosives used in this attack are an exact match to another attack you may be familiar with. One that killed a half dozen law enforcement officers."

"In Miami?" Schultz asked. "Martin was cleared of that."

"I thought so too," Johnson said. "But the ATF says it's an exact match. You should have that report shortly. If I recall, it was never conclusively proven who did it, correct?"

"That's correct, sir," Schultz admitted. "But our agents exonerated Mr. Martin based on the evidence."

"I think we have a pattern here, Director," Johnson said. "I'm sure if you go back to the explosion he was involved with on the boat in Key Largo, you'll find similar results."

"I'll have to look into it, sir," Schultz replied reluctantly.

"So why Senator Wilson, Kerry?" Clifton asked.

"I'm sure the FBI will thoroughly investigate it, but the rumor I heard on the Hill was that Wilson had been using Martin as his own personal investigator to get dirt on people. Maybe Martin finally turned on him," Kerry said with a shrug.

President Clifton let out a long sigh. "So how do we deal with this? I pinned medals on Martin and Decker and now they're implicated in the murder of a U.S. Senator."

"With the truth," Kerry said. "Martin confessed. We can't control what people do when they snap. Let the investigation run its course and I'm sure the rest will come to light."

"Fine," Clifton said. "Does anyone have anything else?"

Clifton waited as the members around the room shook their heads. "Good," she said as she stood to walk out. Everyone stood with her before she exited the room, followed by Johnson and Bradley.

Johnson and Bradley headed to the Vice Presidential office in the West Wing. When they were safely behind closed doors, Johnson leaned back in the chair behind his desk and smiled.

"That worked well," Bradley said.

"The President is still on the fence," Johnson said with furrowed brow. "She'll need more convincing."

"Don't worry, sir," Bradley reassured him. "Marks will point to the tension between the two in the days leading up to this, and his confession seals it."

"Why is he still alive?" Johnson asked. "You said you would take care of both of them."

Bradley shrugged. "We didn't expect him to do what he did, but our guys are very good at what they do. It will all come together soon, sir," Bradley said with a grin. "Martin is not as smart as he thinks he is. His day will come very soon."

"You're sure?" Johnson asked. "Martin has been a thorn in my side for years now. He just won't go away."

Bradley's grin turned to a smile. "Prison is a very dangerous place, sir. I'm sure of it."

"And the girl?"

"Minor setback," Bradley replied confidently. "They'll both be a distant memory by Monday."

"You're a good man, Marvin," Johnson said as his frown turned to a crooked smile.

"Thank you, sir," Bradley replied. "I try."

CHAPTER EIGHTEEN

Jackson, MS
0708 Local Time

The trees lining the gravel road blocked out the rising sun as the lone pair of headlights made its way around the winding road. The four-door sedan bounced along at a leisurely pace as it made its way toward the darkened mosque.

"Comm check," the front passenger said as he pressed two fingers against his inner ear communication device.

"Got you loud and clear, Kruger, how me?" a voice responded.

"Got you same, Coolio," Kruger replied. "How's it looking?"

"No movement," Meeks replied as he piloted the micro-UAV using a secure datalink from his office in Virginia. "One vehicle out front, none anywhere else."

"Copy that," Kruger said. "Keep us updated."

"Will do, boss," Meeks replied.

Kruger adjusted his black tie over his yellow short sleeve shirt and looked at Tuna. "You ready, bub?" he asked.

Tuna looked over and smiled. "I'm just here for the entertainment value of you trying to spread the good word," Tuna said, laughing as he nodded to the Holy Bible sitting on Kruger's lap.

"Stay frosty," Kruger said as he stroked his now-trimmed beard. Qafir and his group were dangerous and had been very successful to date. Kruger was sure that Qafir had been behind the F-35 crash in Florida, and the chatter Meeks had found confirmed it. Somehow, the NSA had done an above average job of censoring their celebration, probably for some political reasons. Kruger didn't really care. Qafir had eluded them for too long.

They had found Qafir's location after one of his aliases was flagged at a rental car location in Jackson. Meeks had used his cyber-wizardry to track Qafir back to the Mosque the day prior. Although they had been too late to stop Qafir in Florida, Kruger intended to put an immediate end to Qafir's trail of terror.

"Looks like they know you're there," Meeks announced. "One contact just walked out the front door."

"Copy that," Kruger replied. The isolation of the mosque posed many tactical challenges. It was secluded in the woods with only one access road that was surrounded by trees. In doing surveillance, they had found fencing surrounding the area and infrared cameras and motion sensors along the fence line. This group was well funded and ready for intruders. Kruger was sure that there were booby traps in the woods as well. It was a tactical nightmare.

Kruger was sure that they could overcome it, but during their team meeting, they decided that the best approach was the most direct. Kruger would have to rely more on spy craft than direct action. He hated it.

"Contact," Tuna announced as they turned into the driveway. A large bearded man was standing near the car Meeks had mentioned. His arms were folded as he watched Tuna and Kruger stop in front of him.

"You've got him," Kruger said to Tuna before getting out of the car.

"Gee, thanks," Tuna replied as he killed the engine.

The man stood motionless as Kruger approached. Kruger estimated him to be at least 6'4" and two hundred and forty pounds. He was dressed in all black. Kruger spotted a handgun printing beneath the man's shirt. He smiled as the man eyed him.

"Good morning, friend. Peace be with you," Kruger said, flashing a smile beneath his reddish beard.

"What is your business here?" the man asked.

"We are with The Mississippi Divine Outreach Ministries Muslim Outreach Program," Kruger said, doing his best to keep smiling as he held up the Bible. "Do you have a minute to talk about our Lord and Savior?"

The man laughed derisively. "This is a Mosque. Do you not see the sign that says no solicitors? Why are you here at this hour?"

"We start our day early, friend, and we have many mosques to visit," Kruger replied. "We just want a moment of your time. Even if you don't wish to hear about God's love for Muslims and the similarities between Islam and the teachings of Jesus, we also like to reach out at community events."

"Are you the Imam here, sir?" Tuna asked. He had positioned himself into a tactical "L" 90 degrees off from Kruger so that the man had to turn away from Kruger to talk to him.

"No, he is inside," the man said. "You must leave now."

"May we speak to him?" Kruger asked, drawing the man's attention back toward him.

"This is private property," the man said. "If you don't leave, I will be forced to remove you and call the police."

Kruger held up his left hand. "Easy, friend. We just want to talk. Perhaps we could make an appointment with your Imam?"

"No appointment! Go!" the man shouted.

Kruger nodded at Tuna. As he started for the man, Kruger immediately shook his head for Tuna to stand down as the large wooden door behind the man opened. A much smaller man with black robes and a turban appeared. His beard was much grayer.

"It is ok, Farah," the Imam said as he walked up to them. "I'm sorry, you must excuse us, but with the Islamophobia these days, we are wary of uninvited visitors. Especially at this hour."

"Imam, thank you for speaking with us," Kruger said, bowing his head. "We only wish to share the good news of Jesus Christ and reach out to you and your brothers and sisters. I am only a humble messenger."

"Copy that, Bravo Team inbound," Meeks said over their earpieces, acknowledging the code word to send in the secondary team that was standing by just outside the mosque property.

"I'm afraid a mosque is not the place for such a thing," the Imam replied. "And even if it were, you would find no one else here at this hour."

"No one?" Tuna asked. He had widened the "L" as they talked, positioning himself to the right of the Imam.

"I'm afraid not," the Imam said. "Morning prayer does not begin for another hour."

Tuna and Kruger exchanged a look before Kruger said, "What about Tariq Qafir?"

The Imam tried to hide his surprise as he and his bodyguard simultaneously stepped toward Kruger. "Excuse me?" he asked, feigning ignorance.

With the two men focused on Kruger, Tuna shot into action, grabbing the Imam in a rear choke with his left arm as he drew his Taser with his right. The prongs fired from the Taser X26 with a pop as they connected with the large bodyguard and dropped him.

Instantly, Kruger was on top of the larger man as his body convulsed on the way to the ground. Kruger pulled out a pair of zip ties and secured the man's hands and feet, as Tuna did the same with the Imam.

"Coolio, give me an update," Kruger said on the tactical frequency as he looked up to see a black panel van speeding toward them.

"No other movement," Meeks replied.

"Copy that," Kruger said as he drew his Glock 17 and stepped over the bodyguard toward the Imam.

"Where's Tariq Qafir?" Kruger growled as he pointed the Glock at the Imam's forehead.

"I do not know who you speak of!" the Imam shrieked as he looked up to see a van stop near the four door sedan. Four men with rifles, body armor, and tactical clothing emerged and headed toward them. "Who are you? Are you government? We have rights!"

"Hit him," Kruger said, nodding at Tuna. Tuna released the cartridge that connected the prongs still in the bodyguard to the Taser and drove the Taser into the side of the Imam as he pulled the trigger. The shock caused the Imam to jerk and yell out in pain. Kruger kept watch through the open door for any others.

As the tactical team approached, Tuna pulled out his Glock 17, handed Kruger the Taser and took up a cover position near the doorway.

"You don't want to do this with me, bub," Kruger warned.

The tactical team stacked up on the front door with Rage in the lead. He nodded at Kruger before kicking the partially open door open and entering.

"It will be much worse for you if they find him," Kruger said as he holstered his Glock and held the Taser in front of the Imam's face.

"Who are you?" the Imam demanded. "Do you have a warrant?"

"Wrong answer," Kruger said, jamming the Taser into the man's neck and squeezing the trigger.

The man screamed out in pain as he tried to jerk away from the electric shock.

"Last chance, where's Tariq Qafir?" Kruger asked.

"He's gone!" the Imam said, trying to catch his breath. "They left earlier this morning."

"Where did they go, dipshit?" Tuna asked from his position of cover as he overheard the field interrogation.

The Imam looked away. Kruger used his free hand to grab the man's face, looking directly into the man's cold, dark eyes.

"I'm only going to say this one more time, bub," Kruger said. "You're a small fish to me. I am only looking for Tariq. But if you don't start talking, I'm going to take you to a very dark place where you will experience pain you can't even begin to imagine. And no matter how strong you think you are, or how much you think Allah will help you, I will make you talk."

"Heads up, local law enforcement picked up a residential burglary alarm call at your location," Meeks announced over the tactical frequency. "ETA seven minutes."

Kruger didn't respond as he heard the warning. He looked into the Imam's eyes, seemingly staring into an abyss of evil. He watched as the Imam seemed to weigh his options.

"Last chance," Kruger said as he tucked the Taser into his back pocket and pulled out the Glock.

"They went to a training compound in Utica!" the Imam said finally. Kruger looked over at his bodyguard, who seemed displeased that the Imam had squealed.

"Where?" Kruger said, pressing the barrel of the Glock into the man's shoulder.

"I don't know!" the Imam replied.

"Three minutes, boss," Meeks announced. "You guys need to get out of there."

Rage emerged with the tactical team as Kruger considered his options. "House is clear, got what we could," he said, holding up a digital camera.

"Ok, let's roll," Kruger said as he removed the gun from the Imam's shoulder and stood.

"What about these two?" Tuna asked.

"Leave them," Kruger said as he went to the driver's side of the sedan. Tuna gave Kruger a confused look as he jumped into the passenger seat and they sped off behind the tactical team's van.

"Seriously?" Tuna asked as they tore down the gravel road, kicking rocks and dust up as they tried to beat the approaching police cars.

"We'll have him lead us to the compound," Kruger said with a knowing smile.

"What makes you think he won't be spooked?" Tuna asked.

"Trust me," said.

As they made it onto the main highway, Kruger's phone rang. He pulled out his in-ear transmitter and answered as he split off from the tactical team van so they could do independent surveillance detection routes.

"Mack," he said gruffly.

"No, sir, we've been working something more pressing, I haven't," Kruger said as Tuna watched for hints. Kruger mouthed 'It's the boss' as he listened to the other end.

"When was this?" Kruger asked as he continued to listen.

"Shit!" he said finally. "Copy that, sir, we'll work it."

Kruger hung up the call and threw the phone down as he yelled, "Fuck!"

"What's going on?" Tuna asked.

"That was Lyons," Kruger said, referring to one of the financiers of their covert mercenary organization. He was the great-grandson of the founder of Odin, an international group that operated outside the rules of governments, financed by Lyons and three other billionaires. Odin consisted of Former American Tier One operators, British SAS, Israeli Mista'arvim, Aussies, Spetsnaz, and even Philippine Special Forces Regiment members.

"Senator Wilson was killed last night," Kruger said. "It was his son that was shot down in the F-35."

"Do we think these fuckers did it? How is that even possible? They were here," Tuna said, trying to make sense of it.

Kruger shook his head. "They don't know who did it, but they know who it's being pinned on."

"Who?"

"Cal Martin."

"Spectre?" Tuna asked.

Kruger nodded and then slammed his fist against the steering wheel. "Goddammit!"

"So what are we going to do?" Tuna asked.

"We have to stop this threat first," Kruger said, shaking his head. "No more innocent lives."

CHAPTER NINETEEN

FBI Fort Walton Field Office
0800 Local Time

Decker grimaced as she took a sip of the black coffee they had given her. Her restraints pulled tightly against her wrist as she brought the cup up to her face. The orange from the jumpsuit they had given her reflected off the stainless steel table. She had been sitting in the tiny interview room for thirty minutes, having made the trip from her isolated holding cell at the Okaloosa County Sheriff's Office an hour earlier.

She was still confused by what had happened at the Air Force Base. She had no idea why Spectre had taken her hostage or what he hoped to accomplish by doing so. If he had at least discussed his plan with her beforehand, she could have told him that such a plan would never work. If his goal were to take the heat off her, taking her as a hostage wouldn't stop them from arresting her as an accessory if their goal was to frame him for the murder of Senator Wilson.

And that was exactly what they had done. After giving her medical attention, she had been taken into custody and processed at the county jail. She had no idea what had happened to Spectre in the interim. She hadn't seen him since the agents had him face down at gunpoint. She hoped he was ok.

It was just like Cal to do something like that. She had seen him time and time again throw himself to the wolves in order to save the people he loved. It was something she loved about him, but it was also incredibly frustrating. She loved him, but she feared it would get him killed one day – if he ever got out of jail.

The agents escorting her had said very few words to her during processing, but the charges were steep, and based on her own experience as a prosecutor and agent, they were in for a long legal battle.

As Decker finished the last of the coffee, she set aside the Styrofoam cup. The room temperature had been slightly elevated, causing her to sweat. They were trying to remove her sense of time by keeping her waiting and ease her tension by affording her basic things like coffee. It was all part of a game Decker had played many times before.

The door finally opened and a short, middle-aged woman appeared carrying a file. She walked with a purpose, brushing aside her short hair as she pulled her glasses down from atop her head and sat down across the interview table from Decker. She pretended to read Decker's file as Decker examined her.

"Michelle Decker," the woman said as she closed the file. "Correct?"

Decker nodded. She folded her hands in front of her on the table.

"I'm Special Agent Barbara Stewart," she said before reaching across the table and grabbing Decker's empty cup. "Would you like some more coffee?"

"I'm fine, thanks," Decker said with a forced smile.

"Very well," Stewart replied. "Let's get started, shall we?"

Decker remained silent as Agent Stewart waited for a reply.

"Well, first things first," Stewart said as she stood and walked around the small table to Decker. She pulled out her keys, finding the handcuff key and releasing Decker's restraints. "All charges against you have been dropped."

"Excuse me?" Decker asked as she rubbed her wrists.

Agent Stewart took her place across from Decker and opened the manila folder she had brought in with her.

"You're free to go, Michelle," she said as she pushed the file across to Decker. "This is a signed confession from your boyfriend. Should you choose to speak to me at this point, any information you give is as a witness. Your cooperation would be greatly appreciated."

"I don't understand," Decker said as she read through the paperwork.

"It's all in there," Stewart replied with a smile. "Overnight, Cal Martin waived his right to counsel and signed a confession stating that he alone planted the device that killed Senator Wilson in his room. Preliminary forensics confirms that it was his bag that contained trace amounts of the explosives used in the blast. Based on his previous history, we believe this is a pretty airtight case."

"History?" Decker asked, still baffled by what the woman was telling her.

"I'm not sure why you're surprised, Michelle, you were part of the case in Florida last year that killed seven law enforcement officers," Stewart said, shaking her head.

"Cal had nothing to do with that! He confessed to that?" Decker asked frantically.

"No, but the ATF has matched the explosives from this event to what they had on file for that one," Stewart said.

"This is not possible!" Decker yelled. "Cal didn't do any of this!"

Agent Stewart put her hand on Decker's. "I know it's hard to stomach right now, but Martin is a sociopath and a murderer. He duped a lot of people, including the President. I'm sorry."

Decker withdrew her hand in disgust. "I was with him the entire time we were on that base," Decker said angrily. "When would he have planted a bomb?"

"You tell me," Stewart replied with a knowing smile.

"He didn't," Decker snapped. "I was with him from the time we landed until the incident. It didn't happen."

"Read his statement," Stewart said, nodding at the report in front of Decker.

Decker angrily picked up the paper and began to read. "What?"

"That's right. Martin knew that Marks was bringing bags for Senator Wilson and planted the device during the flight from Andrews to Eglin," Stewart said smugly. "Your boyfriend is a cold-blooded murderer."

"This is bullshit!" Decker shouted. "You coerced this confession!"

"Calm down, Michelle," Stewart said, holding up her hands. "I know it's upsetting, but let's get your statement and you can get on with your life. Lots of women fall for psychopaths. It doesn't make you a bad person."

Decker stared the woman down. She wanted to use every Krav Maga move Spectre had taught her to shut the woman down, but she knew she needed space to come up with a plan to fix the mess they were in. If they were letting her go, at least she would have a chance to prove Spectre's innocence.

"I don't think so," Decker said after several deep breaths. "I believe I've said enough today. Am I free to go?"

"Criminally, yes," Stewart replied. "But as an agent, not quite."

"What does that mean?" Decker asked.

"The nearest regional office is Jacksonville. I've been asked to drive you there for an emergency administrative hearing scheduled for nine A.M. tomorrow concerning your fitness for continued duty," Stewart said.

"I want to see Cal," Decker shot back.

Stewart frowned and shook her head. "You don't get it, do you? The man is a *murderer*."

"I want to see him," Decker demanded.

"He is being moved to a federal detention facility in Tallahassee today. He can't have any visitors right now. You may be able to see him tomorrow after the hearing," Stewart said.

"I will be his legal representation," Decker replied. "He has a right to an attorney."

"He waived his right to counsel," Stewart said emphatically. "You can't force legal representation on him."

"Fine," Decker said abruptly. "When do we leave?"

"Your belongings are outside. You can use our locker rooms to get cleaned up and then we'll get on the road," Stewart said as she stood to usher Decker out.

CHAPTER TWENTY

Tallahassee, FL
1335 Local Time

They had just turned onto the on-ramp for I-10E when Agent Stewart finally broke the awkward silence. Decker had been sitting in the front seat, avoiding acknowledging the agent as she tried to make sense of the events of the last twenty-four hours.

Whether improvised on the spot or well ahead of time, it was clear Spectre had a plan of some sort. What that plan was still eluded Decker. If he really had confessed, she could only guess that he was doing so in an attempt to keep the spotlight off her. *But why?*

Decker couldn't understand why they hadn't faced the threat together. Why did Spectre think the only way was to pin it all on himself? They were much more effective as a team, and Spectre had vowed to never let them be apart again after the events on Midway Island. She decided she had to talk to him. She needed to see him.

"You're from Georgia, aren't you?" Stewart asked.

"Savannah," Decker said, still staring aimlessly out the window.

"That's a really nice area," Stewart said. "Not too far of a drive from Jacksonville."

"Ok," Decker said curtly, not wanting to get into a discussion with the woman.

"What year did you go to Quantico?" Stewart asked.

"2009."

"2012 here," Stewart said with a smile. "Listen, I'm sorry about what happened."

"It's ok," Decker said, still halfway ignoring her.

"You'll find someone else. I'm sure of it," Stewart added. "You're far too pretty to stay single."

"If you don't mind, I'd rather not talk about it," Decker said.

"Ok, sorry," Stewart said before reaching up and turning up the radio. She switched to AM talk radio as a female newscaster read the latest headlines.

"… Pentagon officials say the cause of the crash has not yet been determined, but denies reports that the F-35 was shot down by an ISIS terror group, calling the claims 'Completely unfounded with no basis in reality,'" the reporter stated.

"You were helping in that investigation, weren't you?" Stewart asked.

"Wait," Decker said, holding up her hand as the reporter mentioned Senator Wilson's assassination.

"Former winner of the Presidential Medal of Freedom, Cal Martin, is the primary suspect in the Senator's death. A spokesperson for the FBI said that Martin was detained by federal agents shortly after the blast, after a brief hostage standoff. It is unclear who the hostage was at this time, but federal officials say Martin confessed to the crime and has been cooperative with investigators. Martin has been moved to a federal detention facility in Tallahassee while awaiting sentencing. For Tallahassee News Radio, I'm Laura Holt."

"Bullshit," Decker said under her breath.

"How long had you two been together?" Stewart asked.

"Long enough to know that Cal didn't do this," Decker snapped.

"So this is coming out now," a male radio host said as the intro to the Walter Matthews Radio Show finished. "Cal Martin... the man who supposedly saved the President's life and won the highest Presidential medal for a civilian... has not only killed a sitting U.S. Senator and former Presidential candidate, but he had a *history* of it, ladies and gentlemen. That's right; the government knew it and gave him access to the most powerful person in the world. And yet here we're wondering how something like this could happen," Matthews said.

Decker reached over and turned up the radio as the radio host shuffled papers and continued.

"Cal Martin was wanted for the murder of seven law enforcement officers in Miami just over a year ago. After a massive manhunt, Martin was located and the charges were dropped with no further explanation or other suspects. This is a report from the Department of Justice, folks. The agent that was investigating this case resigned after the investigation. Why? And conveniently, six months later, Martin ends up on Air Force One while it's forced down on Midway Island," Matthews continued.

"My sources inside the DOJ and Pentagon are saying that the explosives found in Senator Wilson's room and the Miami blast that killed those brave officers are the same kinds of military grade explosives. Now, folks, I'm no expert, but I think we can safely connect the dots here. The man is a serial killer and deserves the death penalty, but this smells of a much bigger conspiracy. Who was he working for? Who else was part of this? We'll take your calls after a brief break. This is the Walter Matthews Radio Show where the truth is king," Matthews said before the music started playing again.

Decker angrily shut the radio off. Stewart looked at her, not sure what to say as she saw the rage in Decker's face.

"I'm—"

"Shut up," Decker growled.

Stewart's pale face reddened as she redirected her attention back to the road. They drove the rest of the way to Jacksonville in silence. Stewart dropped Decker off at the hotel, telling her that she'd pick her back up early in the morning and to call if she needed anything. Decker grabbed her bag out of the trunk and didn't say a word.

After checking in with the front desk attendant, Decker found her room on the third floor. She entered, tossed her bag on a nearby chair, and collapsed on the bed. Tears began to roll down her face. She was exhausted and felt trapped. Despite everything that she had been through with Spectre over the last two years, she had never felt so hopeless.

As Decker drifted off to sleep, a loud banging on the door jolted her awake. She immediately jumped up, searching for a weapon as she considered her options. The banging grew softer as she slowly approached the door, having found nothing to use as an improvised weapon.

Decker cautiously stepped in front of the door as the knocking continued. When she looked out the peephole, her adrenaline surged, and she gasped as she jumped back and braced herself against the wall.

Regaining her composure, Decker checked the peephole one more time. She took a deep breath and opened the door.

"What are you doing here?" she asked.

CHAPTER TWENTY-ONE

Tallahassee Federal Detention Facility
1852 Local Time

The heavy thud of the steel door's lock releasing jarred Spectre awake. He sat up on his bunk as he saw the portly guard at the window. The short nap had been the most he'd slept since Washington. He was still exhausted.

Spectre stepped into the slippers they had issued to him as he stood and stretched. He put his hands out in front of him, wrists touching, as the guard opened the door. In the twenty-four hours he had been part of the prison system, he had already grown used to the routine.

The guard walked in as another guard stood ready to assist in the entryway. He methodically went to work, wrapping a belt around Spectre's waist that connected to arm and leg shackles.

They had treated him well for the most part. The roughest he had been handled had been during the initial arrest. Although he could tell the guards despised him, they had been nothing but professional in their dealings with him. Spectre relied on his military training, remembering his days as a simulated P.O.W. in survival school. He knew that his stay would be much more pleasant if he cooperated, relatively speaking.

"Let's go, you have a visitor," the guard announced as he finished securing Spectre's restraints and grabbed Spectre's arm.

"Who is it?" Spectre asked, trying to sound as humble as possible.

"They didn't tell me," the guard said.

Spectre's mind raced as they led him down the row of solitary cells. He wanted more than anything for it to be Decker. He had no idea how she was or if his plan had even worked. He hoped she understood. In the heat of the moment, he had formulated a plan and stuck with it. It might not have been the best plan, but as Patton had once said, a good plan executed violently now is better than a perfect plan executed next week.

But on the other hand, he wanted her to stay as far away as possible. She was safest away from him and the people he had dealt with. Spectre knew Decker was more than capable of taking care of herself, but it wasn't worth risking her safety and freedom just to see each other one more time. He didn't trust the people he had dealt with to keep their word.

The guards led him out of the pod he had been held in toward another secure area. They escorted Spectre through a series of steel doors that led out of the maximum-security facility where he was being held and into a gated corridor through a courtyard.

Although it was humid and muggy, the fresh night air felt good to Spectre. There was something different and stale about the air inside his tiny cell. It was something Spectre knew he would just have to get used to. It would likely be all he would know for the rest of his life.

They guided him into another building and through another set of steel doors until finally they escorted him into an interview

room. There was a round stainless steel table in the middle with
bench seats on either side.

The guards helped Spectre sit down and then chained him
to the attachment points on the concrete floor. Spectre looked
back as the guard reattached his keys to his belt and then walked
out, slamming the door behind him.

It seemed like hours passed before the door finally opened
again. Spectre looked back over his shoulder, hoping to see
blonde hair as he strained to look around the portly guard that
was escorting his visitor into the room.

His hopes were met with disappointment as a middle-aged
man with dark black hair and blue eyes entered the room. The
man was wearing a suit with a blue shirt and dark tie. He was
carrying a briefcase in his right hand, taking a quick glance at his
Rolex watch on his left wrist as he approached.

He put the briefcase down next to the bench seat and sat
down across from Spectre. He motioned to the guard who
nodded and walked out, closing the door behind him.

Spectre watched the man in silence as he picked up the
briefcase and placed it on the table. He spun the combination
locks and opened it, pulling out a folder before closing the
briefcase and putting it back on the floor.

The man had the appearance of a lawyer, but there was
something about his demeanor that sent chills down Spectre's
spine. He had scars on his face and neck. Spectre could see what
appeared to be burn marks on his hands as the man flipped
through the papers in the folder. He was anything but a lawyer,
Spectre was sure of it.

"Who are you?" Spectre asked, finally breaking the silence.

"That's not important," the man said sternly.

There was something in his voice. He didn't have an accent
of any kind, but in just a few words, Spectre noticed a certain
familiarity of the man's tone. It was monotone, almost like a

tactical debrief. *Military.* The man's chiseled features, obvious scars, and matter-of-fact demeanor screamed career war fighter.

"Who do you work for?" Spectre asked.

"Also not your concern," the man said, still shuffling through the papers. Spectre was now sure of it. He was definitely an operator of some sort.

"Well, alright then," Spectre said with a shrug. "I've had worse first dates, but not many."

The man ignored Spectre as he found the paper he was looking for and slid it across the table to Spectre. Spectre picked it up, confused as he saw the header listing a hotel.

"You're billing me for staying here?" Spectre asked.

"Read the name," the man replied.

Spectre scanned the paper. It appeared to be a reservation confirmation for a hotel in Jacksonville. His eyes widened as he saw Decker's name and room listed.

"What do you want?" Spectre asked nervously as he put the paper down and stared into the man's expressionless face.

"Your cooperation," the man said as he retrieved the paper.

"Well, assuming you work for the same lovely people I met at Eglin, you should know that I'm already cooperating. I gave you the signed confession. You have me," Spectre said. He rubbed his hands together and realized he was sweating profusely. The man across from him was starting to get to him. "We had a deal."

"You're right, Mr. Martin," the man said. "But I'm sure my associates told you that your deal was contingent upon your continued cooperation."

"I'm not sure how much more I could cooperate, sir," Spectre said, holding up his hands. "Here I am."

"You can start by answering a few questions for me. If you are honest with me, your deal will stand. If you are not, I will see to it that you die a slow and painful death at the hands of some very nasty men in ways that can only be described as… graphic. And as for your girlfriend, well…" The man smiled.

"If you touch her—"

The man held up a crooked finger. "Choose your words carefully, Mr. Martin. You don't want to get on my bad side."

"What do you want to know?"

"Let's start with Victor Alvarez," the man said after referencing his notes. "What do you know about him?"

"Who?" Spectre asked.

"Perhaps a name on a piece of paper wasn't good enough," the man said as he pulled out his phone. He unlocked it and swiped right several times before spinning the phone around in his hand and showing it to Spectre. It was a picture of Decker entering her room taken by an overhead security camera outside her room. "Does this make it more real?"

"You mean the Cuban?" Spectre asked. "That *Victor*?"

"Don't play games with me," the man warned.

"He was a Cuban Intelligence agent that convinced my slutty ex-fiancée to steal an F-16 and fly it to Cuba. He was sponsored by the Chinese – or at least that's what he told me. He also killed some people very close to me and also tried to kill me," Spectre said.

"What else did he tell you?"

"Nothing. He told me that some guy named Zhang was his handler. I killed him, by the way. Both of them, actually," Spectre said with a look of satisfaction.

"I'm sure you did," the man said as he took notes. "Who was he working with?

"You mean the assassin? I forgot that asshole's name. Lin. Chin. *Xin* maybe?"

"Did you speak to him?" the man asked.

"Yeah, but it was kind of like this. He was doing most of the questioning," Spectre said with a shrug.

"What did you tell him?"

"Nothing, actually. He wanted to know what I knew, same as you. I killed him too, you see," Spectre said with a sly smile. "Happens a lot these days."

The man looked up and stared Spectre down. "Don't test me. You won't win."

"Oh, no, sir! Not a test. Just cooperating with your questioning," Spectre said.

"What were you doing aboard Air Force One?" the man asked after referencing his notes again.

"Just wanted to congratulate the President in person on her historic victory," Spectre replied.

"Very well," the man said as he put his notes back in his folder and put it back in the briefcase.

"What?" Spectre asked innocently.

"I warned you about cooperating," the man said as he stood. "Perhaps you don't think I'm serious. Maybe your girlfriend will be more cooperative."

"Ok, stop, I'll tell you what you want to know," Spectre said.

"It's too late, Mr. Martin," the man said as he started to walk out. "I'll come back in a few days when you've had some time to reconsider your options."

"What does that mean?" Spectre asked.

"Don't worry, Mr. Martin, I have no doubt that you'll cooperate eventually," the man said. As he walked toward the exit, he suddenly stopped behind Spectre and leaned in. "Brick by brick, I'm going to tear your walls down until you tell me everything I want to know."

Spectre's eyes widened as the man's words hung in the air. Spectre had used those same words in his confrontation with Vice President Johnson during the awards ceremony at the White House. It was no coincidence that the man was now using those words against him.

"Who are you working for?" Spectre demanded as he turned to face the man standing at the door.

The man ignored him as he knocked on the door. A few seconds later, the door opened and the man exited. The same two guards as before walked in and unchained Spectre from his position at the table.

They escorted him out of the interview room. The man was standing just outside the door as they walked Spectre out. He stopped talking to the guard next to him as Spectre eyed him.

"I hope you'll enjoy your new accommodations," the man said with a wry smile. "I'm looking forward to our next chat."

"Fuck you," Spectre grunted under his breath as they continued through a set of steel doors.

CHAPTER TWENTY-TWO

Jaguar Sports Bar and Grill
Jacksonville, FL
1903 Local Time

"I'll admit, you were the last person I thought I would run into here," Decker said as she handed her menu back to the waiter and turned her attention to the lanky man with horn-rimmed glasses sitting across from her.

Carl Simms took a sip of his water and nodded. "You and me both," he said. "When I saw you in the lobby, I had to do a double take. But then the desk agent confirmed it was you. So I had to talk to you."

"What are you doing in Jacksonville?" Decker asked. "Last I heard, you left the Bureau."

"I did," Simms said. "Moved back to Ohio and reopened my old accounting firm in my hometown. After what happened in Tampa with your boyfriend, I was more than happy to go back to crunching numbers. I certainly didn't expect to be recalled."

"Recalled?" Decker asked.

"Martin saved my life," Simms replied. "I don't know what he has gotten himself into this time, but I don't think he's the monster they're making him out to be."

"Why were you recalled?" Decker asked again.

"I was the agent in charge of his investigation in Florida and Louisiana," Simms said before pausing to thank the waiter delivering their appetizers. "I cleared him of all charges before I left. They flew out this morning and picked me up – said I needed to go over the new case with the new agent in charge. It's kind of high priority since it was a sitting U.S. Senator, you know?"

Decker lost her appetite as she listened to Simms. Whoever was behind the attack was pulling out all the stops to bury Spectre. Although she had never gotten along with Simms while trying to save Spectre from Simms's hard-nosed approach, she believed Simms genuinely cared about doing the right thing. She didn't quite trust him, but she didn't feel like he was necessarily an enemy either.

"What did they tell you?" Decker asked.

Simms inhaled a cheese stick before washing it down with the light beer he'd ordered. He held up a slender finger as he drank. "Your boyfriend confessed to killing a sitting U.S. Senator using the same type of explosive we found in Homestead."

"I've heard that a thousand times already. Didn't happen. What else?" Decker asked.

"Easy," Simms said in response to Decker's terse tone. "I didn't say I believed it. You just asked what they told me. They sent the Director's plane to pick me up. This case has gotten traction all the way to the White House. They want closure as soon as possible. I think you're in their crosshairs too."

"Why do you say that?" Decker asked.

"First, you tell me why you're in Jacksonville," Simms said with a grin.

"Emergency administrative hearing tomorrow morning," Decker said.

"Exactly!" Simms replied. "I overheard them talking about yanking someone's credentials on the drive from the airport to the rental car place. I didn't even think about it until I saw you in the lobby."

"I really don't care about the agency anymore," Decker said snappily. "I've got more important things to worry about."

"Fair enough, but I don't think they'll be happy with that," Simms said.

"What does that mean?"

"Martin is an easy scapegoat. Even though my investigation conclusively proved that he had nothing to do with the bombings in Florida, they'll reopen it and link the two. And from what I understand through the news, he confessed anyway. They're going to bury him in charges and give him the death penalty," Simms replied.

Decker cringed. The visual of Spectre being executed sent chills down her spine. After all they had been through together, she just couldn't let that happen.

"I never read your report," Decker said as she shook off the image of Spectre and lethal injection. "What was your conclusion?"

"First report or the final report?"

"What?" Decker asked. A waiter delivered their entrees. Decker ignored the sizzling fajitas in front of her as she waited impatiently for Simms to explain. "Two reports?"

"My initial report included everything – how we tracked him to Louisiana, our captivity in Tampa, and even your role," Simms explained as he cut into his steak. "It was a fairly detailed and thorough report. One of my best."

"What changed?"

Simms shrugged. "Fields kicked it back. He said it was too speculative and told me to chop it down. I did, but it wasn't good enough. He chopped it down for me, taking out everything involving the Chinese and Tampa. It was turned into a skeleton report."

"What about the farmhouse explosion in Homestead?" Decker asked. Special Agent Fields was the Special Agent in Charge for the Miami office. He had been Decker's boss her entire time in Miami.

"You mean what did the final report say? It said the cause of the blast was unknown," Simms said before finishing his steak.

Decker's meal remained untouched as she listened to Simms. "How long after I got out of the hospital did this happen?"

"Six months, maybe more," Simms said. "It was around January. That's what held me up from getting out. They put me in an administrative position until the report was finalized and approved. It took me a month to get it all together once I finished my treatment and physical therapy. It was a big case."

"So when did they kick it back the first time? What month?"

"Well, let me think," Simms said as he downed the rest of his beer. "I guess it was probably early November maybe."

"After the election?"

"Yeah, that sounds right," Simms said with a shrug. "Why?"

"No reason," Decker said. "Are you ready to go?"

"You didn't even touch your food," Simms said, eyeing her plate. "Do you want to get it to go?"

"No, I'm fine," Decker said.

"Ok, I'll get the check," Simms said. "I can expense this meal. You need someone to do your taxes, right?"

Simms paid for the meal and then walked Decker out of the restaurant. As they made it to the gravel parking lot, the hair on the back of Decker's neck was standing up. She couldn't put her finger on it, but something just didn't feel right.

Decker looked around cautiously as they approached the car. There was no one else around, but the feeling just wouldn't go away.

"What's wrong?" Simms asked as he stopped at the driver's door of his rental sedan.

"Are we being followed?" Decker asked as she looked around.

"I don't think so," Simms said as he opened the door. "Maybe you just need to get some rest."

"Do you have a weapon in the car?" Decker asked, still standing at the passenger door.

"How would I? I'm just an accountant now, remember?"

Decker continued her scan around the parking lot and nearby street. Nothing seemed out of place, but her intuition told her something was very wrong.

"Can we go now?" Simms asked impatiently.

"Do you mind if I drive?" Decker asked.

Simms stepped out of the driver's side and handed Decker the keys. "If it means we can finally leave, sure."

Decker started the car. Simms took his place in the passenger seat and buckled in. After adjusting her mirrors, Decker pulled out of the parking lot and made a left, watching her mirrors as she drove slowly down the side street.

Reaching a stop sign, Decker came to a complete stop, still watching her mirrors before she made a right turn. As she turned onto the four-lane road, Decker picked up a white SUV behind them.

"What is it?" Simms asked as he watched Decker.

"Not sure," Decker said. She made another right onto a side street back toward the parking lot. As she reached another stop sign, she saw the same white SUV at a distance behind her turning onto the same street.

"We're being followed," Decker said as she turned back toward the four-lane road to her right and punched it. With the pedal to the floor, Decker accelerated through eighty on the four-lane road. Approaching the interstate on-ramp, Decker eased slightly as the tires screeched and the back end of the car kicked out briefly.

"Oh shit!" Simms screamed as he grabbed the handle above his head. "Not this again!"

Decker ignored him as she floored the throttle again while looking for the SUV. It had given up the pretenses and was now struggling to keep up with the faster sedan as Decker pushed it past one hundred twenty miles per hour.

"Where are you going?" Simms yelped. "The hotel is the other way!"

"We're not going back there," Decker said as she merged onto I-95S and lost the SUV tailing them.

CHAPTER TWENTY-THREE

Utica, MS
0141 Local Time

The team moved slowly in single file through the thick brush and trees, barely illuminated by the half-moon that helped their Panoramic Night Vision Goggles turn the dark night into a monochrome green day.

Their objective was buried deep within the Mississippi woods, accessible only by a small dirt road that snaked for two miles from the main highway. They approached from the east, having found an access road to an adjacent abandoned property that gave them a quarter mile hike to the compound.

"Two tangos, north and south side of the house, stationary," Meeks announced over their tactical frequency. He was piloting the micro-UAV that Tuna had launched from his backpack shortly before the six-man team began their trek into the dark woods. The remotely piloted aircraft's infrared camera had picked up two men guarding the main structure.

"Copy," Kruger said as he continued to lead the team of operators toward the objective.

Reaching a group of fence posts, Kruger stopped and took a knee as he held up a fist. His teammates took up defensive positions as Kruger examined the five-foot tall barbed wire fence in front of him.

He looked for motion sensors or cameras on the posts and indications of buried mines in the nearby vicinity. When he was satisfied there were none, he pulled out a pair of snips from his bag and went to work cutting the wires so the team could continue through. Kruger could see a clearing and light from the main building just a hundred or so yards ahead.

Kruger raised his hand and pointed with two fingers to the left. Per their pre-mission briefing, Rage took Axe and Cuda with him to the south as Tuna and Beast followed Kruger to the north side of the compound.

The north side of the compound looked much like the compound they had raided in Iraq while searching for Qafir. It had several paper targets set up throughout the compound, a physical training area, and what appeared to be a burn pile. There was also a shell of an old school bus, its front door had been removed, and it was sitting on its axles.

Kruger found the northern guard as he made his way through the tree line. The man was leaning against the side of the house, smoking a cigarette. Kruger picked up a loose tree limb with his left hand while keeping his suppressed H&K 416 rifle up with his right as he watched the oblivious guard.

"South tango down, Bravo Team in position," Rage announced, indicating he had dispatched the guard at the front entrance of the house. His team had moved to the west side of the house. It was where they had found a diesel generator powering the compound during their limited aerial reconnaissance earlier in the evening.

"Alpha One copies," Kruger said as he snapped the tree limb, causing the north guard to turn toward him.

Kruger waited. The man approached slowly and walked toward an inner perimeter metal fence with his rifle up and pointing at the tree line. After dropping the limb, Kruger brought his left hand up to steady his aim, and dispatched three subsonic rounds into the man's chest as he walked forward out of the tree line.

"North tango down," Kruger said as the man crumbled in front of them. Kruger opened the waist-high metal gate and sidestepped the man's body as they moved to the house and stacked up on the northern door. After clearing the rear, Beast tapped Tuna's shoulder. Tuna, in turn, squeezed Kruger's shoulder with his left hand to indicate they were ready to move.

"Execute," Kruger said in a low tone over the tactical frequency. Seconds later, Kruger heard the diesel generator die and saw lights in and around the single story house go out.

With his rifle up, Kruger pushed open the door and bolted in. Tuna stayed close on his heels, peeling off to the right as Kruger and Beast went left to clear the immediate entryway. They were in what looked to be a planning room of some sort. There were corkboards with pictures and maps on the walls and chemical bottles strewn about.

Kruger continued forward, turning right down a hallway. A man exited, seemingly confused by the power outage, but unaware of Kruger's presence. Kruger fired two rounds, hitting the man in the center of the chest and throat and causing him to collapse.

The team stepped over the lifeless body and stopped at a closed doorway. Kruger and Tuna each took a side of the door while Beast covered the hallway. After a silent countdown, Tuna opened the door and Kruger entered, button-hooking left as Tuna went right this time.

As Tuna entered, he came face to face with a man who fired wildly toward the door. The rounds missed, but Tuna shot twice, hitting the man center of mass. Tuna and Kruger finished clearing the room and ID'd the corpse before moving back out to the hallway. *Negative contact.*

As they entered the hallway and continued toward the next room, the door opened and a man appeared. Kruger instantly recognized Qafir. He was holding a Glock 17 against his head as he walked toward them.

"Drop your weapon!" Kruger shouted. He wanted very badly to put a bullet in the man's head, but he knew Qafir was planning something much worse than the F-35 attack. He was worth more alive than dead – at least until they could figure out what he had planned.

"You are too late, infidels," Qafir said with a wicked laugh. "The hour of vengeance for the sins of your people is upon us. Your children will burn as you have burned the children of Allah for so many decades."

"Drop it!" Kruger said.

"Allahu Ak—" Qafir said as he started to squeeze the trigger.

Before he could finish, Kruger fired, hitting Qafir in the shoulder with a suppressed round. The hit forced Qafir to drop his weapon just as he pulled the trigger. The 9MM round narrowly missed Qafir's head as the Glock fell to the ground and Qafir screamed out in pain.

Tuna was instantly on top of him, flipping Qafir onto his belly and Flexcuffing his hands behind his back before he could present a struggle. Qafir screamed out in pain as Tuna dragged him to his feet.

"You will never defeat the Islamic State!" Qafir yelled defiantly. Without warning, Beast sent his rifle butt crashing into Qafir's nose, causing it to gush with blood as the defiant terrorist yelped in pain.

"West side of the house is clear," Rage announced over the tactical frequency.

"Copy that, we have one in custody, coming out the front door," Kruger replied on the radio.

As they walked out into the night air, Kruger and his team regrouped with Rage.

"We took down two," Rage said.

"And our three makes five," Kruger said.

"Shouldn't there be more?" Rage asked.

Before Kruger could answer, he looked back to see Qafir suddenly wrestle away from Tuna's grip and take off in a sprint toward the north side of the house.

As the team gave chase, they heard Qafir yell "Allahu Akbar" and then watched him jump forward into the spiked metal fence that surrounded the house.

Tuna caught up to Qafir first and tried to pull him off the fence. As he did, he realized that Qafir had managed to impale himself on the metal spikes, having driven one of them through his neck. Qafir's body seized violently as blood gushed everywhere. With the help of Rage, Tuna tried to pull him off to resuscitate him.

"He's dead," Tuna said as he knelt over Qafir's lifeless body after giving up on CPR.

"Fuck!" Kruger yelled. Qafir's lifeless eyes were still open, almost staring through Kruger as he tried to come up with another solution. Their only hope of figuring out Qafir's plot was dead.

"Fuck him," Rage said, spitting on Qafir's body.

"We need to get whatever Intel we can find out of that house. There's a mockup of a school bus in the back. We need to figure out what their target is," Kruger said as his fists clenched with anger.

They returned to the house. Beast turned the generator back on, giving them light as they scoured the house for intel.

Kruger returned to the first room where he had seen the corkboards with maps.

With the light on and his night vision goggles off, he could see maps of Louisiana, Mississippi, Tennessee, and Texas. There was a diagram of a mall somewhere near the Mississippi-Tennessee border and hundreds of school schedules.

They had found a treasure trove of information, but without Qafir, Kruger knew they had little chance of identifying probable targets before it was too late. They had reached a dead end at the worst possible time.

CHAPTER TWENTY-FOUR

Tallahassee Federal Detention Facility
0515 Local Time

"Wake up, princess!" a booming voice said as the cell door was flung open. Spectre's eyes fluttered open. He felt like he had just barely fallen asleep after a night of tossing and turning on the non-existent mattress.

"Hands together," the guard ordered as he grabbed Spectre. He complied, clasping his hands in front of him as the guard went to work putting the chain belt around Spectre that secured his hands and feet.

"What's going on?" Spectre asked, trying to regain his senses.

"You've been transferred," the guard replied. "Congratulations, you're going to Level Three."

"What does that mean?" Spectre asked as the guard guided him out of his cell and a second guard shut the door behind them.

"It means you're going to make some new friends today," the guard said with a knowing smile. "No more solitary unless you don't behave yourself."

"Great," Spectre said. He had been expecting something similar since his mysterious interrogator had made thinly veiled threats for not cooperating during their interview, but when they took him back to his cell, he thought he might have been mistaken. Solitary confinement was good for Spectre's continued survival. Being mixed amongst the general population, where anyone could be working for Johnson and his goons, was not.

"Don't worry, you'll love your new roommate," the guard said.

They guided him out of his pod and back into the courtyard. It was still dark out. Spectre still looked for possible avenues of escape out of habit. If he were to attempt an escape, it wouldn't be easy. There were multiple rows of fences with coiled barbed wire and signs that Spectre was pretty sure indicated an electric current running through the fencing. It would take a much higher level of resourcefulness to escape.

After passing through the empty courtyard, the guards stopped and swiped their access badges on the building marked LEVEL THREE. Entering through two sets of doors, Spectre found a lone guard sitting at a control station. His escorts said something to the man before another set of doors opened.

Unlike the pod he had previously called home, this one had an open area in the middle of the two-man cells. It had stainless steel tables and LED TVs on the walls. It appeared to be much less restrictive than his old accommodations.

The guards led him up a flight of stairs to the third level and stopped him in front of his new cell. Spectre heard a buzz and a metallic click as the guard sitting at the control station released the lock. The guard opened the door and turned the light on, revealing a set of bunk beds on one side and a desk on the other with a toilet in the corner of the room. Compared to his last cell, it was much more spacious.

"Antonio, wake up," the guard said as the man in the top bunk stirred. "You have a new roommate."

Antonio slowly sat up and slid down from his bed. Out of habit, he assumed a position of attention with his hands together in front of him. His eyes were barely open as he waited for the guards to restrain him.

The guards walked Spectre into the room and started releasing his restraints. Spectre watched Antonio. He appeared to be in his late forties with jet-black hair and gray streaks on either side. He was a few inches shorter than Spectre, but appeared to be in good physical condition. Spectre noticed a spider tattoo on the man's lower neck, and multiple other tattoos on his arms.

"Antonio, this is Cal. Cal, Antonio" the guard said. "You two kids have fun. Breakfast is in an hour." The guard left, closing the door behind him.

"Top bunk is mine, don't touch my things," Antonio said as he returned to the top bunk.

Spectre didn't bother setting up his bed. Instead, he just crawled into the narrow space and rested his head against the folded pillows and blankets, lying awake as he waited for the breakfast notification. He knew there was no way he could sleep for an hour with Antonio above him.

Antonio began to snore as Spectre lay silently. His mind began to wander back to Decker. He wondered how she was doing. He hoped she understood what he had done.

It had been a split-second decision. After seeing the agents raiding their room, Spectre knew they were there to frame the bombing on them, and being on a military base, there would be no escape – at least not without killing more innocent people. They had Spectre and Decker cornered.

So Spectre improvised. It wasn't the best of plans, but it was the only plan he could think of to take the heat off Decker. He would take her hostage and then confess to whatever they wanted him to, as long as Decker was let off the hook. At least that way, she still had a chance to take Johnson down and put an end to his reign of terror. They would be helpless if they both went to prison. In Spectre's mind, it was the only way.

Surprisingly, it had worked. The agents questioning him were more than willing to go along with it. Spectre was sure at least a few of them were reporting directly to Johnson. They seemed less interested in finding out what happened and more interested in putting Spectre away. So he made a deal – full confession for Decker's freedom.

But what Spectre hadn't considered was that they didn't just want them dead, they wanted to know what information Spectre and Decker had on Johnson. That was what the man in the interrogation room had been fishing for. They needed to know just how much Spectre and Decker knew so they could perform damage control and bury the damning information. Spectre had played it off, but he knew it wouldn't last long. They would eventually lose their patience and try to kill them anyway.

As Spectre started to drift off to sleep, an alarm sounded, followed by a public address system announcement that inmates were to report to the chow hall for breakfast. The doors clicked open as the announcement was repeated.

Antonio descended from his bed and put on his slippers. "You coming to breakfast or what?"

"Yeah," Spectre said as he did the same.

"Where you from?" Antonio asked as Spectre followed him out of the cell and they both fell in line toward the cafeteria.

"Louisiana," Spectre said. He kept his head on a swivel, watching each inmate's hands as he looked for improvised weapons.

"I like New Orleans," Antonio replied as he casually walked in front of Spectre. "I'm from Arizona. This your first stint?"

"Yeah," Spectre said softly.

"You gotta be careful here, man," Antonio said. "It's not the worst joint I've ever been in, but there are some groups you gotta watch out for. Especially a guy like you."

"A guy like me?" Spectre asked, still alertly keeping track of every inmate around him.

"Pretty boy," Antonio said as he turned back to wink at Spectre. "You ain't hard and people can smell it. It's the law of the jungle in here, man."

"I can hold my own," Spectre said as they walked into the cafeteria. Spectre could feel the eyes upon him as he grabbed his tray and got in line.

"Everybody thinks that," Antonio said with a chuckle. "I know I did too at first. But there are some bad dudes in here. Real bad."

"Are you one of them?" Spectre asked as he eyed the watery slop on his plate and continued moving with the line.

"Nah, son, I'm cool," Antonio replied. "I got Jesus. You saved?"

"Me?" Spectre asked. "I think God's been sitting the last few plays out."

"We can work on that," Antonio said.

Spectre followed him to a table and sat down across from him. He downed the milk and then went to work on the food. As bland as it was, he was still hungry and knew that he'd have to keep his energy up if he expected to survive in this place.

"You see that guy getting milk over there?" Antonio said, nodding to his left.

"The big bald-headed guy?" Spectre asked. The man appeared to be over 6'4" and solid muscle. He could've been an NFL linebacker, Spectre thought.

"Yeah, that's DeSean," Antonio said. "He runs one of the gangs in here. You don't want to get on his bad side. And if he wants to make you his bitch, you do it. No questions."

"Noted," Spectre said.

"Lucky for you, though, he doesn't usually like white dudes," Antonio said. "But *he* does."

"Who?" Spectre asked.

Antonio nodded behind Spectre. He turned around to see a much shorter Hispanic man with face tattoos walk in surrounded by a group with their pants sagging down. "Him?" Spectre asked.

"That's Jorge. Be careful around him," Antonio whispered. "They all have shanks, but if you need a score, they're the dudes to go to."

"A score?"

"Cigarettes. You smoke?"

"I thought that wasn't allowed here," Spectre said.

"There are a lot of things not allowed here," Antonio said. "Doesn't mean much."

"Can you get me a cell phone?" Spectre asked.

"Can it be done? Yes. Can I? No," Antonio said, shaking his head. "But I know who can."

"Jorge?"

Antonio shook his head again and lowered his voice to a whisper, "You're going to want to talk to the Italian. He can get anything. He's got connections."

"Where can I find him?" Spectre asked.

"I'll introduce you later," Antonio said. "You ready to go?"

"Sure," Spectre said.

Spectre followed Antonio to turn in his tray. As they turned to walk out, Antonio froze. "Shit," he hissed as he turned back to face Spectre.

"What?"

"Skinheads," Antonio said in a hushed tone.

Spectre looked up to see a group of three pasty white men walk in. Their heads were shaved and the apparent leader had a tattoo of a swastika on his face. He appeared to be of average height and build. Spectre didn't see what the problem was.

"Those guys?" Spectre asked.

"Yes!"

"What about them?"

"They can't see me!"

"Why?"

"Let's just say I got into it with one of them yesterday talking about Scripture in the yard and they want payback," Antonio said nervously. "Plus they hate Cubans."

"You'll be fine," Spectre said. "They won't do anything here."

The group noticed Antonio and eyed him as he and Spectre walked toward the exit they were standing near. Antonio looked away, trying to avoid eye contact.

"What are you looking at, nigger lover?" one of the minions said.

"What?" Spectre asked as he stopped a few feet from them.

"You're a traitor to your own kind, hanging out with *him*," the skinhead replied.

"He's Cuban!" Spectre replied.

"Ok, wetback lover then," the skinhead replied. "You're still a traitor."

The apparent leader held up his hand. "Now, boys, that's no way to treat a newcomer. We are all God's children here," he said with a thick southern accent.

"That wetback was talking shit to me yesterday," the other skinhead said.

"I'm sorry," Antonio said, still avoiding eye contact. "I am sorry."

"What's your name, friend?" the leader asked.

"Cal Martin," Spectre replied brusquely.

"That's a nice southern name, Calvin. I'm Harlan Montgomery and these here are Jimmy Edwards and Tanner Crowe, pleased to meet you," Harlan said as he extended his hand.

Spectre looked at Harlan's extended hand and then back at Antonio who shook his head subtly.

"We can be friends, can't we?" Harlan asked, looking at his hand.

Spectre shook Harlan's hand. Harlan flashed a smile, showing his stained teeth as he stared down Spectre.

"If I catch you with this nigger again, I'm going to shank you myself, do you understand, boy?" Harlan asked. His grip suddenly tightened around Spectre's hand.

Spectre tried to pull his hand away, but Harlan's grip tightened.

"Do you understand, boy?" Harlan asked as his two lackeys started laughing hysterically.

"Since we're friends and all, I'm going to give you the chance to let go of my hand and take back the mean things you said about my friend Antonio," Spectre said, holding eye contact with Harlan.

The laughter suddenly stopped. Harlan's grip loosened slightly as he sized up Spectre. "Is that a threat, boy?"

"Try me," Spectre replied.

Harlan squeezed down on Spectre's hand as hard as he could as he lifted up his shirt, revealing an improvised knife in his waistband.

As Harlan started to speak, Spectre grabbed Harlan's hand with his left and tightened his own grip. With a secure grip on Harlan's right hand, he shot forward, pushing Harlan's hand upward as he stepped underneath it and turned, snapping Harlan's wrist as Spectre spun around to face Harlan and twisted his hand around. Harlan screamed out in pain before Spectre released Harlan's right hand and grabbed the knife out of Harlan's waistband.

Spectre turned to see Tanner approaching. He kicked backward, striking Tanner in the gut with the heel of his foot. As Spectre reset, he spun the blade around in his hand until the blade pointed downward. Tanner fell to the ground as Jimmy produced his own blade and attempted to stab Spectre from above.

Moving forward to intercept the blade, Spectre blocked the descending knife with his left hand while sweeping Jimmy's feet from underneath him. As he followed Jimmy to the ground, he kept his own knife against Jimmy's throat.

"Apologize to my friend," Spectre said as Jimmy impacted the ground and dropped his knife.

"What?" Jimmy squealed as he caught his breath.

"Say you're sorry," Spectre said.

"I'm sorry!" Jimmy cried.

As Spectre stood, he heard loud sirens and turned to see guards in riot gear appear. He dropped the knife and held his hands up as the first of the tear gas canisters hit his feet.

Prison sucks, Spectre thought to himself.

CHAPTER TWENTY-FIVE

FBI Miami Regional Office
0655 Local Time

"You're not seriously going to do this are you?" Simms asked nervously as Decker pulled into a parking lot and backed into a spot under an oak tree near the back of the lot.

"We're just going to talk," Decker said as she put the rental car in park and checked her watch.

"And what if he doesn't? Are you going to kidnap him too?"

"You're not kidnapped," Decker said as she rolled her eyes. Simms was always so dramatic.

"Well, I didn't exactly choose to spend all night driving down to Miami," Simms replied.

"Would you rather go back and chat with the people chasing us last night?" Decker asked angrily.

"I just want to go home," Simms said with a resigned sigh. "I thought I was done with this life."

Decker put her hand on Simms's shoulder. Her voice softened. "I think that's what we all want, but it can't happen until we put a stop to the people behind all of this. Help me clear Cal's name and I promise you can go back home and no one will bother you again."

"Are you sure?" Simms asked timidly.

Decker nodded. "I don't think there's any other way," she replied. Her attention turned back to the parking lot as a black pickup entered and backed into a spot. "There he is, right on time."

"What's your plan?" Simms asked.

"I'm going to go talk to him," Decker said. "Stay in the car and be ready to go."

"Just talk?" Simms asked.

"Just talk," Decker replied as she exited the car.

As Decker approached Fields's truck, Simms got out and ran around the back of the car to get in the driver's seat. After buckling in, he watched as she casually approached Fields, who had just slammed the door shut on his truck and headed for the entrance.

Fields caught Decker's reflection in the window of a nearby car as she neared him. Spinning around, his eyes widened as he realized who it was. "Michelle?"

"Hi, Rick," Decker said as she stopped a few feet from the Special Agent in Charge of the Miami Office. He was carrying a travel mug, wearing a white polo shirt with an FBI badge embroidered on the chest and khaki tactical pants. "Long time no see."

"Aren't you supposed to be in Jacksonville this morning?" Fields asked.

"I thought I might pay you a visit instead," Decker replied. "Why?"

"I just had a few questions for you," Decker said as she moved to within a few feet of Fields.

"About what?" Fields asked nervously as he looked around the parking lot.

"Cal's case."

"You could've just called," Fields said. "Why don't you come inside and we'll talk."

"That's ok," Decker said, eyeing Fields's right hand as it slowly moved toward his holstered Glock. "Out here will be fine."

"Then you leave me no choice. I'm sorry, Michelle," Fields said as his right hand drew his Glock 17.

The training Spectre had spent hours on over the summer with her instantly kicked in. With her left hand, Decker grabbed Fields's wrist and sidestepped, pushing the line of fire away from her body as Fields fired a shot and shattered the window of a nearby car. Grabbing the top of the Glock with her right hand, Decker simultaneously pulled Fields's wrist toward her body with her left hand and pushed the Glock toward Fields with her right. The gun slipped free of his grip, but not before his finger was caught in the trigger guard. It snapped as Decker ripped the gun away and struck Fields in the temple with the barrel.

Stunned by the blow, Fields stumbled forward. Decker used his momentum to drive his head into the quarter panel of a nearby parked car. She tucked the Glock into her waistband and went to work using Fields's cuffs to secure his hands as Simms pulled up and lowered the passenger side window.

"What happened to *just talk*?" he yelled as he exited the car to help her.

"He chose Option B. Help me get him in the back," Decker said as she started to drag the dazed and bleeding Fields toward the sedan.

Simms grunted and strained to lift Fields into the back seat with his scrawny arms as Decker grabbed Fields's legs. They could hear sirens off in the distance as they finally got him in and slammed the door.

"You drive!" Simms said as he jumped into the passenger seat.

Decker jumped behind the wheel and spun the sedan's front wheels as she floored it out of the parking lot and turned right. The tires screamed as she hit the side street and headed toward the interstate.

"Where to now?" Simms asked as he eyed Fields in the back seat. "Holy shit I can't believe you kidnapped him!"

"That son of a bitch shot at me!" Decker said angrily. "He's lucky this is all we're doing."

"Let me go," Fields groaned slowly from the back seat.

"*We?*" Simms asked.

Decker glared at Simms. "You're going to have to get used to the fact that you're in this too now. Got it?"

"Ok, ok," Simms said, holding up his hands. "What do you want me to do?"

"Keep an eye on him," Decker said.

"Yes, ma'am," Simms replied.

Decker merged into the morning traffic on I-95 and headed south toward Homestead. She kept an eye out for tails as she worked her way south. She took side roads, eventually traveling through the farmlands of the Redlands until they reached their destination.

After traveling down a mile of dirt roads, Decker stopped the sedan in an open field surrounded by trees. It was the same field she had dropped Spectre and his friends off at to rendezvous with the Blackhawk helicopter that took them into Cuba to rescue Spectre's ex-fiancée.

She killed the engine and opened the back door, dragging Fields out as he fell onto the grass. Decker pulled out the Glock and pointed it at him as he rolled to his knees and faced her.

"You're going to kill me?" Fields asked. His face was stained with blood from his mouth and forehead.

"That's up to you," Decker replied. "Are you going to be honest with me?"

"Fuck you, Michelle!" Fields said defiantly. "I am not afraid to die!"

"No?" Decker asked.

"I'm not telling you shit!"

"How's Teresa doing, by the way?" Decker asked as she lowered the Glock.

"What?" Fields asked.

"Teresa. You know, your wife. The one that caught you fucking the babysitter. The one you begged to take you back. How's that going?" Decker asked.

"Leave my wife out of it," Fields warned.

Decker tucked the Glock into her jeans and squatted down next to Fields. She patted down his cargo pockets, pulling his cell phone out of the left pocket before stepping back.

"So you guys are doing better? No trust issues?" Decker asked, holding up the phone.

"What the fuck are you talking about?" Fields asked nervously.

"I'm just making conversation," Decker replied. "I seem to remember the drama when you came to the office asking my advice. You didn't think she'd ever trust you again, but you wanted to make it work. Remember?"

"Yeah…"

"Hell hath no fury like a woman scorned, right?" Decker asked, as she unlocked his smartphone and scrolled through his contacts.

Fields stared at Decker.

"After all that work to fix things, it would be a shame if she found out about us," Decker said with a chuckle.

"What the fuck are you talking about? There has never been an *us*, you crazy bitch!" Fields yelled.

"You and I know that," Decker said. She selected his wife's contact and turned the phone around so he could see. "But *she* doesn't."

"You're crazy!"

"Am I?" Decker asked as she hit the CALL button and held the phone up to her ear.

"Stop! What do you want to know?" Fields asked frantically. "Shit!"

Decker ended the call before it connected. "Be honest with me or the next time, I ruin your fragile marriage."

"Goddammit, Michelle," Fields said as he leaned back on his heels.

The phone rang in Decker's hand. It was Fields's wife calling him back. She turned the screen around to show him. "This is your only warning. Tell me the truth or I tell her that the reason you're always early to work and late to leave is that we've been fucking."

"Fine," Fields said with a look of resignation.

"You made Simms change the final report on Cal's case, correct?" Decker asked.

"Yes."

"Why?" Decker asked.

"It came from higher up," Fields said. "I was just doing what I was told. Believe me, I didn't want to."

"Who?" Decker pushed.

"I don't know!" Fields replied.

Decker frowned and looked at the phone.

"Wait!" Fields said.

"Didn't we already go over what would happen if you lie to me?"

"They'll kill my family," Fields cried.

"Who?"

Fields looked around, searching for anyone that could be listening in the empty area. When he found none, he exhaled slowly and closed his eyes.

"Larry Engall," Fields said.

"The Attorney General?"

"He wasn't the Attorney General back then. He was still just a U.S. Attorney in Miami," Fields said, shaking his head.

"But why—"

"I hear vehicles approaching," Simms warned, interrupting Decker.

"They're here, we have to get out of here," Fields added.

"Who's here? Who told you they'd hurt your family?" Decker asked as she put away the phone and drew her weapon from her waistband.

"We need to get going," Simms said as he tried to look around the car at the approaching dust cloud on the gravel road.

Decker helped Fields to his feet as Simms held the door open.

"Can you uncuff me?" Fields asked.

Decker and Simms exchanged a look.

"Look, if these guys are here to hurt you, I'll be more helpful without my hands behind my back. I'm not a bad guy, Michelle," Fields argued.

"Fine," Decker said as she pulled out the keys she had taken from Fields and released the handcuffs. "But if you cross me, I will shoot you."

"Fair enough," Fields said as he rubbed his wrists and jumped into the back seat.

Decker took her place in the driver's seat and started the engine. As she backed out, she saw what appeared to be a large SUV approaching about a half mile down the road. The field they were on was a dead end. The only way out was to pass the approaching vehicle. They would have to take their chances.

Putting the car in drive, Decker proceeded slowly down the road. The SUV grew closer, leaving a cloud of dust behind it as it approached. Decker slowed to a crawl as the SUV came within a hundred feet, waiting for the SUV to pass as she hugged the side of the narrow road.

As the SUV neared to within a few dozen feet, it suddenly stopped. Armed men emerged with their weapons up. Decker floored it, kicking rocks and dust up from the sedan's front wheels as she sped toward them and then hooked right into a nearby field she had picked as her bug-out route.

The armed men fired off several rounds before returning to the SUV and giving chase. Unlike the open field they had come from, this field was freshly plowed. Decker followed a perimeter dirt road around it as the SUV pursued, firing another volley of rounds at them as the mercenaries gave chase.

"We're trapped!" Simms yelled. "They're shooting at us!"

While steering with one hand, Decker pulled out the Glock and handed it to Simms. "Well, shoot back!" she yelled as she sped down the dirt road searching for a place to bail.

Rounds peppered the car as Simms lowered his window. He fired blindly at them, ducking as the glass shattered in the back seat.

"You ok back there, Fields?" Decker asked as she looked up in the rear view mirror. To her horror, she saw Fields doubled over, clutching his neck as blood poured from his jugular. "Fields? Fields? Shit! He's hit!"

"You have to get us out of here!" Simms screamed.

"Just keep shooting!" Decker yelled as she made a hard left over a small dirt pile that sent the car airborne. The car landed, ripping off the front fascia as Decker turned into an adjacent field. In the distance, she found what she was looking for. The car's check engine light suddenly illuminated and a warning chimed. Decker could see steam coming from the engine. It wouldn't last much longer.

"I can't shoot with you driving like this!" Simms complained.

"Conserve the ammo, I've got a plan," Decker said. "See about Fields."

"It's not good!" Simms replied as he looked back to see Fields doubled over with blood gurgling from his mouth. "He needs a hospital!"

Decker sped toward the open barn she had found. It wasn't much, but it could offer cover as they fought back. She sped through the open front doors and skidded to a stop. She had barely put the car in park when she exited, running toward the doors.

"Help me close these doors!" Decker yelled.

Simms ran to catch up. They each took a side of the opening and pushed the sliding doors closed. The SUV was right on their heels, sliding to a stop in front of the barn as they managed to close the doors.

"Now what?" Simms asked as he surveyed the barn.

Decker looked around the barn, hoping to find a vehicle or even large tractor to escape in. Having grown up in a farm town in Georgia, she was somewhat familiar with their operation. She found nothing except implements and carts as she frantically scanned the large barn.

"We hold this barn," Decker said.

"We're so fucked," Simms said dejectedly.

CHAPTER TWENTY-SIX

Tallahassee Federal Detention Facility
0725 Local Time

His eyes were still puffy and burning, but the blurry vision had finally started to subside. After subduing him, they had taken him to the infirmary along with several other inmates to get treatment. Spectre, however, was the first to be removed.

He had thought he was going back to solitary as punishment, but instead they took him right back to the interview room where he expected the mysterious man from the night prior to enter at any moment. As he sat shackled to the chair, he daydreamed of Decker walking in, kissing him, and telling him it was all over instead. But Spectre knew it couldn't be that easy. In fact, he had resigned himself to the idea that he would die in prison.

After what seemed like an eternity of waiting, suddenly the door flew open. Spectre looked over his shoulder to see the same man dressed in a suit and tie enter. This time he was carrying a smart tablet of some sort instead of a briefcase. Spectre turned back to face forward as the man walked in and took his seat across from him.

"I must say, I didn't expect to be seeing you so soon, Martin," the man said. "You're already making friends and influencing people in there."

"What can I say? I'm a people person," Spectre replied with a sly grin.

"We'll see about that," the man replied coolly. "It's no matter, though. Your timing is excellent. I wanted you to see this."

The man opened the protective cover of the tablet and swiped the screen to unlock it. He flipped it around on the table so that Spectre could see the black and white video feed. It appeared to be aerial footage of a sedan traveling down a gravel road.

"What's this?" Spectre asked as he studied the screen.

"UAV footage," the man said. "As in an Unmanned Aerial Vehicle – a surveillance drone."

"I know what a UAV is," Spectre said as he watched the sedan turn off a dirt road and into an open field.

The man smiled. "That's right. Hot shit fighter pilot, I forgot."

"I think you mean *shit hot*," Spectre quipped.

"You were shot down on your last flight, weren't you?" the man asked with a raised eyebrow.

"Who is this?" Spectre asked, ignoring the jab as he watched the video. The sedan stopped in the field. Two people exited the front and then pulled a third out of the sedan. The image zoomed in. Spectre could tell it was a female and two males.

"That's your girlfriend," the man said. "You see, Cal – if I may I call you Cal – anyway, technology has changed this job.

Just five years ago, I would have had to deal with cumbersome phone calls or mailing body parts or other tedious ways of providing proof of life to someone stubborn like you. But now? Now I can show you the whole thing in real time."

"If you hurt her—"

"You're going to do what?" the man asked. "You're in no position to do anything."

Spectre watched as the drone video zoomed in, confirming that it was Decker holding a gun pointed at a hostage on his knees.

"She's pretty ruthless isn't she?" the man asked as he pointed at the screen. "Kidnapping a Federal Agent? I think her balls are bigger than yours."

"Leave her alone," Spectre growled.

The man shook his head as he waved his hand. "I'm sorry, Cal, but that option is off the table. I gave you a chance to cooperate last night, remember?"

"I will tell you what you want to know," Spectre said dejectedly. "Just don't hurt her."

"That's not up to me," the man said.

Spectre watched as Decker uncuffed her hostage and the three got back into the sedan, heading back down the same road they had just entered on. The drone image panned down the road to an approaching SUV.

"Who is that?" Spectre asked.

"Oh, them?" the man asked innocently as he picked up the tablet and tapped the screen several times. He put the tablet back down. The video was now streaming from what appeared to be a body cam of a man sitting in the front passenger seat of a vehicle while holding an AK-74 rifle.

"Do you know how hard it is to get a team together on such short notice? I mean, sure, we tracked your girlfriend all the way to the FBI office from Miami, but to get a team together like this takes some work. She didn't make it easy on us," the man said smugly.

The audio was a bit garbled, but Spectre thought he heard them speaking Spanish to each other. "Cubans?"

The man laughed. "You'd think since it's Miami, but no, they are far too unreliable for this sort of thing. I prefer Colombians. They're a little meaner, but they get the job done. It's nice to have friends."

"Call them off," Spectre said.

The man pulled out his phone and placed it on the table. "I could, but what fun would that be? Besides, I still don't think you're taking me seriously enough, and that's a problem."

Spectre watched as the approaching sedan came into view and stopped. The vehicle the Colombians were in also stopped and the man exited with rifle up. As he approached Decker's car, Spectre could see Decker's face. He felt sick to his stomach as he realized what was happening.

"Please!" Spectre shouted. "I'll tell you anything you want."

"Of course you will, Cal," the man said with an evil smile.

Spectre heard more yelling in Spanish before the vehicle Decker was in made a hard right. The Colombian raised his rifle and fired several shots at them.

"Make them stop!" Spectre cried.

"It's not up to me anymore," the man said. "For your girlfriend's sake, I should hope she surrenders soon. Adrenaline makes these hot heads horny and… well, she's hot."

"Fuck you!" Spectre yelled angrily as he pulled against his restraints.

Spectre watched as the man reentered the vehicle and they gave chase. As they entered a field, the man leaned out of the window and started firing at Decker's car. Her car swerved erratically around the field. The video feed from the man's body cam was jittery as his vehicle pursued, hitting bumps and swerving as well. Spectre could barely tell what was going on.

As the chase continued, what appeared to be a barn came into view in the distance. Spectre silently cheered Decker on, knowing she was perfectly capable of getting herself out of the situation. The sedan entered the barn. Seconds later, the Colombians stopped twenty or so yards away as the doors closed.

"She's pretty resourceful," the man said. "I admire that in a woman."

"Please let her go," Spectre pleaded. "I'll tell you what you want to know. Just don't touch her."

"Ok, Cal, I'll make you a deal," the man said. "I'll have them take her alive if you answer my next question. They might use her for their own purposes in the interim, but that's just part of it. I can't control that and neither can you. But if you lie to me or try to fuck with me, I'm going to have them burn that barn down with her in it. Deal?"

Spectre watched the body cam feed. The man's rifle was up and pointed at the barn as the other man yelled something to him in Spanish. Seconds later, the man appeared to spin around and turn toward a tree line with his rifle pointed skyward. There was a loud noise that washed out the tablet's speakers and suddenly the man fired his weapon toward the sky before spinning and falling face down into the dirt.

"What the fuck?" the man across from Spectre said.

He tried to switch to the UAV feed. It was nothing but static. He then switched to another man's body cam. The man appeared to be sitting on the ground and moving slowly, dragging his feet in the dirt as he moved backward. Moments later, he tried to hold his handgun up weakly.

Spectre watched as a man in the distance approached with rifle up wearing full tactical gear. He fired, hitting the Colombian on the ground and causing him to fall backward until the image was nothing but sky.

After a few seconds, the man appeared, standing over the Colombian. He was holding a handgun as he seemed to pause and look into the camera. He pointed the gun toward the camera and fired, causing the camera to shake violently. The image of the bearded man was once again replaced with blue sky. As Spectre saw the backwards ball cap with INFIDEL inscribed on it in English and Arabic and recognized the familiar red beard, he knew exactly who had come to Decker's aid.

"No deal!" Spectre said triumphantly.

The man across from him frantically cycled through the cameras, each of the four body cams showed blue sky, dirt, or static. The wet work team had been neutralized. Spectre knew he would owe Kruger a truckload full of beer when this was all over.

Spectre eyed the man across from him as he stared blankly at the tablet. "Didn't see that one coming, did ya? I told you, I'm a people person," he said. Spectre was suddenly more confident. "It's good to have friends, right?"

"I'm not sure what you think you've done, but I can assure you that you won't win," the man said angrily.

Spectre laughed before suddenly turning serious. "I've seen this look before. You're no different from any of Johnson's other goons – Xin, Zhang, Alvarez. You're all the same. You think you own the world until someone starts tearing it down, and then you panic," Spectre said as he leaned forward.

"I want you to get used to that image – the one of the man with the beard standing over you. Because if I don't kill you, he will. And while you may think your friends are mean, mine are the meanest," Spectre said confidently. "As you reminded me yesterday, I told your boss that I'm going to bring his castle down brick by brick and bury him in the rubble. Well, I'm going to start with you."

In a fit of rage, the man leapt across the table, punching Spectre in the face. Spectre laughed, spitting blood to the side as the man punched him two more times. "Fuck you!" the man yelled angrily.

"Get it out now, buddy," Spectre said defiantly as he recovered from the blows and spat more blood.

"You won't get out of this place alive, I assure you," the man said as he regained his composure and picked up the tablet from the table. "And I will make it my mission in life to hate-fuck your pretty little girlfriend before I kill her."

"Good luck," Spectre said as the man stormed out and slammed the door behind him.

*　*　*

Decker could feel the vibration of the helicopter's rotor blades before she heard it. As they took inventory of the possible weapons around them, Decker heard the helicopter fly low over the barn followed by what sounded like a mini-gun firing. She managed to make it to a dusted-over window on the side of the barn in time to see four men rappelling from the hovering helicopter before it cut the lines away and flew away.

"Who is here?" Simms asked nervously. "More of them?"

"I don't think so," Decker said softly as she heard an exchange of gunfire followed by silence.

"Great, more to fight," Simms said.

Decker held up her finger. "Shhh," she said. "Listen."

She could hear voices in the distance. They seemed to be approaching. She thought she heard her name as the voices grew closer.

"What are you doing?" Simms asked.

"I know him," Decker said as she removed the wooden barricade they had set up for the door.

"You can't be sure!" Simms said.

"Decker, it's Kruger!" the voice from outside yelled. "Friendlies!"

"See?" Decker asked as she started to push the door open.

As the light entered the dusty barn, she saw Kruger standing with a rifle slung across his body armor. She immediately hugged him.

"Thank God you're here!" Decker said as she squeezed him.

Decker looked out into the field. The men with Kruger had set up a defensive perimeter. Decker saw the bodies of the men that had been chasing them scattered around the SUV. It too had been severely damaged in the firefight.

Kruger pushed her off him. "Are you all ok?" he asked. "We have a medic."

"Fields is dead in the car," Simms said timidly. "Who are you?"

"Friends," Kruger said as he directed Axe to go take a look.

"How did you find us?" Decker asked.

"You'll have to ask Coolio," Kruger said. He keyed his radio and gave the code word that they were ready for extraction by the orbiting helicopter.

"Coolio?" Decker asked.

"He's our computer guru. He found out you were going from Eglin to Jacksonville, but I don't know how he figured it out from there. You can ask him yourself when we get there because right now we have a more important crisis on our hands."

"Get where? What crisis?" Simms asked nervously.

"Is he cool?" Kruger asked suspiciously, gesturing to Simms.

"Carl Simms, this is Kruger – sorry I don't know your real name," Decker said. "Kruger, you might remember Carl. He was the agent in the hospital in Tampa."

"Whatever, we have to go," Kruger said. "We're tracking down an imminent terror attack on U.S. soil. I could probably use your help."

Decker frowned. "As much as my sense of duty outweighs just about anything else, Cal is sitting in federal prison right now. I have to figure out how to get him out," she said.

As the helicopter landed in the field behind the barn, Axe walked back from checking on Fields, shaking his head.

"Alright, let's get out of here. My boss is at the airport. You can meet him and then we can discuss a way forward, fair?" Kruger asked.

"Fair enough," Decker said.

Simms whimpered softly as he followed them out. "I just want to go home."

CHAPTER TWENTY-SEVEN

Opa Locka, FL
0807 Local Time

The Blackhawk touched down and a line worker wearing khaki shorts and a blue polo shirt marshaled it to its parking spot. The pilots had replaced the Odin patches on their tan flight suit with Customs and Border Protection Air Branch patches, a cover they had used time and again at civilian fields to avoid questions about a non-military Blackhawk helicopter stopping in.

Kruger was out of the side door and headed toward the Fixed Base Operator (FBO) building before the rotors spooled down.

"Why is he in such a hurry?" Simms asked one of the men in the back. They had all changed out of their tactical gear and were wearing tactical pants and polo shirts to pass as federal agents.

"Kruger's always in a hurry," Tuna replied as he started to help Decker out of the helicopter. Decker politely thanked him, but declined as she stepped into the hot Florida heat. She saw Kruger meeting a woman wearing dark pants and a button-down white shirt standing next to a stocky man with a shaved head and tactical pants.

She approached slowly, studying the man and woman cautiously. Although she knew Kruger was a friend, she had grown to be wary of new faces, especially in the wake of shootouts. She kept an eye out for potential escape routes as she neared them.

"Michelle, I'd like you to meet Mr. Jeff Lyons," Kruger said as he turned to greet her. Lyons extended his hand and flashed a warm smile. He was nearly eye level with the five foot, six inch Decker. She guessed he had to be five eight or five nine, dwarfed by the much larger bearded Kruger standing next to him.

"Michelle Decker," Decker said as she shook his hand. She turned and nodded at Simms, who was walking slowly across the ramp with two of the operators that had saved them. "That's Carl Simms."

"It's a pleasure to finally meet you," Lyons said. "I hope you're doing well."

"I'm fine, thanks," Decker said. "But I'm afraid I don't know anything about you."

"My apologies," Lyons said. "For the time being, think of me as a fan of your work. You have quite the story that I'd love to hear. These men work for my company as contractors doing security work."

"That's pretty cryptic," Decker said with a raised eyebrow.

"In this line of work, one has to be," Lyons replied. "I'm sure you understand."

"He's legit," Kruger said gruffly. "I wouldn't be here if he weren't."

"Oh man!" Simms yelled as he approached the group and headed straight for Lyons. "Jeff Lyons! I loved your videos!"

"So you're the one viewer?" Lyons replied with a hearty laugh.

"I'm Carl Simms," Simms said as he shook Lyons's hand. "I used to love your YouTube Channel on guns and tactical stuff. I was an agent with the FBI and your techniques really helped."

"Videos?" Decker asked as she looked at Kruger.

"I used to have a YouTube Channel reviewing guns, covering shooting techniques, and discussing new equipment for the field. It was kind of a video blog," Lyons explained.

"Ok, then," Decker said before glaring at Kruger. *A vlogger? Holy shit, I don't have time for this,* Decker thought as her eyes shot daggers at Kruger.

"I'll explain later," Kruger whispered as he leaned toward her.

"Well, now that we know each other, I think we can get airborne. I would like to personally invite you both to my offices in Virginia and then we can take you wherever you want," Lyons said.

"I just need to make sure they finished servicing the oxygen and do a quick preflight and we'll be ready," the female pilot said.

"Michelle, this is 'Jenny' Craig," Kruger said. "She used to fly with Spectre."

"With the Gators?" Decker asked.

"After that," Kruger said.

Decker got the hint. They weren't just contractors. If they flew with Spectre after his tour in the Air Force, they had been part of the top-secret group known as Project Archangel. Decker felt a bit more at ease as she put the pieces together.

"It's a pleasure to finally meet you," Jenny said. "I've heard a lot about you. Spectre was a good pilot."

"Thanks," Decker said.

"The APU is running on the jet. You should have cold air conditioning if you want to wait on board while I finish the walk around," Jenny said.

"Right this way," Lyons said.

"What about the others?" Decker asked as they walked back out on the ramp.

"Shorty, Tango, and Beast are going to take the Blackhawk back to its hangar in Miami," Kruger said. "Tuna and Axe are just getting their gear off the helo and then they'll join us."

"You have a hangar in Miami?" Decker asked, trying to grasp the scope of their operation.

"We have hangars in a lot of places," Kruger said with a boyish grin.

"But seriously, 'Shorty', 'Beast', 'Tuna'?" Decker asked using air quotes with her hands. "Does anyone have a real name around here?"

"Well, we have real names," Kruger said with a shrug. "But no one knows them. We tried a 'First Name Fridays' once, but it didn't really work out. It was mass confusion."

"If you say so," Decker said.

They walked out to a black and white Gulfstream G-IV business jet sitting on the ramp. Lyons led the way up the stairs as Jenny conducted the preflight. As they entered, Lyons invited them to make themselves comfortable as he went to the cockpit.

"He flies too?" Decker asked.

"He's the boss," Kruger replied. "He does what he wants."

Axe and company entered the cockpit and took their seats. Tuna offered Decker and Simms each a bottle of water before sitting down and reclining the plush leather chair to take a nap.

As Decker watched the Blackhawk start its engines, Jenny suddenly raced up the stairs and headed straight for the cockpit. Seconds later, Lyons emerged with her and headed down the air stairs. "Are you sure?" he asked as he followed her.

"What's going on?" Simms asked nervously. "Is there a problem with the plane?"

Decker strained to look out the window to see what they were looking at underneath the right side of the airplane. Before she could figure out what was going on, Lyons returned and waved for Kruger to join them.

"What's up, boss?" Kruger asked as he descended the stairs.

"I asked for fuel and nothing else," Jenny said, holding up what appeared to be a circuit board

"What's that?" Decker asked as she and Simms joined them.

"Well, it used to be the Cabin Pressure Acquisition Module," Jenny said, shaking her head.

"The what?" Decker asked.

"It's the microprocessor that controls the cabin pressurization system of the aircraft," Lyons explained.

"Ok, I get that something is fucked up here, but talk to me like I spent most of my life crawling through weeds and eating snakes," Kruger interjected. "What does this mean?"

"I was doing the walk around and noticed the access panel to the CPAM wasn't secured. So I opened it up and found that the CPAM module had been taken apart and this was attached to it," Jenny said. "Someone was trying to depressurize the plane."

"Who?" Kruger asked.

Jenny shrugged. "Any of the line guys that serviced the plane."

Kruger looked back at the FBO, searching for anyone that looked out of place or appeared to be watching them. As he saw the "WELCOME TO OPA LOCKA AIRPORT" sign, it hit him.

"Michelle, did Spectre ever mention a guy named Tom Jane to you?" Kruger asked.

"Wasn't he the guy who helped you get on that oil rig?" Decker replied.

"Yeah," Kruger said. "A few months later, his plane crashed and no one could figure out why. It was all over the news."

"I do remember that," Decker said. "Hypoxia?"

"It took off from *this* airport," Kruger said as he turned to walk toward the FBO.

"Where are you going?" Lyons asked.

"To have a chat with the nice folks that put gas in our airplane," Kruger replied.

"I think I'll just stay here," Simms said meekly as he headed back up the stairs into the cabin.

Decker gave chase, following Kruger into the FBO as Kruger headed straight for the desk.

"Excuse me; do you know who serviced our aircraft?" Kruger asked the petite young blonde sitting behind the desk. "The Gulfstream on the ramp."

"Let's see," the girl said as she shuffled through fuel receipts. "It looks like Wayne did it. Is there a problem, sir?"

"No problem, just have a few questions to ask him," Kruger said. Decker knew he wasn't lying per se, but she had a feeling the grizzled ginger would do more than just politely ask a few questions.

"Yes, sir," the woman said as she paged the line attendant. Moments later, a younger man in his twenties appeared with long hair, khaki shorts, and a yellow reflective vest over his polo shirt. His eyes widened as he saw Kruger.

"Wayne, these—" the girl began, but before she could finish, Wayne took off running toward the flight line.

Kruger hurdled the marble countertop and gave chase as Wayne ran through an employee lounge and out onto the flight line. Decker stayed behind, discouraging the startled girl from calling the police as she flashed her FBI credentials.

Wayne sprinted across the flight line, but soon realized that Kruger was easily running him down. He slid to a stop and turned to fight Kruger, bringing his hands up to defend himself as he backpedaled. Kruger closed the distance between them in an instant. His right hand grabbed Wayne's throat as he used his own momentum to drive the line attendant backward. As the two slowed, Kruger kicked Wayne's leg out from under him, driving him straight into the asphalt and knocking the wind out of him.

As Wayne hit the ground, Kruger flipped him over and put a knee on the back of his neck, driving Wayne's face into the asphalt and holding him there. Tuna and Axe ran out to assist, having seen the foot pursuit from their jet a hundred yards away. Axe brought with him a pair of Flexcuffs and secured Wayne's hands before dragging him to his feet.

"Please don't kill me!" Wayne cried as he caught his breath.

"We're just going to talk, bub," Kruger said as he walked Wayne toward the plane. He patted Wayne down, finding a handheld programmer in his right cargo shorts pocket. "Specifically about this."

"I can explain!" Wayne pleaded.

"Oh, you will," Kruger growled.

Decker joined them at the jet as Kruger forced Wayne up the stairs and into one of the nearby chairs in the front part of the cabin.

"I showed the girl my credentials," Decker said. "That should buy us some time, but we should probably hurry."

"This won't take long," Kruger said as he walked to the aircraft's sleeping area. He returned with a pair of needle-nose pliers and two bath towels that he placed on the floor in front of Wayne.

"Oh Jesus, Lord God, please don't!" Wayne begged as he stared at the pliers.

"Here's the deal, bub," Kruger said as he leaned in close. "I don't have a lot of time here, so your chances to leave here with your fingers and testicles still attached are dwindling. Are you tracking?"

"God, please help me," Wayne said as he started to sob.

Kruger grabbed him by his long hair, coming face to face with the disheveled line attendant. "God won't help you here," Kruger said. "Only the truth will save you."

"I'm sorry!" Wayne cried. "I just needed the money."

"Let's start with what you did," Kruger said as he took a step back.

"I swapped out the CPAM with the one they gave me," Wayne said as he stared at the floor.

Kruger placed the pliers under Wayne's chin and pushed his head up to face him. "Look at me when you talk, bub," Kruger growled. "Who gave it to you?"

"His name is Mark Terry," Wayne said. "Please, I just did it for the money."

"How did you meet him? What did he ask you to do?" Kruger asked.

"I met him last year. He gave me five grand to let him out on the flight line when some oil fat cat's jet was out here. He said he'd kill my parents if I said anything. I thought I was going to jail when I heard that the plane crashed, but no one ever talked to me about it. I thought the guy was out of my life and I'd never hear from him again. But this morning he called me and asked if I was working. When I said no, he told me to go in," Wayne said nervously.

"Then what happened?"

"He was waiting outside, man!" Wayne said. "Came from out of nowhere. Told me he'd double the money if I swapped the CPAM. I told him I had no idea how, but he showed me a diagram and told me how to do it. That dude was serious."

"How did you know what airplane you were looking for?" Jenny asked as she leaned against the cockpit door, having overheard the interrogation.

"Terry gave me a tail number. November Two Eight Five Victor Kilo, said it was a G-IV," Wayne said as his eyes darted nervously between Jenny and Kruger. "I'm telling you the truth, I swear."

Kruger snapped his fingers in front of Wayne. "Look at me, Wayne," he barked. "How do I find this man?"

"I don't know man!" Wayne cried. "He found me!"

"You said he called you, correct?" Decker asked.

Wayne nodded nervously. His legs started to shake.

"Where's your phone?" Decker asked.

"In the FBO," Wayne replied.

"Then let's go get your phone," Kruger said as he grabbed Wayne by his shirt and pulled him to his feet.

CHAPTER TWENTY-EIGHT

Washington, D.C.
1155 Local Time

Jason Travis sat on a park bench in Constitution Gardens overlooking The Three Soldiers memorial. He watched as tourists took selfies and then moved on, some headed to the Vietnam Memorial Wall just across the park, while others continued on to the Lincoln Memorial to his left.

The soldiers in the monument seemed to look toward the wall, solemnly paying tribute to their fallen comrades listed there. It was a fitting place to meet, a metaphor of the war he had been fighting for the last decade. A tribute to the sacrifices a country gives when it fights a war, either publicly or covertly.

Travis had fought many wars for his country. He had joined the Army at age nineteen, just a few days after the attacks of September 11th. He had given up a scholarship to the University of Texas, instead vowing revenge against the terrorists that killed so many innocent Americans.

A year later, he got his first and only taste of combat as an American rifleman. On March 2, 2002, Private First Class Travis joined the 1st Battalion, 87th Infantry Regiment in eastern Afghanistan as part of Operation Anaconda.

His unit received heavy fire from the vastly underestimated Taliban forces in the valley where they were dropped off by Chinook helicopters. They were forced to run for cover in what became known as "Hell's Halfpipe" where they were shot at from heavy machine gun fire from above. Travis lost three close friends that day and took a bullet just beneath his body armor that ended his short military career.

Upon returning to Texas, Travis was angry and disgruntled. He blamed terrible leadership at every level for the death of his friends and the loss of his career. It took him nearly two years to learn how to live a normal life again.

As he struggled to find work, Travis felt that the government had abandoned him just as he regained his strength and recovered. He battled depression and survivor's guilt. Then one day his dad introduced him to a business partner in the oil industry named Kerry Johnson, who hired him to help with oil field security. He credited Johnson with saving his life.

Johnson had given him a purpose when he had found none elsewhere. Travis eventually became Johnson's most trusted man, doing the jobs that no one else could be trusted with and influencing deals when needed. Travis proved that he could do whatever was necessary to ensure mission success, without moral reservations.

Their only hiccup had been when Johnson became Secretary of Defense. As a public figure, Johnson couldn't be associated with a man of Travis's talents, so he stashed Travis away in a group called Project Archangel. Travis had been excited to get a second chance at going to war.

But just as had happened with his first attempt at fighting for his country, Travis's tenure with the covert group was short-lived. The group's leader, Charles Steele, thought Travis was too vicious and lacked a moral compass when fighting the enemy. He convinced Johnson to move Travis out of the elite unacknowledged unit after just two deployments. Travis was glad to hear that the Chinese had killed Steele. He had been a weak leader.

In the wake of his severance from the organization, Travis went back to doing what he was most comfortable doing – leading wet work teams. It was a fancy term for hired guns who took care of people who knew too much or posed too much of a threat. Travis enjoyed it and was compensated well for it. It was the least he could do, he thought, for the man that had pulled him out of the ashes of depression like a phoenix.

"Were you followed?" he asked as Johnson's feeble Chief of Staff, Marvin Bradley, arrived and sat next to him.

"No, were you?" Bradley asked as he cautiously looked around the crowd of tourists.

Travis scowled at Bradley. "You know me better than that."

"Of course," Bradley said as he unwrapped a sub sandwich he had brought. "Hungry?" he asked as he offered Travis half.

"Let's keep this short," Travis said.

"Has it been taken care of?" Bradley asked before taking a bite of his chicken sandwich.

"There have been bumps in the road," Travis said, shaking his head. "But we've taken care of another problem."

"Which problem?" Bradley asked with a raised eyebrow.

"Lyons," Travis replied.

"What?" Bradley asked as he nearly choked on his sandwich. "You found him?"

"I found his private jet. It was registered through one of his shell corporations. Just happened to go to the Opa Locka airport where I have a guy. He's taking care of it just like the oil guy," Travis whispered.

Lyons had been on Travis's "To Do List" for nearly a year. The billionaire YouTube star had been a strong financial supporter of Senator Wilson's Presidential campaign against Clifton and Johnson. More recently, he had moved up on the list after Lyons publicly stated that he thought Johnson's handling of the attack on Midway had been weak and that he thought Johnson needed to resign as a result. He was far too influential in the public eye to be allowed to live.

"The same way?" Bradley asked cautiously.

Travis nodded. Oil CEO Tom Jane had been dispatched the same way he had planned for Lyons. They had found his plane landing at the Opa Locka airport and paid off a line attendant for access to the plane. The crash had been ruled an accident, and the media was none-the-wiser that a man who could have taken down Johnson had been assassinated over the Gulf of Mexico. It was a near perfect plan, in Travis's mind.

"Shit!" Bradley hissed.

"What?" Travis asked. "You said you wanted him silenced."

"I said he would be a problem that might need to be dealt with *later*," Bradley replied angrily. "Not *now*, you idiot."

"What?" Travis asked as he leaned away from the fuming Bradley.

"We just had a former Presidential candidate killed in a terror attack, an F-35 crash, and now you're going to have a famous billionaire killed in a crash? You don't think that will raise a few eyebrows? Jesus fuck!" Bradley said. "Call it off."

"I can't," Travis said. "It's already done."

Bradley rubbed the bridge of his nose and closed his eyes. "When?"

"A couple of hours ago," Travis replied.

Bradley let out an exasperated sigh. "Fine, ok. We can deal with this. What about the other two?"

Travis frowned. "Martin knows about the boss. He wouldn't give up how much he knew, but I would say he has more information. I suspect the girl does, too, but I don't know what she knows yet."

"Why not?" Bradley asked.

"Martin wouldn't tell me and we have yet to be able to detain her," Travis whispered.

"Unable to detain? And just what *the fuck* does that mean?" Bradley hissed.

"She fled from Jacksonville to Miami. We tried to grab her, but a third party intervened," Travis said. "We were not expecting that."

"Third party? Who?" Bradley asked.

"We're working that now. Facial recognition drew a blank. I know I've seen him before, but we can't find anything on him. The video was too grainy," Travis said.

"What about Martin?" Bradley asked.

"Don't worry about Martin," Travis said. "He'll be dead by Monday."

Bradley finished his sandwich and rolled up the paper, putting it in the trash can next to him as he stood.

"Make sure they're both dead," Bradley said. "Can you handle that?"

"I can," Travis replied.

"Good, because if you can't, I will find someone else who can. Understand?"

Travis stood to face Bradley. He was several inches taller, and although they were both wearing suits, it was clear that Travis had double the muscle mass of the Vice President's wormy chief of staff.

"I understand," Travis said. "But know that my loyalty is to Mr. Johnson, not *you*. You should watch how you say things."

Bradley didn't flinch at the thinly veiled threat. He stood his ground, staring down the much larger man in front of him.

"Fix this problem or I will," Bradley replied. "Have a nice day."

Travis watched Bradley as he walked away. He clenched his fists, resisting the very primal urge to intercept Bradley and beat him to within inches of his life. He vowed to kill the smug little prick as soon as he finished with Martin and company.

"Fuck you," he said under his breath as Bradley blended into the crowd of tourists.

CHAPTER TWENTY-NINE

Tallahassee Federal Detention Facility
1230 Local Time

After leaving the interrogation room with the unknown man, Spectre had been taken straight to the cafeteria. He ate alone, feeling the stares of those that had witnessed the morning fight. By their body language, he could tell that some were afraid of him while others looked at him as a challenge that they were more than willing to accept.

Antonio was sitting at the desk in their tiny cell when Spectre finally made it back. He was reading with eyeglasses perched on the bridge of his nose. The back cover of the book was torn off. Antonio appeared to be roughly halfway through.

"I didn't think I would see you again," Antonio said as he smiled and placed a bookmark before putting the book on the desk.

"I'm sure I'll be here a while," Spectre said as he sat down on his bunk bed. "Good book?"

"You have to keep your mind active in this place," Antonio said as he took his glasses off. "It's the third time I've read it."

"What is it?" Spectre asked as he leaned back against the cinderblock wall.

"Lone Survivor by Marcus Luttrell," Antonio replied. "Have you read it?"

"I've heard of it, but never got around to reading it. I heard the movie was pretty good too," Spectre said.

"Oh, it's a great book. I'll loan it to you when I'm done. You kind of remind me of Marcus," Antonio said.

"How's that?" Spectre asked.

"You do the right thing. You're not afraid to stand up for what you believe in.," Antonio said with a smile. "And you're a survivor."

"I guess," Spectre replied. "It didn't help me stay out of this place."

"What are you in for?" Antonio asked.

"It's complicated," Spectre said.

"It always is, my friend," Antonio said. "We've all made mistakes."

Spectre closed his eyes and exhaled softly. "If it's ok with you, I think I'll just take a nap now."

"Suit yourself," Antonio said as he returned to his book.

As Spectre tried to relax on the rock hard mattress, his mind drifted off. He wondered how Kruger had found Decker in time to save her. The intense stare behind the red beard was unmistakable on the camera. There was no doubt that she would be in good hands as she tried to prove his innocence.

He thought about the man in the interrogation room. He was working for Vice President Johnson at some level, Spectre was sure of it. He knew too many details that were tied to Johnson. What the man didn't know was how much Decker and Spectre knew. Spectre thought that could be leveraged later. Johnson was fighting an unknown enemy.

Spectre fell into a deep sleep. He dreamed about being with Decker. They were sitting at the lake where he had proposed during an evening picnic. *She was so beautiful.* They were happy together.

But the happiness was suddenly shattered. Suddenly the man from the interrogation room appeared, holding a knife to Decker's throat. Spectre tried to move, but he felt like his feet were stuck in cement. He could see the fear in her eyes as she looked at the helpless Spectre. She called out to Spectre before the man sliced through her throat.

Spectre screamed out, shooting upright in his bed as he awoke. As he realized he had just awakened from a terrible nightmare, Spectre saw Antonio standing over him and grabbed Antonio's arm defensively.

"It's ok, Cal," Antonio said as he was pulled down by Spectre's grip. "You were dreaming."

Spectre slowly released his hold on Antonio as his mind caught up with his actual situation. "Sorry," Spectre said faintly.

"It's ok," Antonio said as he withdrew his right arm and rubbed it. "I was just trying to wake you. They're about to call for the yard."

"The yard?" Spectre asked as he swung his feet onto the floor.

"Exercise time," Antonio said. "We get one hour of fresh air in the yard in the morning and an hour in the afternoon."

As if on cue, an alarm sounded and a voice came over the public address system, announcing that all inmates should line up for the yard. Spectre stood as he put on his slippers. Antonio grabbed a pair of sneakers from beneath the bed.

"You're going to want to wear shoes," Antonio said as he pointed at Spectre's feet.

"These are all they let me have," Spectre said. "Why do I need shoes?"

"Those slippers aren't good for fighting," Antonio said.

"I don't plan on fighting," Spectre replied.

"We shall see, friend," Antonio said as he lined up at the door. "Let's go."

After the alarm sounded again, there was a metallic click and the doors automatically opened. Spectre followed Antonio as they made their way out of the cell pod and into a corridor where a corrections officer stopped each inmate and did a quick pat down for weapons. Once cleared, they made their way into an outdoor courtyard with bleachers, several weight benches, and a basketball court.

Spectre took a seat on the second level of the bleachers, watching as Antonio exchanged greetings with several other inmates. As the yard filled with people, Spectre watched for the different players Antonio had mentioned earlier. He could see the segregation of the various factions and gangs. It was like high school cliques on steroids.

As Spectre observed the crowd, he noticed the large linebacker named DeSean approach with a small group of friends. Spectre looked around to find no one around him as DeSean and his group surrounded Spectre, trapping him in his spot on the bleachers.

"You da white boy that caused all the problems this morning?" DeSean asked as he folded his arms, flexing his massive biceps.

"I'm sorry," Spectre said, holding up his hands. "I didn't mean to."

"You ruined my breakfast," DeSean said sternly.

"I'm really sorry," Spectre replied, trying to avoid eye contact.

"I should beat your little pasty white ass," DeSean said menacingly as he put his foot up on the bleacher in front of Spectre.

"I would rather you didn't," Spectre said, still holding up his hands.

"But you beat those KKK motherfuckers down," DeSean replied. "I like that."

"Thanks?" Spectre replied cautiously.

"Bring your breakfast to me tomorrow and we good," DeSean said before turning to walk away.

Members of his entourage stayed and eyed Spectre as he sat dumbfounded by what he had just heard. One of the men winked at him before following DeSean to the weight benches. As fascinating as the social dynamic of prison was, Spectre wasn't looking forward to navigating the social hierarchy for an extended period of time. He hoped Decker came through for him soon.

"What was that all about?" Antonio asked as he approached Spectre.

"I owe him breakfast tomorrow," Spectre replied. His eyes were still scanning the other inmates as he looked for new threats.

"You're lucky that's all he wants," Antonio replied.

"What?" Spectre asked.

"It looks like he's taken a special interest in you," Antonio replied with a shrug. "Be careful."

As Spectre thought up a witty reply, another group near the basketball court caught his eye. They were clean cut and muscular with light hair. Of the four men in the group, three of them seemed to be staring right at Spectre.

"Who are they?" Spectre asked, nodding toward the court. "I don't remember them from breakfast."

Antonio turned to see the group eyeing Spectre. "That's odd," he said as he scratched his head.

"What?"

"I've never seen them before," Antonio said. "Must be new."

"Is that normal?" Spectre asked.

"One or two, maybe," Antonio replied.

"Four?"

"I don't know," Antonio said. "Nothing has been normal around here since you showed up."

CHAPTER THIRTY

Fort Lauderdale, FL
1620 Local Time

Wayne Lawson nervously wiped his hands on his oil-stained khaki cargo shorts as he sat in the booth in the small diner. He felt like a field mouse, trapped between two very vicious predators. He just wanted to go home, toke up, and forget he had ever met the angry man with the red beard.

He looked nervously out the window as the waitress poured a glass of water and put it down in front of him. He had no idea how he would make it through this meeting. He knew he would never get paid for the job he'd done. He was merely acting for his own survival.

"Can I get you anything or are you still waiting?" the waitress asked.

Lawson's head jerked toward her. As he rubbed his hands on his shorts, he realized his knees were bouncing up and down rapidly. He tried to calm himself as he smiled at her.

"He'll be here in a minute, thanks," he managed. The woman smiled and walked off. He felt like his heart was going to explode in his chest.

As he watched a girl on rollerblades in short shorts and a bikini top skate by on the nearby sidewalk, a deep voice called from behind. "You should never sit with your back to the door," the man said.

Lawson looked up. Mark Terry stood behind him. He was wearing a gray polo shirt with the words DRUG ENFORCEMENT AGENCY and a badge embroidered in gold on the left breast. Before Lawson could say anything, Terry took his seat across from him.

"You're a fucking *fed?*" Lawson whispered frantically.

"Relax," Terry said, flashing a gold Rolex as he waved his left hand casually. "You have nothing to worry about as long as you keep your mouth shut."

"Jesus Christ," Lawson said under his breath.

"Now, why did you need to meet in person so badly? Did you do what I asked?" Terry asked as he casually picked up a menu.

"It's done," Lawson said. His eyes darted nervously around the room as Terry studied the menu. "They're supposed to take off in an hour."

"Where are they going?" Terry asked, looking up from the menu.

"Ronald Reagan International in D.C.," Lawson replied.

"Good," Terry said, returning to the menu.

Lawson stared at him, waiting for him to finish reading the menu. He cleared his throat, causing Terry to look up.

"So what's the problem?" Terry asked finally.

"They picked up some people," Lawson said.

Terry folded the menu and put it down on the table. "Who?"

Terry looked around the diner before leaning forward. "A blonde girl. Real famous. The one that saved the President," he whispered.

Terry's eyes widened. "Michelle Decker?"

"Yeah... Yeah, I think that's her name!" Lawson replied. "She got on the plane with the rich guy. I didn't know what to do. I couldn't undo it. Jesus, you have to help me."

"Settle down," Terry said. "You'll be fine."

"If they find out that I..." Lawson stopped before leaning back and looking over his shoulder. "*You know.* They'll give me the chair!"

"Then it's best that no one finds out," Terry said with a sinister grin.

"You gotta get me out of here," Lawson pleaded. "I can't stay in Florida."

"Just relax," Terry said. "Who else was on the plane?"

"Well," Lawson began as his foot started tapping the floor again. "There was a short bald guy. I don't know his name. I think I've seen him on TV too, but I don't know his name."

"Very good," Terry said. "Who else?"

"Real rough looking guys," Lawson said as he leaned back in. "They looked like bikers. One had a red beard. Real mean looking guy."

"And you're sure they got on the plane?" Terry asked.

Lawson nodded enthusiastically. "They were boarding when I sent you the text. That's why I needed to see you. I didn't sign up for this many people. Last time it was just one guy and his pilot."

"You'd be wise not to talk about last time," Terry warned.

"Sorry," Lawson replied. "But this is way different."

Terry pulled out his billfold and dropped a twenty on the table. "Buy yourself an early dinner. Go home. Your money will be at the drop tomorrow," Terry whispered.

"Where are you going?" Lawson asked.

"Don't worry about me," Terry said as he slid out of the booth. He stood and started to walk out, stopping next to Lawson. "Keep your mouth shut and everything will be fine," he whispered as he put his large hand on Lawson's shoulder.

As Terry walked off, Lawson watched him in the reflection on the window. When he was sure Terry was gone, he exhaled as he slouched in his seat.

"Did you get all of that?" he whispered.

The in-ear transmitter he was wearing suddenly crackled to life, "We did. Good work," the red-bearded man responded.

* * *

They were sitting around two laptops as they watched and listened to Lawson's meeting. Kruger had given Lawson a wireless camera hidden in a pen and an in-ear transmitter. As the meeting progressed, Meeks pulled everything he could on the Federal Agent that had tried to kill their boss.

"Special Agent Mark Terry has been with the DEA for fifteen years," Meeks said through their Skype chat. "He's been assigned to their Fort Lauderdale field office for the last three years. Before that, he was in Louisiana. Former Army Ranger, but was only in for four years. No wife. No kids. Parents live in Galveston, Texas."

"Can you get his financials?" Decker asked as she hovered over Kruger's shoulder in the front of the luxury jet.

"Nothing stands out. Several 401(k) accounts and IRAs. His net worth has to be in the high six figures," Meeks replied.

"Is that normal for a Fed?" Kruger asked Decker.

"Fifteen years? Maybe," Decker replied. "If he lived in a cardboard box and never spent any money."

"Any offshore accounts?" Kruger asked as he turned back to the laptop.

"If he has anything, it's not under his name," Meeks replied. "It'll take me some time to run that down. The only thing I can see is that his primary checking account received a transfer today for five thousand. The routing and account number traces back to a holding company out of Houston."

"Good job, Coolio," Kruger said. "Do you still have a track on him?"

"Good ping on the phone," Meeks said. "It looks like he's headed back to his house."

"Then let's pay him a visit," Kruger said.

CHAPTER THIRTY-ONE

Fort Lauderdale, FL
1715 Local Time

Terry parked his BMW M4 in the single car garage as the door closed behind him. He killed the engine and walked into his house overlooking Sunrise Bay. Tossing his keys on the marble countertop in the kitchen, he walked to his office.

As he sat down, he opened the top right drawer of his desk, pulled out a cell phone, and powered it on. It was a cheap prepaid flip-phone he used only to call his old friend. He dialed the number from memory, holding the phone up to his ear as the phone connected through the various proxy-IPs to the person at the other end.

"Jason, it's me," he said as the line connected. "I have good news."

"Is it done?" Jason asked.

"It's done and then some," Terry said proudly.

"What do you mean?"

Terry leaned back in his executive office chair and propped his feet up on the desk as he watched an MJM 50z Yacht cruise toward the yacht club across the bay.

"Remember the woman you were looking for?" Terry asked.

"You found her?"

"She got on the plane!" Terry replied with a hearty laugh.

"You're sure?" Jason asked cautiously.

"My guy confirmed it," Terry said proudly. "That should be worth a bonus at Christmas time."

"Wait, was there someone with her?" Jason asked.

"A couple of biker looking guys, why?" Terry asked.

"Red beard?"

"Yeah, that's what my guy said," Terry replied.

"And you're sure they took off?"

Terry looked at his watch. "I confirmed their flight plan. They should be taking off in twenty minutes," he said.

"Where were they going?"

"Washington, D.C.," Terry said. "Look buddy, relax. It's done."

"We need to clear this line," Jason said suddenly. "I'll be in touch."

"Talk to you soon," Terry said.

"Good work, Ranger," Jason said before the line disconnected.

Terry smiled as he turned off the phone and closed it. He put it back in the top drawer and walked to the kitchen. He grabbed a glass from the cabinet and put it on the counter before pouring himself two fingers of scotch. He took a sip, feeling the warmth as it eased down his throat. *Today was a good day.*

He walked over to his living room and turned on his 80" 4K LED TV as he unlaced his boots and kicked them off. He thought about how he would spend his extra allowance as he watched highlights from the Dolphins preseason game.

As he started to doze off on his plush leather couch, his doorbell rang. Groaning as he stood, he put the scotch down and walked barefoot to his front door. As he peered through the peephole, he saw an attractive young blonde standing on his doorstep. He quickly checked his hair and teeth in the nearby mirror before unlocking the door.

"Whatever you're selling, I'm buying," he said as he opened the door.

"Good," the woman said. As he looked down, he saw the Taser she had been holding close to her body. He heard a loud pop and then felt two prongs enter his chest and abdomen as his body tensed up and he fell backward into the doorway.

As Terry rode the lightning, two men dragged him inside, securing his hands behind him as they rolled him onto his belly. As the five-second shock ended, Terry tried to speak, but before he could, Kruger had duct-taped his mouth and placed a hood over his head. He felt another prick in his neck and lost consciousness seconds later.

* * *

As Terry came to, he found himself sitting in a plush leather chair. His hands were now bound in front of him, but the duct tape and hood were gone. Looking around, he realized he was in the front cabin of a luxury jet. The cockpit door was just a few feet in front of him.

"Glad you're awake," a voice from behind him said. He looked back, seeing a man with a red beard wearing a black jumpsuit. The man approached him, stopping just a few feet in front of him.

"Who are you?" Terry asked groggily.

"You can call me Kruger, bub," he said as he squatted next to Terry. "Not that it matters."

"What do you mean?" Terry asked. "Where am I?"

"You're on a business jet at thirty thousand feet," Kruger replied. "Sound familiar?"

"Oh God!" Terry cried as he made the connection between the red beard and being on a plane and realized what jet he was on. "We have to land. This plane isn't safe."

"Funny you should mention that," Kruger said. "Let's talk about that."

"I'll tell you anything!" Terry said. "Just please land this plane."

"What did you do?" Kruger asked innocently.

"I had the line attendant swap the pressurization computer. It's set to slowly depressurize the plane thirty minutes after takeoff," Terry said frantically. "Please!"

"Good to know," Kruger said. "Why?"

"What do you mean? *Why?*"

Kruger stood and moved to a chair across from Terry. He casually sat down, leaning back as he crossed his right leg over his left knee. "Why would you do such a thing?"

"We can talk about that when we land!"

"Let's talk about that now," Kruger said. "If what you say is true, we've only got a few minutes left."

"I was paid to do it!"

"To do what?"

"I already told you!"

"Yes, but I want to hear you tell me what exactly you hoped to accomplish," Kruger said as he looked at his watch calmly. "Five minutes."

"Jeff Lyons! I was paid to kill him!" Terry said.

"Why?"

"I didn't ask why!" Terry said nervously. "I was just told to make sure he was on the plane and make sure the part gets swapped."

"Who?"

"Who?" Terry asked.

"We're not owls here, bub. You know what I'm asking," Kruger said as he looked at his watch again. "Three minutes now, better make it quick."

"I'm a Federal Agent! You can't do this!" Terry cried out.

"Oh, I know all about you, *Special Agent* Terry, DEA," Kruger said. "But if I were you, I'd stop wasting time. You're down to two minutes."

"Ok! Ok!" Terry shouted. "His name is Jason Travis."

"Go on," Kruger said, motioning for Terry to continue.

"We were in the Army together in Afghanistan. I've done odd jobs here and there for him since I joined the DEA," Terry said, nervously looking forward as the cockpit door opened.

A woman wearing the same black jumpsuit appeared. She was attractive, but not the same as the woman that had tricked him into opening the door at his house.

"It's time," she said as she approached Kruger.

"You see that?" Kruger asked. "I told you that you should hurry."

"Wait, what's happening?" Terry asked.

"Last question," Kruger said as he uncrossed his legs and leaned forward. "And this one's important."

"Please! We have to land!"

"Just one more question," Kruger said calmly as he held up a finger.

"What? What is it?" Terry cried.

"Who does Jason Travis work for?" Kruger asked.

"I think you mean *for whom does Jason Travis work?*" the woman interjected.

"Right," Kruger said. "For whom does Jason Travis work?"

"What the fuck is going on here?" Terry asked.

"Answer the question, please, bub," Kruger said.

"I don't know!"

"Are you sure?" Kruger said.

"I swear! Jason never told me. Said it was better that way. I just did the jobs he asked me to do and took the money when I finished," Terry responded. "Please!"

Kruger stood and approached Terry. "Ok, I believe you."

"Thank God! Now please, land this plane!" Terry pleaded.

"Sure thing," Kruger said. He pulled Terry up to his feet and started walking him toward the cockpit.

"Where are we going?" Terry asked nervously.

"To land the plane," Kruger replied as he walked him into the empty cockpit.

"What?" Terry screamed. "Who's going to land the plane?"

"You are, bub," Kruger said.

"What? I can't fly a plane! What are you doing?" Terry cried as Kruger cut his restraints and sat him down in the left seat.

"Well then you've got the rest of your life to figure it out," Kruger said as he pulled out a pair of leg restraints and shackled Terry's feet behind the column of the yoke. "Good luck."

"Wait! No! Please!" Terry screamed.

Kruger walked out and closed the cockpit door without saying another word. As he did, Jenny was standing waiting for him with her hands on her hips.

"This is a terrible idea," Jenny said.

"You'll do fine," Kruger reassured her as he walked her to the rear of the cabin.

"I've only done this once in training," Jenny said.

"And you did fine," Kruger said as they stopped in the rear cabin where their jump gear was waiting. "Just stick with me."

"What about the jet?" Jenny asked.

"I'm sure he has insurance," Kruger said.

They put on their parachutes, oxygen equipment, gloves, goggles, helmets, and oxygen masks. When they were finished checking each other over, they exchanged thumbs up and opened the baggage area access compartment.

Crawling through the four-foot access area, they reached the specially designed cargo door. Kruger gave Jenny another thumbs up and flipped a switch, depressurizing the aircraft before sliding the door open.

Jenny walked to the door first. After a slight hesitation and a soft push from Kruger, she was on her way. Kruger followed moments later.

If everything went as planned, Terry would be unconscious within minutes, and they would be touching down on the beach just in time to be picked up by the rest of the team.

CHAPTER THIRTY-TWO

Andrews AFB
2105 Local Time

The blue and white Boeing 757 pulled to a stop in front of the motorcade of black SUVs and limousines. Marvin Bradley watched from the rear of the armored limousine as a truck with air stairs pulled up to the Vice President's aircraft. A few minutes later, the Vice President emerged.

Bradley straightened his blue silk tie as he exited the limousine and accompanied the head of the Vice President's ground security detail to the foot of the stairs. As Vice President Johnson descended toward them, Bradley smiled. The anticipation was just too much to maintain his usual stoic demeanor. He felt like a kid at Christmas.

"You look happy," Johnson said as he cleared the last step and kept walking toward his limousine.

"I have news," Bradley said enthusiastically. He turned to follow Johnson, who made no attempt to stop or acknowledge his giddy chief of staff.

Johnson ignored the Secret Service Agent holding the door open for him as he entered the limousine. He slid across the leather seat to the minibar, retrieving a glass and a bottle of Crown Royal as he sat back and loosened his tie. He poured three fingers and then took a pull straight from the bottle before letting out an exasperated sigh.

As he put the bottle back, he looked over as the door closed behind Bradley. He was still grinning from ear to ear. "What a goddamned day, Marvin," Johnson said before taking another sip.

"How did it go, sir?" Bradley asked, trying to hide his enthusiasm. One of the escort vehicles sounded its siren and the motorcade started to roll. Johnson closed his eyes and leaned his head back against the headrest.

"Awful," Johnson replied without moving. "All these people acting like Wilson and his son were these big national heroes. Grieving widows. *God*. Wilson's wife is insufferable."

Bradley picked up a file from his bag and placed it in his lap. Johnson had flown to Indianapolis for the day to be there for the arrival of the bodies of Wilson and his son. Bradley had stayed behind to meet with their off-the-books associate, but he knew Johnson would detest going. Johnson hated everything about Senator Wilson and his family.

"They put flags on their caskets and everything," Johnson continued. "Goddamned American heroes, people kept saying. *I had to* say that too. Do you know how stupid that sounds, Marvin? Wilson, a *hero*. Can you imagine? His decrepit wife even tried to hug me."

Johnson opened his eyes and waited for a response from Bradley. "Why are you smiling so much?" he asked as he finally noticed Bradley. "Did you take too many Prozac pills?

"I have something that I think will make you feel better," Bradley said, holding up the file marked SECRET.

"What is it?" Johnson asked before downing the rest of his drink. He leaned over to the bar and grabbed the Crown Royal once more, this time adding three ice cubes as he poured his drink to the top of the glass.

"Here," Bradley said as he happily tried to hand the file to Johnson.

Johnson held up his crooked fingers and closed his eyes. "Marvin, I'm in no mood to read. Just read it to me or tell me what's going on."

Bradley opened the file and began reading. "At approximately 1800 hours Eastern Time, a Gulfstream G-IV, tail number November Two Eight Five Victor Kilo registered to Tacticorp Holdings, LLC departed the Opa Locka Airport with four souls on board en route to Ronald Reagan International."

"Marvin, what the fuck are you reading?" Johnson asked impatiently. "If this is another terror attack..."

"Even better, sir," Bradley said as he continued reading. "After departure, the flight checked in with Miami Center and was cleared to its cruising altitude of thirty-one thousand feet. At approximately 1830 hours, the flight was directed to switch frequencies to Jacksonville Center. The pilot checked in on frequency and was cleared on course. Four minutes later, the controller attempted to give the flight a new routing, but was unable to reestablish contact."

Bradley flipped the page before continuing. "The Jacksonville Center controller made five more attempts on frequency before attempting the emergency frequency and relaying through other aircraft. As the flight headed through a warning area where Jacksonville Air National Guard F-15s were conducting training, the controller requested the F-15s intercept it.

"The flight of two F-15s rejoined on the Gulfstream, noting that the interior windows were fogged over, but that they could see at least one occupant slumped over at the controls. The wingman noted that the baggage compartment door on the rear of the aircraft was missing and suspected that the plane had depressurized. They shadowed the aircraft until F-16s sitting alert at Langley could intercept as the aircraft continued its course on a northeasterly heading over the Atlantic," Bradley continued, pausing as he flipped the page again.

"The F-16s continued to follow the aircraft while attempting radio and visual communications. At approximately 1945 hours, the F-16s were forced to return to Langley due to fuel limitations. The aircraft was tracked until approximately 2015 hours when the primary transponder return was lost over the Atlantic Ocean. At approximately 2040 hours, a debris field was noted by a Coast Guard HC-144 in the area and a search and rescue effort was launched. That effort is still ongoing, but has been severely limited due to Tropical Storm Helen."

"Marvin, holy shit, I don't care," Johnson said impatiently. "Why are you telling me all of this?"

Bradley pulled out another piece of paper from his file and dramatically held it up. "Passenger manifest," he said as he started reading the names. "Darlene Craig, Frederick Mack, Jeffrey Lyons, and Michelle Decker."

Johnson nearly choked on his drink as he sat straight up in his seat. "You didn't!"

"I did!" Bradley replied enthusiastically.

Johnson put his drink aside and clapped, laughing as he jerked the paper out of Bradley's hands and studied it. "Michelle Decker *and* Lyons?" he asked as he shook his head. "You slippery son of a bitch! How?"

"Well, sir—"

"Wait, wait, wait," Johnson said as he held up his fingers. "No. Don't tell me. Plausible deniability and all that."

"Right, sir," Bradley replied. "Prudent."

"I could hug you, you sly son of a bitch!" Johnson said. He handed the paper back to Bradley and squeezed Bradley's knee. "Both of them? I never expected *this*."

"Well, sir, the opportunity presented itself and I made it happen," Bradley said proudly.

"You sure did!" Johnson said. "Oh man, this just made my night."

"I'm glad, sir," Bradley replied.

"And this is legit, right? Confirmed and everything? No traces?" Johnson asked as his smile vanished.

"I know you always say you don't need to know how the bologna's made, but let's just say the information in this Air Force report has been verified by external sources and has been confirmed, sir," Bradley replied. "That part of the problem is done."

Johnson smiled again as he leaned back and rubbed his hands together. "This is perfect, Marvin. Great job!"

"Thank you, sir," Bradley said as he put the files away. "I try."

Johnson leaned forward and grabbed another glass, chunking three pieces of ice in and pouring a healthy serving before offering it to Bradley. "Here! Have a drink, you've earned it my friend," he said with a smile.

"Thank you, sir," Bradley replied as he graciously accepted it.

As they toasted to the small victory, Johnson suddenly became serious again. He leaned in close to Bradley as his voice lowered. "But what about Martin?" he asked.

Bradley smiled. "Taken care of, sir," he replied. "By Monday, he'll be but a distant memory. A speed bump, if you will."

The sinister smile returned to Johnson's face as he raised his glass to toast Bradley once again. "Perfect," he said as their glasses clinked.

"But wait," Johnson said with a pensive expression.

"Yes, sir?"

"Weren't he and Decker lovers? Engaged or some such nonsense?" Johnson asked.

"I believe they were, sir," Bradley said. "What are you thinking?"

"After everything he's put us through, Marvin, he has been more than just a speed bump," Johnson replied.

"Yes, sir," Bradley said. "That's true."

"Let him suffer a bit first," Johnson said with a wicked smile.

"How so, sir?" Bradley asked.

"I don't care how you do it, Marvin," Johnson replied. "Just make sure he gets the news. After all, a national hero deserves to know that his fiancée was killed in a plane crash, doesn't he?"

Bradley grinned, seeing the genius in his boss's plan. "Yes, sir, he does," Bradley replied.

Johnson leaned back in his seat and closed his eyes. "Good, now, when we get home, I don't want to be disturbed. It's been a long day and I'm exhausted."

"Yes, sir," Bradley replied.

CHAPTER THIRTY-THREE

Tallahassee Federal Detention Facility
0610 Local Time
Present Day

Spectre shuffled through the breakfast line with Antonio following in close trail. The servers wasted no time in shoveling the milky-gray slop onto Spectre's tray and sending him along. It was a main course supplemented only with bread and a fruit salad. Prison food certainly wasn't like deployment food, Spectre had learned.

Spectre and Antonio sat at a table as far away from the entrance as Spectre could find. As he took a sip of his water and picked up his spoon, Antonio stopped him.

"What are you doing?" Antonio asked as he grabbed Spectre's wrist.

"What?" Spectre replied, cautiously eyeing Antonio's hand.

"You can't eat that!" Antonio said.

"Well, it may be barely edible, but I have to eat something," Spectre said, withdrawing from Antonio's grasp.

"No, no, no," Antonio replied, wagging his finger. "That tray belongs to DeSean now, remember?"

"You can't be serious," Spectre said.

Antonio looked over his shoulder, searching for DeSean and his crew. When he didn't find him, he turned back to Spectre and lowered his voice. "He told you to give him your breakfast today, didn't he?"

"Yeah, but—"

"But nothing!" Antonio hissed. "You don't get what it's like in here, man. You *do not* want to be making enemies like this. Even though you're a Kung Fu badass, you can't survive like this."

"You really think he cares?"

"I *know* he cares," Antonio whispered. "This place has a memory. Months, years, decades even. You don't know how long you're going to be here, but do you really want to piss him off over this grub?"

"Fair point," Spectre said. He looked up and saw the burley DeSean walking in with his usual group. "There he is."

"Do whatever you want," Antonio said. "But I've been here long enough to know that you gotta pick your battles."

Avoid. Negotiate. Kill. Antonio was right. It had been part of his training in Krav Maga. The best way to win a fight was to avoid it altogether. If it couldn't be avoided, then the second best way was to talk one's way out of it. Finally, if all else failed and all other options had been exhausted, it was important to kill. Kill the attacker's will to fight. Kill the attacker's ability to fight. Or, if necessary, kill the attacker.

Spectre nodded as he watched DeSean sit down at a table near the door. "I guess you're right," he said as he stood.

"You know I'm right," Antonio said. "Good luck."

Spectre walked across the crowded cafeteria. He passed Harlan and his merry band of racists. They watched him intently but said nothing as he approached DeSean's table. He saw two guards also take notice. It felt like all eyes were turned on Spectre as he neared DeSean.

Arriving at the table, one of DeSean's associates stopped him. His pants were baggy and worn low, exposing his white boxers. He was wearing a white tank top under his partially buttoned orange shirt. Spectre tried to present himself as unthreateningly as possible.

"What you want, cracka?" DeSean's bouncer asked.

"Just here to pay a debt," Spectre said.

The bouncer turned back toward DeSean who nodded his approval. Spectre thanked him and walked the final three steps to the table. He put the tray on the table, pushing it across to DeSean as he stepped back.

"I'm sorry for what happened," Spectre said.

DeSean smiled, revealing several gold teeth. "Sit," he ordered.

"I really need to get back," Spectre said.

"*Sit*," DeSean said sternly.

Spectre reluctantly sat across from DeSean. He hated the submissive nature of this game, but he knew Antonio was correct. His best chance of survival was to placate the various power-mongers, striking only when necessary. The day prior had been a mistake in the long run.

"Cal Martin, right?" DeSean asked as his look turned serious.

Spectre's face felt flush as he heard his name. "How did you know?" he asked timidly.

DeSean laughed. "I know everything that goes on here, son. You a pretty boy, but you ain't no unique cracka."

"I don't want any trouble," Spectre said.

"You got plenty of that," DeSean said. "But it ain't with me."

"Yesterday was a misunderstanding," Spectre said innocently.

DeSean let out a hearty laugh. "A 'misunderstanding?' That's what you crackas are calling ass whoopings these days? I done heard it all!"

"Won't happen again," Spectre said.

"I ain't talking about dem fools," DeSean said as the smile vanished from his face. "You got other problems."

"Story of my life," Spectre replied quickly.

"You saw dem boys that showed up yesterday, huh?" DeSean asked. "Buncha new crackas. Army types."

"You know them?" Spectre asked. He remembered a group of four fairly clean cut prisoners eyeing him in the courtyard the day prior.

"They been asking about you," DeSean replied. "Transferred here from New York or some shit. Bad news."

"What did they ask?" Spectre asked.

"They want to know who your boys are," DeSean said. "Whatever you did, they want to fuck you up."

"Good to know," Spectre replied. "But I should probably get going."

"I could get your back," DeSean said. "I need a new boo."

"Excuse me?" Spectre asked.

"This place can be dangerous without a big brother to watch your back," DeSean said.

Spectre stood, shaking his head. "I appreciate it. I really do. But I don't think I'm ready for that kind of commitment. It's not you, it's me. Sorry."

"Suit yourself, white boy," DeSean said as Spectre pushed his way out of the group surrounding the table.

Antonio had been watching Spectre's attempt at making new friends the entire time. As Spectre walked away from

DeSean's table, Antonio joined him, and together they started across the cafeteria, heading for their cell.

"How'd it go?" Antonio asked.

"I'm pretty sure he wants me to be his boyfriend," Spectre said with a sour look.

Antonio laughed. "You should feel special; he usually doesn't like your type. Plus, it's free protection."

"I'd rather take my chances," Spectre replied as he shuddered. "Speaking of which."

Spectre stopped at a table near the cafeteria door. The four men from the courtyard were sitting and eating, pretending to ignore Spectre as he walked by.

"You boys looking for me?" Spectre asked as he stopped at the table.

"Who are you?" the man nearest Spectre asked. He had a thick Russian accent.

"Don't act like you don't already know me," Spectre said with a grin. "You've been asking about me since you four showed up. I know why you're here."

"Look at this American Cowboy!" the man said, causing the three others to laugh. "Everything is about you. Are you here to challenge me to a showdown at the K-O corral?"

"I think you mean O-K corral," Spectre replied. "And no, I'm just here to let you put a face to a name, in case there's any confusion."

"There's no confusion here, cowboy," the man said. "But you should watch what you say. You might not like the results."

Spectre leaned in toward the Russian. "I'm your huckleberry," he said, quoting his favorite line from Doc Holliday in Tombstone.

The Russians laughed nervously. "Can you believe this guy?"

"Say when," Spectre said, rounding out his Doc Holliday tribute as he walked off.

"Holy shit!" Antonio screeched. "What was that? What happened to just getting along?"

"Those men aren't here to just get along," Spectre said as he headed back to the cell.

"Well, not anymore they're not! You have to cool it, friend," Antonio warned.

"They never were," Spectre said. "They were sent here to kill me. Did you see the tattoo on the talkative one's neck?"

"No, I missed it," Antonio said. "What was it?"

"Spetznaz, Russian Special Forces," Spectre replied. "And DeSean told me they've been asking about me. I don't believe in coincidences."

"So what are you going to do?" Antonio asked as they reached their cell and walked in.

"The only thing I can do, I—" Spectre stopped in his tracks. Someone had put a folded up newspaper on his pillow. He walked over to it and opened it. There was a sticky note attached inside that read, "I WARNED YOU."

Spectre's heart started racing as he scanned the headlines. It was the Tallahassee paper with today's date. The article on the right column was circled with a red marker. The headline read, "BILLIONAIRE CRASHES AT SEA, SEARCH CONTINUES."

Spectre was confused as he read the article. He had no idea who Jeffrey Lyons was, but the article explained how he was the heir to a billion-dollar company and had started his own tactical companies. As he read through the article, his stomach turned. *Frederick Mack, Darlene Craig, Michelle Decker.* Her name was underlined in red. He dropped the paper to the floor.

"Oh my God," Spectre said as his eyes began to water. "God, please, no."

"What's wrong?" Antonio said, picking up the paper. "What is this? How did this get in here?"

"They're all dead," Spectre said. He was stunned.

"Who?" Antonio asked. "What does this mean to you?"

Spectre had no words. The love of his life was gone. He was sure of it. The evil son of a bitch in the interrogation room had succeeded in taking her and Kruger out. A wave of guilt suddenly came over Spectre. *If I had just cooperated*, he thought. He felt like vomiting.

"Why is this name underlined? Talk to me, Cal," Antonio said.

"He killed her," Spectre said as he started to sob. "She was my fiancée."

"Oh Jesus man," Antonio said. "I'm so sorry."

Spectre buried his face in his hands. He felt like a caged animal, but at the same time, he wanted to curl up and die. The pain was infinitely worse than anything he'd ever felt, including the loss of Chloe and his best friend Joe Carpenter. Decker had been his best friend and lover. She was his entire world.

"Maybe they're not dead," Antonio offered. "It says here that they just located debris, but haven't been able to get to it yet due to bad weather."

"They wanted her dead, and they succeeded," Spectre said between sobs. "They won."

"Who won?" Antonio asked.

Spectre said nothing. Antonio finally gave up on Spectre after an hour went by. Spectre lay in the fetal position in the corner of his lower bunk, staring at the wall as he mourned the biggest loss of his life. After everything they had been through together, from captivity at the hands of ruthless assassins to a nuclear bomb on Midway Island, Spectre had almost started believing they were invincible.

But the truth was staring him in the face. Johnson and his despicable foot soldiers had won. They had gotten away with the murder of all of Spectre's friends, a U.S. Senator, and now, Decker. His world had ended. There was nothing left to care about. *God. Why didn't we just stay off the radar? Why did we go back?*

Two hours after breakfast, the public address system announced their courtyard time. Antonio helped Spectre out of the bed and forced him to walk with him. Spectre droned along like a zombie, numb to the world as he followed the herd out into the blinding sunlight.

Antonio sat Spectre down on the same bleachers he had occupied the day prior. Spectre said nothing; his thousand-yard stare said it all. He was just gone.

A few minutes after sitting down, Antonio stood. The four Russians approached and surrounded the two as Spectre stared at the dirt.

"Where is your fighting spirit, cowboy?" the Russian asked. "It has only been a few hours."

"The guards are watching, guys," Antonio warned. "Not now."

"Of course they are," the Russian said with a chuckle. "Why do you think we are here?"

Spectre looked up from the dirt. The Russian pulled out a switchblade knife and flicked it open, holding it close to his side.

Spectre stood, his face expressionless as he stared through the Russian. He held his arms out and said, "Do it."

"You should leave now," the Russian warned Antonio. "You are not of our concern."

"He's my friend," Antonio said, stepping in front of Spectre.

"Suit yourself," the Russian said. Flipping the blade around in his hand, he stabbed Antonio between the neck and collarbone. Antonio collapsed as the Russian followed up with another stab before turning to Spectre.

Spectre stood motionless with his eyes closed. He felt the blade slice through his skin and into his gut. His world seemed to slow down as he fell to his knees. The pain was immense, but numbed slightly by his desire to die. As he dropped to his knees, he felt the blade withdraw before it pierced his chest.

He fell forward as his face went into the dirt. He saw what appeared to be a dozen feet as he lay in the dirt. They were shuffling and kicking up dust. They were screaming. He saw Antonio on the ground, his lifeless eyes staring back at him. He felt someone grab his shoulders.

Someone flipped him over onto his back as he drifted away into darkness.

CHAPTER THIRTY-FOUR

Falls Church, Virginia
1209 Local Time

"**I** think I have something, boss," Meeks said as he stared at the array of computer monitors in front of him. He had recently adapted to the frigid cold of his isolated office, wearing fingerless gloves and a New England Patriots Starter jacket.

"Good work, Coolio," Kruger said as he and Decker sat in the chairs behind Meeks, waiting for him to find what he could on Jason Travis.

"This is everything I could find on him – service records, employment history, criminal record, medical history," Coolio said, pointing at the screen. "But there's something else."

"What's that?" Kruger asked.

"You may already know him," Coolio said as he paused for dramatic effect before opening a new window that showed a picture of Jason Travis.

"Holy shit!" Kruger said as he stared at the ruthless man staring back at him on the screen. "Are you sure?"

"What?" Decker asked, feeling like she was missing out on an insider conversation. "Who is he?"

Kruger studied the picture. "We knew him as Gabriel Cooks, but he made everyone call him 'Punisher' because he thought he was some kind of vigilante hero."

"You knew him?" Decker asked.

"He was gone before I got here," Meeks replied. "But I think the boss did."

"Gone from where?" Decker asked with a look of frustration. "Can we stop with the secrets already? I think we're deep enough in this now to be honest with each other."

"That's fair," Lyons said as he walked up behind them. "We can start with where you are."

"Thank you," Decker said as she turned to face the billionaire.

"Your friends are part of a group called Odin, named for the Norse god of war. It was a group formed by my Great-Grandfather and several of his friends in response to the sinking of the Lusitania before World War I. Over the years, the group has grown from mercenaries on a path to vengeance, to an established clandestine organization that answers to no government and lives by its own code."

"Wait a second," Decker interrupted. "So you're rogue?"

"Not exactly, Ms. Decker," Lyons replied with a sheepish grin. "We live by our own moral code. There are three others like me, and we have joined together to do what's right in the face of evil."

"And what happens if that code conflicts with the U.S. Government?"

"When my great grandfather started Odin a hundred years ago, he gave his men three rules. First, never kill or harm an innocent or civilian. Second, do not steal or pillage from noncombatants. And finally, always cover and fight for the man next to you. In the hundred years Odin has been working behind the scenes, these rules have carried and worked for every man and woman that has worked for us," Lyons replied.

"You didn't answer my question," Decker said, keying off on the obviously rehearsed reply.

"So long as the U.S. Government's interests do not interfere with those three rules, we are synergistic in our operations, Ms. Decker. But at times, we have been at odds. We support every government's right to sovereignty and its people's right to freedom and justice," Lyons replied.

"You're ok with this?" Decker asked Kruger. "It could be treason."

"It was a decision my team and I had to consider carefully, Michelle," Kruger said. "I had seen their work and heard about them in Afghanistan and Iraq. Their existence was rumored, but the rumors always pointed to an organization that could get beyond the bureaucracy and achieve results. I like results."

"Results against your own government?" Decker asked.

"I took an oath to support and defend the Constitution of the United States against all enemies," Kruger said before pausing. "Foreign *and domestic*."

"Historically, there have been few times where this has been a factor, Michelle. We have almost always been there to supplement the United States and its allies," Lyons interjected.

"*Almost?*" Decker asked suspiciously.

Lyons smiled. "You're very perceptive, Ms. Decker. But, yes, there have been times in our history when we have been forced to act against U.S. citizens, but rest assured they were not innocent."

"So you're the judge, jury, and executioner? What about rights? Due process?" Decker asked.

"Do you think the people trying to kill you today deserved due process?" Kruger asked. "What about the Chinese mercenaries on Midway Island?"

"If they had been captured, yes," Decker said. "And how did you know they were Chinese?"

"It's a very altruistic notion, Ms. Decker – to think that even the worst of our society can be reformed," Lyons replied.

"I didn't say that," Decker interrupted.

"But you really did. You see, the justice system is all about corrections, but some people just can't be corrected no matter how hard you try. For them, the only answer is death. We just happen to bypass the middle man," Lyons explained casually.

"I understand how the system works," Decker shot back. "But how do *you* determine guilt? What happened to being judged by a jury of your peers?"

"The people we go after have no peers," Kruger said. "They're not accountants who have a few too many drinks and get pulled over or a meth-head who robs a liquor store. These are people who want to massacre thousands of innocent people or disrupt governments or destroy freedom."

Lyons nodded. "We have lived by our founding principles for over a hundred years now. That's a century of being unknown to the public, but for a few select individuals. You are now one of those trusted few. I hope you will respect that trust. We are here to help you."

"Help me do what, exactly?" Decker asked. "How did you even find me?"

"I did that, ma'am," Meeks said. "After we found out about the bombing at Eglin, Kruger had me try to track you and Mr. Martin down. I found your hotel reservation in Jacksonville and used the hotel's IP security cameras to confirm it. When I saw you leave with Mr. Simms, I found his rental car reservation and set up an ALPR hit to alert me if he left the area. I was surprised to see it leave the area, so I pinged his phone and realized I wasn't the only one pinging it. Someone else was doing a similar search, coincident with a UAV mission from NSA. That's why Mr. Kruger decided to pick you up."

"That's a little creepy, but ok," Decker said. "Thank you."

"And Mr. Simms is comfortably on his way home now," Lyons said. "Don't worry, he'll be protected."

"But still. Why us? Why now?" Decker pressed.

"Spectre is a good dude," Kruger said. "I had my doubts about him at first, but he really proved himself after Ironman was killed."

"That's why I'm marrying him," Decker said with a smile.

"I consider you both friends. And when I heard about the attack, I knew you were being set up. That just happens to be something we can help with," Kruger said.

"You're going to go up against the Vice President?" Decker asked.

"Is that who you think set you up?" Lyons asked. "Martin did confess."

Decker scoffed. "He did that to save me. Cal didn't do anything. This has Johnson written all over it."

"What makes you say that?" Lyons asked.

"Well, since we're all friends here," Decker began. "After I was discharged from the hospital in Tampa, Cal and I went to a storage unit Charles Steele had given me the key to. In it was a thumb drive that contained files, audio recordings, and other incriminating evidence linking then Secretary of Defense Johnson to the Chinese. Apparently he had used them to try to kill Cal when he worked for Project Archangel in Syria."

"That was the trace route Ironman made me run," Meeks interjected. "The Chinese had been behind Spectre's radio encryption failure and the fake messages to rendezvous. They had also scrambled fighters to intercept our mission."

"Go on," Kruger said. Decker could see his jaw clench beneath his thick red beard as his eyes narrowed.

"Johnson had threatened Steele's family and given him hush money. He was working with a Chinese intelligence operative and an assassin to tie up loose ends. Steele knew he wouldn't live and created the thumb drive as an insurance policy for his family," Decker continued. "I have a close college friend at the State Department that got us an audience with President Clifton. That's why we were on Air Force One when it went down."

"Where is the thumb drive now?" Kruger asked.

Decker shook her head. "Gone. They took it from Cal when they took us all hostage."

"Did you make copies?" Meeks asked.

"No," Decker said. "With something this big, we didn't want to risk putting it on a laptop and it somehow getting into the wrong hands and manipulated."

"That's not a very solid lead," Lyons said.

Suddenly Meeks spun back around in his chair, hastily clicking through the info he had picked up on Travis. "That's it!"

"What?" Decker asked.

"Travis worked for Cajun Oil and Gas; I remembered seeing it in his civilian employment history. They hired him to do security," Meeks said excitedly.

"So?" Lyons asked.

"When we were on that mission in New Orleans," Meeks said, looking at Kruger. "Mr. Jane told me that Johnson had owned forty percent and helped run the company until he got into politics. Some Chinese company bought him out."

"Coolio, don't you think you could've mentioned that earlier?" Kruger asked with a scowl.

Meeks retreated into his chair. "Sorry, boss, but I didn't even think of it at the time. I just thought our boss was a business guy. It never dawned on me that he might be crooked, even after we were disbanded."

"So Travis is connected to Johnson through his old oil company," Decker said as she tried to piece it together. "What about the other thing? How did you know him as Gabriel?"

"That actually explains a lot," Kruger said as he leaned forward and rested his elbows on his knees. "You see, when Project Archangel was first thought up, it was a pretty selective process. We only picked up operators and pilots that had stellar reputations, and even then, there was a six-month interview process where we vetted them. There were only two people that I ever knew of that bypassed the process – Gabriel Cooks and Spectre."

Kruger could see Decker frowning and leaned over to put his hand on hers. "No offense to Spectre. He turned out to be a great dude, but everyone was surprised when he showed up one day. Rumor was that it was political and the order came from above, but Gabriel... Gabriel was something else."

"How so?" Decker asked.

"Well, we, at least, got to see his personnel record before he showed up. It said he had been a Ranger before going to Special Forces Operational Detachment-A or SFOD-A. That was the first red flag. I was SFOD-D, also known as Delta, and I had never heard of him. No one had ever heard of him. This world is pretty tight-knit, so it was uncommon to not have at least heard of a guy," Kruger explained.

"And then there was training. One of the things that set us apart from other covert groups was that we had our own 'zero-to-hero' training program. Even the pilots went through it. Spectre was a natural. I helped with his resistance training. He was good and picked it up quickly. But Cooks was a slow learner, and for a guy with an operator background, he should've been more like Spectre," Kruger continued.

"Again, that's why I'm marrying him," Decker said with a grin.

"Well, Cooks eventually picked it up and graduated, but the issues didn't end there. His first deployment was a train wreck. I wasn't with his team, but from what I was told, he was just ruthless. They were in the Horn of Africa and he wanted to kill everyone. His team leader had to keep him on a tight leash. He was identified as a risk and Ironman wanted to remove him, but from what I heard someone above him intervened," Kruger said.

"It wasn't until his second deployment that I got to experience it first-hand. We were in eastern Afghanistan. He had even told me he had been in the battle of Takur Gahr, but I had no idea he was holding on so tight. I was leading a six-man team to capture a Taliban commander that had fled to Pakistan to avoid capture. U.S. ROE didn't allow missions into Pakistan at the time, so obviously that's a job better suited for an unacknowledged organization than a traditional unit.

"But as we were skirting around a village, a man with his wife and kid were traveling on the mountain path we were using. It slowed us down, but I decided to wait them out before we kept on since the alternate route wouldn't be any faster. Cooks killed all three of them before I could stop him. I almost killed that son of a bitch when I found out," Kruger said.

"Jesus," Decker said as she sat captivated by the story. "What did you do?"

"We scrubbed the mission and brought him back. I told Ironman that if I ever saw that sick fuck again, I'd kill him. Ironman had him sent home and we never saw him again," Kruger said, shaking his head.

"Well, he's your top priority now," Lyons said. "Especially if he knows about our organization."

Kruger shook his head. "As much as I'd like to snatch the life out of him, there's still a threat of an attack on U.S. soil right now, boss. I can't let that happen."

"We don't have any actionable intelligence on that, Kruger," Lyons replied. "What we do have, Meeks can hand off to the FBI to run down, but this is more important."

"They had plans to attack school kids," Kruger said as he stood. "They're not done yet and neither am I."

"But if this Travis guy knows about Odin, we're all done," Lyons said. "You already took down the cell leader that we knew about. Yes, there could be more, but we don't know that for sure and the FBI is more than capable of handling that lead. We have to focus on the nearest alligator to the boat, and right now, that's maintaining the integrity of this organization."

Kruger's fists clenched. "I don't like it."

"I know you don't," Lyons said. "But I don't think we have a choice here."

"The FBI has a very good counterterrorism unit, Kruger," Decker offered.

As they tried to talk Kruger down, Meeks's computer sounded an alert. He spun around to open the alert. "Uh, oh," he said as he read the info.

"What's going on, Coolio?" Kruger asked.

Meeks looked back over his shoulder at Decker and then turned back to the screen. Sensing something was wrong, she jumped up and walked up to him. "What?" she asked.

"I have an alert set up on my system for anything related to Spectre where he's being held. Apparently there was a riot today," Meeks said as he lowered his voice. "It's not good."

"What's not good?" Decker asked frantically. "What happened? What's going on?"

Meeks pulled up a report and read through it quickly. "This is just a preliminary report. It doesn't say what happened – just that there was a riot and three inmates were stabbed. It lists the patients that were transported for medical care as Antonio Lopez, Dmitri Molanov, and Cal Martin," Meeks said."

"What else?" Decker asked. "Where is he?"

"I'll have to dig into their system more," Meeks said. "This is all I have right now."

Decker turned to Kruger. "We have to get him!"

"You're right," Kruger said as he turned to Lyons. "We recover Spectre and then we take down Travis."

"Fair enough," Lyons said, seeing the determination in Kruger's eyes.

CHAPTER THIRTY-FIVE

White House
1345 Local Time

"Sir, before we go into this meeting, there's something you should know," Bradley said in a hushed tone as he pulled the Vice President aside and allowed his entourage to keep going.

"What is it, Marvin?" Vice President Johnson asked as they stepped into a nearby vacant staffer's office and closed the door.

"I had a talk with Chapman before this meeting, but I'm not sure he's willing to play ball," Bradley whispered.

"I thought we took care of him?" Johnson grunted. As the Director of Central Intelligence, Chapman had been a key part of the Midway Island crisis, but unlike others, he had been hesitant to accept Johnson's leadership. He was a staunch supporter of Senator Wilson and had been the first to question whether Islamic terrorists or Chinese operatives were behind the attack. At the time, Johnson had silenced him, but that hadn't been the end of it.

In the aftermath of the attacks and secret hearings that followed, Johnson learned that Chapman had been researching Johnson's former business connections with the Chinese, suspicious of Johnson's potential involvement in the event. With the help of Travis, Bradley had taken care of it, or at least Johnson thought he had. He didn't want to know the details, but Bradley had reported that Chapman had dropped his inquiries and would be on their side going forward.

"We did, sir," Bradley whispered. "*Very* convincingly."

"What's his plan here?" Johnson asked.

"He has data confirming that the F-35 was taken down by terrorists," Bradley replied. "I tried talking to him, but—"

"Did you tell him what would happen?"

"Yes, sir, but he said he thinks the President should decide how the information is handled."

Johnson turned and opened the door. "Thanks, Marvin. Let's go before we're late."

They walked into the Situation Room and took their places to the right of where the President would be sitting. Joining them were FBI Director Schultz, DCI Chapman, Secretary of Defense Hunt, and the newly appointed Secretary of State Oliver Dunning. They remained standing as President Clifton walked in followed by her Chief of Staff Plonski.

"Please, take your seats," Clifton said as she took her place at the head of the conference table. "Thank you all for coming on such short notice."

As they all took their seats, Clifton leaned to her right to Johnson and asked, "How did it go in Ohio?"

"It was very sad," Johnson said. "They were both loved by the community."

"We should both go to their funeral," she replied as she looked at her chief of staff. Plonski nodded in acknowledgment as he jotted down a note in his ledger.

Clifton put her glasses on and turned to the classified folder in front of her. "Now," she said as she picked up the folder. "Let's get started. What do you have, David?"

"Yes, ma'am," Chapman replied. "What you have in front of you is our intelligence assessment of the F-35 crash in Florida. Based on our intelligence sources and intercepts of internal ISIS chatter, we believe that the group is correctly taking responsibility for the downing of this aircraft."

"How?" Clifton asked. "How does a rag-tag group of insurgents take down our newest and most advanced fighter?"

"Based on our assessments, ma'am, with a Russian SA-24 shoulder-fired surface to air missile that was smuggled in through Mexico," Chapman replied. "The dossier in front of you is of Tariq Qafir, a Pakistani national that we believe orchestrated the attack. We believe there may be another attack on the horizon."

"Secretary Hunt, does the Air Force have anything to support this based on the current investigation?" Johnson interrupted.

Hunt cleared his throat. "No, sir, we do not. In fact, we are confident that it was caused by a failure of the pilot's helmet and electronic displays which led to spatial disorientation at low altitude."

"Director Schultz?" Johnson asked as he made eye contact with the Director of the FBI. Schultz immediately looked away. He had been another that Bradley had *convinced* to get in line. His convincing, however, had required much less effort.

"This is the first we're hearing about it," Schultz replied. "We do have a credible threat of lone-wolf style attacks against soft targets, but nothing on military targets. Past or future."

"Please finish," Clifton said, ignoring the sidebar discussion.

Johnson glared at Chapman, hoping the DCI would take the hint and stand down. Chapman shuffled through his notes as he ignored the Vice President and continued.

"From our communication intercepts and other sources, Qafir's cell intends to target schools and local malls. They have gone to ground since the attack in Florida, but it is clear that they intend to strike within the coming months. Perhaps by the holidays," Chapman said.

"Do you have a specific region?" Schultz asked.

"That part was unclear. A few days ago the chatter suddenly stopped. We haven't heard anymore, but given Qafir's connections, I'd focus on major metropolitan areas in the Southeast," Chapman said.

"Ma'am, if I may," Hunt interjected after seeing the scowl on Johnson's face.

"Go ahead, Chaz," Clifton said.

"While there may very well be a credible threat of ISIS attacks, I think we should be clear on what has happened with the F-35 mishap. We do not want to associate this program with something that's simply not true," Hunt said.

"With all due respect, the documents are right in front of you, Secretary Hunt," Chapman replied. "We also have a thermal event picked up from satellites at the time of the crash. This is consistent with an explosion."

Hunt shook his head vigorously. "It's simply not true. We pulled the maintenance data from the aircraft. The Distributed Aperture System, which is designed to detect missile launches anywhere around the aircraft, showed no missile or threat warning indicators. Further, it *did* show a display and helmet failure followed by an afterburner initiation as the pilot attempted to recover from the unusual attitude. This boils down to human error and should be treated as such, as unfortunate as it is."

"You can keep your head in the sand on this if you like, but—" Chapman replied.

"What's your angle here, David?" Johnson blurted out angrily.

"Excuse me, sir?" Chapman replied.

"You have evidence that this was clearly an unfortunate accident caused by pilot error, yet you're getting very hostile in your defense of a very damaging narrative. Why?" Johnson asked.

"Sir, I'm just presenting the information we have so that *the President* can make the most informed decision on the matter," Chapman replied.

"Your track record is not the best, Mr. Chapman," Johnson shot back. "You may want to stand down."

"I don't follow," Chapman replied with a look of contempt.

"Due to *your* agency's intelligence failures, the President is lucky to be here today," Johnson said with a raised voice.

"That's not—"

"Gentlemen, enough!" Clifton barked. "I have neither time nor patience for this finger-pointing. Let's get back on track here. David, do you have anything further on this incident?"

"No, ma'am," Chapman said as he tried to stare down Johnson.

"Good," Clifton replied before turning to Director Schultz. "Track down the leads on a pending attack."

"Yes, ma'am," Schultz replied.

"Now, what do you have on the assassination of Senator Wilson?" Clifton asked.

"Well, ma'am, as of right now it's a pretty clear-cut case. Senator Wilson's top aide gave a statement that Cal Martin was left alone with Wilson's baggage. Martin confessed and confirmed that he placed the bag in Wilson's room. Motive is still unclear, but at this point it doesn't matter. The only issue is that Martin is in critical condition in the ICU at Tallahassee Regional Medical Center at this time," Schultz replied.

Johnson's eyes widened as he looked to Bradley for answers. Bradley shrugged as they waited for Schultz to elaborate.

"Why? What happened?" Clifton asked.

"Earlier this morning there was a fight in the prison courtyard and Martin was stabbed twice. From what I understand, he has a partially collapsed lung and one of his kidneys was severely damaged. I believe he's in surgery right now, ma'am, but that's all I know at this time. Two others involved died on arrival to the hospital," Schultz said, reading from his notes.

"I still don't understand why he would do all of this," Clifton said, shaking her head. "He didn't seem like the type."

"You were in a very stressful situation on Midway, Madeline," Johnson said as he put his hand on hers. "There's no way you could've known what kind of monster he would turn out to be."

"And poor Michelle Decker," Clifton said softly. "How have so many bad things happened to this couple? Do we have any updates on that?"

"No, ma'am," Plonski answered. "As of thirty minutes ago, the search and rescue efforts were still suspended due to the severe weather. The aircraft flew right into the tropical storm before it crashed. Sea states and winds are still high in that region. It may be a few days before they can locate any survivors or remains, but pieces of debris have been found."

"Director Schultz, I'd like you to have a team work with the NTSB on that investigation," Clifton said.

"Yes, ma'am," Schultz replied.

"From what I understand, it was just a case of hypoxia," Johnson said. "Why do you want the FBI involved?"

"Something about that whole thing just isn't right," Clifton replied. "Senator Wilson was murdered and then Lyons, who was an active supporter of Wilson's campaign, is killed with Martin's girlfriend two days later?"

"Do you think Martin was somehow involved?" Johnson asked with a raised eyebrow.

"I just want it looked into," Clifton said tersely.

"Not a problem," Schultz replied.

"Does anyone have anything else?" Clifton asked. As the cabinet members around the room shook their heads, she took off her glasses and stood. "Thank you all for coming."

Everyone stood as she left the room. Johnson and Bradley walked out behind her, turning toward Johnson's office as they left the secure area.

"Martin is still alive," Johnson grunted angrily as he stormed down the hallway.

"That will be remedied soon, sir," Bradley said.

"You've said that before," Johnson said.

"It will be covered, sir," Bradley reassured him.

"Chapman is going to be a problem," Johnson said in a low voice.

"I'll take care of it, sir," Bradley said.

"For good," Johnson said. "And make sure Schultz stays in line."

"Yes, sir," Bradley said with a sly smile as they continued down the hall.

CHAPTER THIRTY-SIX

Tallahassee Memorial Healthcare Center
1821 Local Time

The blue and white EuroCopter EC145 helicopter gently touched down on the hospital's roof helipad. The helicopter's side door opened, revealing four armed men wearing black body armor with US MARSHAL embroidered in gold on the front and back. Carrying shotguns, the men escorted the flight nurse wearing his blue flight suit as he pulled the yellow stretcher down the long, narrow ramp to the hospital access doors.

"I'll do the talking," Tuna said as Axe held the door open.

"Suit yourself," Axe said with a shrug as he followed Beast, Cuda, and the flight nurse in behind Tuna.

Entering the complex marked LEVEL G, they took the elevator to the critical care unit two floors down. The elevator doors opened and Axe gestured for Tuna to lead the way as they approached the nurses station.

Tuna smiled at the attractive brunette wearing blue scrubs as he approached. "Excuse me, ma'am, I'm looking for the prisoner, Calvin Martin."

"You're going to want to talk to the shift supervisor," the nurse replied. "I just started here."

"Can you point me to her?" Tuna asked.

The nurse smiled. "*He's* with a patient and should be right back."

"Thank you," Tuna said.

"Real smooth, boss," Axe said, punching him lightly on the shoulder.

The team waited as the shift supervisor finished with his patient and returned to the desk. At first, he ignored the armor-clad warriors, but after Tuna cleared his throat for the third time, the man finally acknowledged them.

"Don't you people just come and go as you please anyway?" the supervisor asked. "Can I help you?"

"We're here to transport the patient, Calvin Martin, to Jacksonville," Tuna said gesturing to the flight nurse. "Chopper's waiting."

"I heard you come in. I was wondering what that was all about. I'm sorry, but we didn't have any transports scheduled today," the supervisor replied.

Tuna pulled out a folded paper from his vest and handed it to him with his gloved hand. "The order just came in an hour ago. You should have it in your system by now as well."

"Wait right here. I am so sick of you feds," the supervisor said before letting out an exasperated sigh and walking to a nearby computer.

"You should've let me talk to him," Axe said as they waited.

"Because he seems like Axe's type," Beast said in his thick Russian accent. The former Spetznaz operator chuckled as Axe flipped him off.

"We're not trying to sell him a used Corolla with two hundred thousand miles, Axe," Tuna said, a jab at Axe's interim job selling cars at a Tampa dealership after Project Archangel disbanded.

"You sure? Because I bet I can get him in a low mileage Mini Cooper," Axe shot back.

"Alright, knock it off, he's coming back," Tuna said as the huffy supervisor returned, shaking his head.

"You're right, the order is there, but I don't think it's a good idea," the supervisor warned. "He's only been out of surgery for an hour. He's not stable enough to transport."

"I just work here," Tuna said as the supervisor handed back the transport order. "Where is he?"

"All the way at the end of the hall, Room 6C," the supervisor said as he pointed to his left. "It's the one with all the war mongers that look like you."

"Thanks," Tuna said.

"Well, he seemed nice," Axe said dryly as they turned toward Spectre's room.

"Your type," Beast said from the rear of the formation.

As they approached, the two armed guards sitting outside Spectre's room turned to face them. They were wearing uniforms marked Federal Bureau of Prisons and carrying holstered handguns instead of the body armor and shotguns Tuna's team wore.

Tuna wasted no time in announcing his purpose as the guard started to query them. "We're here to transport Prisoner Martin to Jacksonville," Tuna said, holding up the paper.

"No one told us anything about this," the guard closest to the door said.

"We just found out about it an hour ago," Tuna said. "Came straight from Washington."

Tuna handed the order to the protesting guard. The man studied it carefully, flipping it over several times before handing it back to Tuna. "I'll need to call my supervisor at the prison," he said calmly.

"Do you hear that?" Axe said, cupping his ear and pointing toward the ceiling. "That's the sound of a helicopter wasting taxpayer money at a thousand dollars an hour. We have to get going."

The guard looked at the other guard for help before shrugging. "I've just never done a transfer like this before. Do we go with you?"

Tuna tapped the tactical shotgun slung across his chest and laughed. "No, I think we can handle it. How is he?"

The guard frowned. "Not good. He has a collapsed lung and they just took out one of his kidneys. Probably won't make it through the night."

"Good riddance," the other guard said. "This scumbag killed an American hero."

"We're wasting time, fellas," Tuna said. "Can we take him or not?"

"I'll make a phone call while you guys prep him," the guard replied.

Tuna nodded to Axe. As they wheeled the stretcher in, another guard was sitting next to Spectre's bed. He stood as they entered. The guard from outside explained that they were transferring Spectre, but that he would need to call back to the facility first to figure out what to do.

"Let me see the order," the guard sitting by Spectre said.

Tuna handed it to him. He studied it carefully before handing it back to Tuna. "I've seen this before, don't bother them. The Marshals own him now."

"You sure?" the outside guard asked.

"Positive. We can go home early tonight, boys," he replied.

Tuna breathed a sigh of relief. Beast and Cuda took positions outside as the flight nurse went to work prepping Spectre to move. The cute brunette from the nurses station walked in and offered to help as they prepped Spectre for transport.

Spectre looked terrible. He was wearing an orange gown and handcuffed and shackled to the bed rail. Blood stained the bed sheets and his gown. He had tubes protruding from his swollen face. Tuna wondered if he would even make the short flight to Jacksonville where a private jet waited to take Spectre and company to Lyons's private medical facility in Virginia.

The men helped transfer Spectre from the bed to the stretcher. One of the prison guards reattached Spectre's handcuff and shackle to his new bed. "Safety first," he said as he double-locked the cuffs and put his key back in his pocket.

"Good to go," the flight nurse said finally, after making the necessary preparations. The prison guards helped push Spectre's bed out of the room and down the hallway. As they reached the elevator, Tuna turned and shook the helpful guard's hand, thanking him for his help.

"Well, that was easy," Axe said as the elevator doors closed behind them.

"We're not in Virginia yet," Tuna warned.

* * *

Jason Travis had watched the helicopter land as he and the two men accompanying him exited the white Chevy Tahoe. It had flown in low and fast, almost making a tactical landing like the helicopters he had flown on in Afghanistan, but he hadn't thought much about it at the time. It was just cool to see.

He was drained from the back and forth travel between Tallahassee and Washington. He hadn't planned on ever going back. The Russian mobsters had assured him that, for the price he had paid, Cal Martin would die a slow, painful death in prison. It was supposed to have been taken care of.

But to Martin's credit, no one had expected him to make friends in prison so quickly, much less friends with one of the most powerful prisoners in the facility. The guards had told Travis that the prisoner named DeSean had come to Spectre's aid, ending the knife attack and killing Martin's attacker. Travis was starting to see why Johnson hated the man so much – he just wouldn't die.

And so he found himself back in the armpit of Florida, finishing the job himself. Johnson's smarmy chief of staff had shit on him enough when he found out that Martin had survived. He didn't need more whining. Why wasn't he happy that he had killed two birds with one stone in taking down Lyons and Decker? Travis dreamt of the day he'd wipe the smug grin off the face of Johnson's whipping boy.

Travis pulled two badges out of his sport coat and handed them to his associates. He had worked with them since Johnson had taken office. Steven Barnhart was a former Marine with a nasty gambling habit. He wasn't the brightest, but he was fiercely loyal and did whatever it took to make things happen. Douglas Cordero, on the other hand, was new. The 6'5" former cage fighter thought he was smarter than he was and had a tendency of trying to do things his own way. Travis liked him, but always kept him on a short leash.

"You both understand what we're doing?" Travis asked as they accepted the badges.

"We're with the Bureau of Prisons Investigations Division here to assess the prisoner, got it?" Travis asked as the two stared blankly at him.

"Got it?" he asked again. They nodded. Travis led them to the elevator, which they took to the third floor critical care unit.

As Travis stepped off the elevator, he looked to his left to see three uniformed men turn as the elevator doors closed.

Travis thought he saw a glimpse of a man wearing tactical gear just before the elevator closed. As he heard the helicopter on the roof, it suddenly hit him.

Holding up his badge, he darted toward the guards. "Who were they?"

"U.S. Marshals," the first guard said. "Transporting the prisoner to Jacksonville."

"You idiots!" Travis shouted as he pushed past them. "No, they're not!"

Travis and his men bypassed the elevator to the stairway. Sprinting up the two flights of stairs, Travis drew his Sig P226 as Cordero and Barnhart followed suit. Reaching the top floor, Travis burst through the door with his gun up and ready.

Travis could see a man standing in the narrow corridor as they held the door open for the stretcher. The man in tactical gear picked his shotgun up to take aim, but Travis fired three shots, hitting him twice in the upper part of his plate carrier and once in the neck. The man dropped his shotgun as he fell and reached toward his throat.

"Axe!" he heard a man yell as the door swung shut.

Travis followed up with another shot to the head as he approached the downed man. The door swung open. Travis and his men spread out, avoiding the return fire as two men entered. One of the men dressed in tactical gear shot at Travis, missing as the other dragged the first man's lifeless body out the door.

As they exited, Travis attempted to follow. A hail of bullets and shotgun pellets peppered the door, causing him to retreat behind the wall. He motioned to Barnhart on the other side of the door. They began a silent countdown before Barnhart burst through the door, followed by Cordero and Travis.

Travis ducked and returned fire, sprinting to the left behind a roof vent as the two men carrying their downed comrade laid down suppressing fire. As he fired back, he could see that

Cordero had been hit and was crawling to where Barnhart had taken cover behind his own vent on the right.

The suppressing fire stopped as they loaded the downed man onto the helicopter and the door slid closed. Travis ran toward it, firing at the fleeing helicopter until the slide of his 9MM handgun locked open as he fired his last round.

"Fuck!" he screamed as he watched the helicopter disappear behind the other buildings.

CHAPTER THIRTY-SEVEN

Falls Church, Virginia
2314 Local Time

Decker was exhausted, but she couldn't sleep. Her eyes were puffy from crying. Her face felt raw. She had been sitting next to Spectre's bed for two hours without moving. She still couldn't believe it.

The last few hours had been torture. She and Kruger had met the plane at the airport. The first stretcher off the aircraft had been a body bag. No one had told her that Axe had been killed in a shootout. What seemed like an eternity later, they followed with Spectre and transported him to Lyons's private medical facility on his three-hundred-acre ranch.

Kruger had been livid. She had never seen anyone so angry. She was afraid to be within ten feet of him as he hovered over the body of his fallen friend. She wasn't sure how long they had known each other, but it was obvious that he meant a lot to everyone on the team. Her relief that it hadn't been Spectre was replaced by empathy.

But that empathy was fleeting. Spectre had been hanging on by a thread when he arrived. The doctor that Lyons used was supposedly one of the best in the country, but he was pessimistic about Spectre's chances. The travel had worsened Spectre's condition from the report the doctor had received after Meeks set up the transfer. His pulse was weak. Even with the ventilator, he was nearly suffocating. Decker wondered if she'd ever see his blue eyes again.

Kruger had gone out with Tuna to be with Axe's family when Spectre took a turn for the worse. Decker had been alone in the hospital room as she watched Spectre's body suddenly convulse before a multitude of alarms went off. She knew she was watching the love of her life slip away.

The doctor and nurses had been quick to rush into the room. One nurse dragged Decker out as she tried to cling to Spectre's hand. She didn't want to let go. *She couldn't let go.* She could barely breathe as the tears streamed down her face amidst her sobs.

When the doctor walked out, she could tell by the look on his face before he even said a word. Spectre had crashed. They had done everything they could to bring him back. After nearly thirty minutes of working on him, they had managed to get a pulse, but there was no guarantee, the doctor said, that they would be able to repeat those results when, *not if*, it happened again.

When it happened again. Lyons's doctor gave Spectre less than twenty percent chance of making it through the night. He was lucky to have even made it this far, he had told her. Most people wouldn't have made the helicopter flight in his condition.

Decker found herself lying with her head resting on Spectre's bed, listening to the rhythmic beeping of his heart monitor. As long as it sounded, he was beating the odds. Decker was convinced he would. He had been through so much in his life. He deserved a second chance. *He deserved a chance at happiness.*

"How is he?" a raspy voice asked from across the room.

Decker picked up her head. In the darkness, she saw Kruger leaning against the doorway, arms folded.

"How long have you been standing there?" Decker asked.

"Long enough," Kruger said softly. He walked up and squatted next to her as she sat up in the chair. Putting his hand on hers, he showed a much softer side than she had ever expected from the bearded operator.

"He's not good," Decker replied with trembling voice as her lip began to quiver.

Kruger stood, pulling her up with him as he gave her a hug. She buried her face in his shoulder, sobbing as he rubbed her back. "It's going to be ok," he said tenderly.

Decker withdrew, wiping her eyes as she leaned away. "The doctor thinks he won't make it through the night," she said with a sniffle. "It's not going to be ok."

"Don't count Spectre out just yet," Kruger said. "Your fiancé is a good man. A fighter. A *warrior.* I don't think he's done yet."

Decker looked back at Spectre and picked up his hand. "I hope you're right," she whispered.

Meeks knocked on the door as he stood in the doorway. "Excuse me, boss, am I interrupting?"

"What's up, Coolio? I thought you had gone home?" Kruger asked. "It's almost midnight."

"I had work to do, boss," Meeks said as he walked in holding a folder. "And I think I have something that might help."

"Did you find it?" Decker asked.

"I did, ma'am," Meeks said.

"Find what?" Kruger asked.

"One of the leads we were running down on Johnson was the circumstances around the murder of the Air Force One pilot's family. We had tracked down surveillance footage from the neighbor's camera, but Senator Wilson sent us to Florida before we could follow up the lead. While we were waiting for Cal, I was thinking about this Travis guy's connection to Johnson. I thought maybe if we could find out what happened with that and who took her hard drive from her, we could track down Travis," Decker said. "I don't believe in coincidences."

"And it worked," Meeks said. "Mrs. Watson used cloud storage for all of her surveillance footage. I was able to pull up the footage from when the two agents took the hard drive."

"Jesus, that's brilliant," Kruger said. "And? What'd you come up with?"

Meeks opened the folder he was holding, pulling out a still shot from the surveillance camera. It showed two men in suits standing in Ethel Watson's driveway. "I started with the day the hard drives were taken. These two men identified themselves as law enforcement, if I understand correctly, but they were nothing of the sort."

"Who were they?" Decker asked.

"Douglas Cordero and Steven Barnhart," Meeks replied. "Barnhart is a former Marine and for Cordero, the only thing I could find is a criminal history of battery, domestic violence, and petty theft. He was also apparently a cage fighter at one point, according to what I found on social media."

"Any connection to Johnson?" Decker asked.

"Nothing direct, *but*, I did manage to pull their W-2s, and they both worked for Cajun Oil and Gas at different times," Meeks replied excitedly.

"Do you have their addresses?" Kruger asked.

"I have three addresses, boss," Meeks replied.

"Three?"

"I have address of record for both of them, but I was able to get a plate on the vehicle they were in when they went to Mrs. Watson's house. I did an ALPR query and found out that they went to an unregistered warehouse in Georgetown shortly after. Not sure if it's anything, but I thought you might want it," Meeks said with a shrug.

Kruger stood and grabbed Meeks by the shoulders. "Great job, Coolio. I owe you a six pack of beer."

"Ouch," Meeks whimpered as Kruger released him. "How's Mr. Martin?"

"It's going to be a long night," Decker replied with a soft sigh.

CHAPTER THIRTY-EIGHT

Washington, D.C.
0615 Local Time

"Wake up, bub," he heard a voice growl in the darkness.

Steven Barnhart rolled onto his back in his bed as the voice registered. His eyes opened to the muzzle of an M4 staring him in the face. He instinctively tried to grab it and disarm the intruder standing over his bed, but instead the bearded apparition jammed the muzzle into Barnhart's forehead with great force.

"Not today, bub," the man said. The pain was blinding. Two other men grabbed Barnhart, dragging him out of bed as they drove him face first into his hardwood floor. They Flexcuffed his hands behind him before duct taping his mouth shut and putting a burlap sack over his head.

He thought back to his survival training in the Marines. They had done similar things to him in training. He tried to keep track of his surroundings and maintain situational awareness. The men dragged him onto the balcony of his apartment.

As he stood there, he felt them rigging him with a harness. He heard the sound of rotor blades off in the distance before he felt a stick in his neck. Seconds later, he was out.

* * *

Kruger cracked his knuckles and exhaled slowly as he walked into the soundproof interrogation room in the sprawling compound. Despite the rage brewing inside, he knew he had to keep his emotions in check.

He wanted nothing more than to walk in and destroy the man sitting in the lone chair. Steven Barnhart was at least partially, if not completely, responsible for the death of one of Kruger's best friends. Just looking at the man made Kruger think of the pain in the faces of Axe's wife and kids as he broke the news.

Kruger had engaged in many interrogations throughout his career, first as a member of the Army's SFOD-D "Delta" team, then as part of Project Archangel, and finally with Odin. Some of it had been personal for him, especially in Afghanistan while interrogating Taliban commanders that had been responsible for the death of his brothers in arms. But this went far beyond anything he had ever encountered. This was deeply personal.

But Kruger knew he'd have to be at the top of his game to succeed. The former Marine in front of him had been through survival and interrogation resistance training. He wasn't a gutless terrorist, but a trained warrior.

Kruger walked in and snatched the hood from Barnhart's head, tossing it aside as he walked behind Barnhart. Barnhart's wrists and ankles were restrained to the metal chair with leather straps. He made no attempt to turn around to look at Kruger.

"I was wondering when you'd show up," Barnhart said smugly. "What has it been? A couple hours? Time deprivation, nice."

Kruger said nothing as he walked to the back of the room. He opened the bottom drawer of the rolling tool box, pulling out a cordless drill and inserting a fresh battery. He found a 5/8 titanium drill bit and inserted it before squeezing the drill's trigger.

"You won't get anything out of me," Barnhart said as he heard the spinning drill. "Drill or not."

Kruger slammed the drawer shut and walked back around to face Barnhart, holding the cordless drill loosely by his side. Barnhart eyed it as Kruger stood there in silence.

"Are you CIA?" Barnhart asked nervously. "Is this the farm? You must be CIA. What do you want from me?"

"When I finish with you, you're going to wish I was CIA, bub," Kruger said ominously.

Barnhart smiled, still staring at the drill. "Yeah, right. I know you're not really going to use that thing."

"What makes you think that?" Kruger asked.

"Because you have rules," Barnhart replied. "That's the problem with you government types – too many rules. This little act might work with Jihadi Mohammed, but you're wasting your time if you think I'm going to shit my pants. Besides, I don't know anything anyway."

"You don't?" Kruger asked.

"Nope," Barnhart said. "In fact, this is kidnapping."

"Fair enough," Kruger replied calmly.

"I'm just a security consultant," Barnhart added. "There are far more interesting people you could be talking to right now."

Without warning, Kruger grabbed Barnhart's right hand. Barnhart tried to withdraw it, but Kruger overpowered him, driving the spinning drill through the top of Barnhart's right hand as he screamed out in pain.

As Kruger withdrew the bit from Barnhart's hand, blood poured onto the floor. Barnhart cried out in agony. "What are you doing? My God!"

"I assumed you were right handed," Kruger said as he pulled out a rag from his pocket and wiped the blood off the bit. "Was I wrong?"

"You're a monster!" Barnhart shouted.

"We haven't even scratched the surface yet, bub," Kruger said as he closed in on the writhing Marine.

"What do you want from me?" Barnhart asked.

"Tell me about your boss," Kruger said.

"My boss? Who's my—"

Before he could finish, Kruger sprang toward him, grabbing Barnhart's throat as he closed to within inches of the Marine's face. "I'm going to move on to knee caps and then eyeballs if you don't start talking, bub. Don't mistake my patience for weakness."

Kruger released the man's throat and stepped back. Barnhart choked and wheezed as he tried to catch his breath.

"Jason Travis. Tell me about him," Kruger said coolly.

Barnhart's eyes widened.

"You think I don't know?" Kruger asked. "I *trained* your boss."

"Holy God," Barnhart said, shaking his head as he closed his eyes.

After a pause, Barnhart opened his eyes and let out a deep breath. "What do you want to know?" he asked finally.

"Who is Travis working for?" Kruger asked.

"His name is Marvin Bradley," Barnhart said as he looked Kruger in the eyes. "A real slimy little prick. Jason hates him, but he makes sure we're well taken care of."

"Who's *we*?" Kruger asked.

"Who isn't?" Barnhart replied. "He has so many people on the payroll; it would be easier to tell you who doesn't work for him."

"Who does he work for?"

"Bradley?" Barnhart asked with a chuckle. "You mean you've never watched the news?"

"Humor me," Kruger said, holding up the drill.

"Alright, geez," Barnhart said weakly. "He's the Vice President's Chief of Staff."

"And Travis reports directly to him?" Kruger asked.

Barnhart nodded. "It didn't always used to be that way. Back in the old days, Johnson used to call the shots. But ever since he got into politics, Bradley has been his shit screen. Plausible deniability or some shit."

"Why did he try to kill Jeff Lyons?"

"*Try?*" Barnhart asked with a raised eyebrow.

"Answer the question, bub."

"Look, man, I don't get into the weeds of the *why*, I just worry about the *how* and the *how much* I'll be pocketing," Barnhart said. "But I heard it was because that spoiled prick was talking shit about Johnson. Johnson hates that sort of thing."

"Why were you at the hospital last night?" Kruger asked. His anger grew just thinking about it.

"Because I was paid to be there," Barnhart said arrogantly.

Kruger punched Barnhart in the solar plexus, causing him to gasp for air. "Try again," Kruger growled.

As Barnhart recovered from the hit, Kruger placed the tip of the drill bit on Barnhart's left knee. "Final warning," he said.

"Ok, ok," Barnhart said. "We were there to finish the job with Cal Martin. He was supposed to die in prison, but some thug took a liking to him and saved him from the Russians."

"Who set him up?" Kruger asked as he removed the drill from Barnhart's knee.

"That was all Jason," Barnhart said. "He loves explosives."

"Ordered by Bradley?"

Barnhart nodded. "Johnson *hates* Martin. He and his hot little girlfriend were poking around with Senator Wilson. I think he's more afraid of Martin than anyone else. We followed him to the old lady's house and realized he was getting too close."

"Ethel Watson?" Kruger asked.

Barnhart nodded once more. "Crazy old lady. I thought we were going to have to take care of her too."

"Why did you take the hard drive from her?" Kruger asked.

"Because when they served the search warrant on that Air Force Lieutenant Colonel's house, we went with them and realized she had cameras pointing at the house," Barnhart said.

"So?"

"So, we were worried that the cameras saw us," Barnhart replied. "Or saw Travis."

"Why? What did he do?"

Barnhart gave Kruger a look of disgust. "That was a nasty one. He was supposed to just take their family and make it look like they were kidnapped so the guy would land Air Force One where we wanted him to, but Travis took it way too far."

"How far?"

"He chopped them up. Even the little boy. Said it would be more believable that way. It was gruesome," Barnhart replied, shaking his head.

"And you went along with it?"

"Hey, I ain't perfect. Sometimes you have to look the other way when the money is this good," Barnhart replied casually. "Job security, ya know?"

"Where can I find Travis?"

"No one really knows where he stays. He's pretty paranoid," Barnhart said. "But we have a warehouse in Georgetown that we work out of. All our gear is there."

Barnhart looked at his hand, trying to shake off the pain. "He probably won't be there, though."

"Why not?"

"We got another job last night," Barnhart said. "I think he was planning on us doing it tonight."

"What was the job?"

"Another hit."

"Who?" Kruger asked impatiently as he put the drill bit back on Barnhart's knee.

"David Chapman."

"The director of the CIA, David Chapman?" Kruger asked.

"You know him?"

"We've met," Kruger replied. "Why?"

Barnhart tried to shrug against his restraints. "Same as anyone else, I guess. He pissed off the boss. That's why I thought you were CIA. I thought maybe they had found out and taken me."

"How is he planning on doing it?"

"No idea," Barnhart replied. "He said he'd call us today with a time to meet up. Doug got shot yesterday at the hospital, so I'm assuming he wanted to deal with that first."

"Douglas Cordero, right?" Kruger asked. "Where is he?"

"I'm guessing at home, or he should be today. The bullet went through and through, so he might even be with Travis tonight," Barnhart said. "That's another sick bastard."

Kruger started toward the rear of the room. Barnhart eyed the drill as Kruger passed him. "What are you going to do with me now?" Barnhart asked. "I've been cooperative."

"One more question," Kruger said, standing behind Barnhart. "And don't even think about lying to me, bub."

"I think we're past that," Barnhart said. "I've already told you everything I know. If Jason or Bradley or Johnson find out that I talked, I'm a dead man. So we need to talk about protection."

"First, answer my question," Kruger said.

"Ask away," Barnhart said.

"On the rooftop of the hospital last night," Kruger began. "You were there, right?"

"Yes, sir, I was," Barnhart replied.

"And you know that one of my guys was shot, right?" Kruger asked.

"That wasn't me!" Barnhart said.

"Who pulled the trigger?" Kruger growled.

"Jason Travis," Barnhart said. "He was the first through the door out of the stairwell. Your people were just getting onto the ramp toward the helipad while the last guy was covering rear security. Travis shot him three times and he fell before he could return fire, but he wasn't dead. Travis shot him execution style before they could pull him to safety."

"You're sure?" Kruger asked.

"I swear on my momma's grave!" Barnhart pleaded. "If you know Jason like you say you do, then you know that's something he'd do."

"You're right," Kruger said. Walking up behind Barnhart, he wrapped his left arm around Barnhart's neck in a chokehold to keep him still.

"What are you doing?" Barnhart protested. "Please! I'm sorry!"

"It's too late for *sorry*, bub," Kruger said. With his right hand, he placed the drill bit against the base of Barnhart's skull and squeezed the trigger, driving the spinning bit into Barnhart's brainstem and killing him instantly.

CHAPTER THIRTY-NINE

Georgetown
1826 Local Time

Jason Travis parked his Lexus in the small empty parking lot behind the warehouse. He checked his phone for messages and found none. He still hadn't heard from Barnhart.

Although it wasn't uncommon for the former Marine to go on a bender with hookers and blow after an op – particularly after one filled with direct action like the one the night prior – Barnhart was nothing if not completely reliable. He never ignored Travis's phone calls or texts, and he was always at least fifteen minutes early, even if he showed up completely hungover.

Travis found Barnhart's number in his contacts and dialed it one more time. As before, the call went straight to voicemail. Travis hung up without leaving a message. *I don't need this shit right now*, he thought.

He had bigger issues to worry about. The trail for Martin had gone cold. Every off-the-books source Travis could tap into had no leads at all. There was no record of any patient of any name with Martin's injuries checking into a hospital anywhere within two thousand miles. Professionals had obviously taken him and stashed him somewhere.

As Travis had returned to his apartment last night, he had gotten a secure message from Bradley through their digital drop. It was another high priority hit. Travis accepted, having decided that Martin could wait. He had barely survived the prison attack, and from all accounts, probably wouldn't survive much longer. He might have even died during the escape. Travis could only hope.

Travis had also decided to hide Martin's escape from Bradley and Johnson. He didn't need the harassment from Johnson's sniveling little whipping boy. Martin would be taken care of soon enough. No one could hide forever, even someone as resilient as Martin.

It wasn't the first time Travis had heard of a hit being put out on Martin. Before the election, Johnson had used the Chinese and a Cuban to do the heavy lifting. They offered Johnson more plausible deniability and allowed Travis to focus on more important things like security and surveillance.

But both the Chinese and the Cuban had failed to seal the deal on numerous occasions. Even when they had him in custody twice, they still failed to finish the job. Travis was determined not to make the same mistake. Travis knew that he was better than the Chinese and smarter than the Cuban. Martin's escape from the hospital was only a minor setback made possible by friends in high places.

Travis found himself wondering how a man like Martin could have so many friends. After replaying the video of the Colombian hit team getting taken out for the hundredth time, Travis had finally recognized the bearded savior of Decker. It had been Kruger, the man that had trained him and worked with him during his brief time at Project Archangel. Travis knew that Kruger was driven by misguided principles and a moral compass that was entirely too sensitive. In Travis's mind, that made Kruger weak.

Although he had never gotten confirmation from Johnson, Travis knew that Kruger had been behind his dismissal from Project Archangel. They had been given the opportunity on a silver platter to kill a ruthless Taliban Commander responsible for the lives of many American servicemen. The only minor roadblock was a small family impeding their route into Pakistan. Time was critical and Travis did exactly what he had to do to make the mission happen. After all, the lives of a few non-combatants were worth far less than the men and women in uniform that would be saved by killing the terrorist scumbag hiding on the other side of the mountains.

But Kruger hadn't seen it that way. He thought Travis was a monster. He didn't have the stomach to do what was necessary and scrubbed the mission, crying to Steele that Travis wasn't a fit for the team. Travis thought Kruger should've been the one dismissed. *He was an arrogant coward.*

Travis was disappointed that Kruger had been killed on the plane that crashed in the Atlantic. He had been looking forward to squaring off with Kruger and killing him – finally a worthy adversary. Kruger would die a coward's death and Travis would emerge as the superior warrior. *Such a shame.*

With Kruger and Decker out of the picture, Kruger wondered who the team was that had beaten them to Martin. The timing of the order to take out Chapman made Travis think that maybe it had been a CIA team. Chapman had been silenced once before. Was he trying to use Martin as leverage? Was that the reason for the rescue?

As he sat in deep thought, Travis looked in his rear view mirror to see Cordero's blue Porsche Carrera GT4 pull into the lot and take the spot beside him. Travis killed the engine and exited his four-door sedan. Cordero limped out of his car toward Travis.

"Have you heard from Barnhart?" Travis asked as Cordero approached.

"I know he went out to the clubs last night, but I didn't talk to him after," Cordero said.

"That's what I thought, but he's not answering," Travis replied.

Cordero shrugged. "Maybe he found another future ex missus Barnhart, who was working her way through law school one dollar at a time?"

"I doubt it. We'll have to do this op without him," Travis said. "Are you up for this?"

"I've fought through worse," Cordero said. "I'll be fine."

Travis nodded as he pulled out his key to the back door of the small warehouse. He opened the door as the alarm beeped. Turning to his left, he entered the six-digit pin into the wall-mounted keypad and the alarm went silent.

Travis turned the lights on, revealing several armored SUVs, stacked crates of military-grade weapons, an interrogation cage, and a computer workstation lined with monitors and servers.

"Let's get what we need, brief up a plan, and get moving," Travis ordered as Cordero limped in behind him.

Travis headed straight for the safes near the computers. He spun the combination and opened the safe, pulling out the hard drives. As he did, he heard Cordero yell something from the other side of the building.

Drawing his Sig Sauer P226, Travis put the hard drive back in the drawer and slammed it shut before spinning the lock. "What's going on, Cordero?" he asked as he turned toward the sound of Cordero's voice.

"Jesus Christ!" Cordero yelled.

Travis picked up his pace, sweeping left and right for threats as he maneuvered through the maze of vehicles and equipment. As he quickly moved through the obstacles toward Cordero, he searched high and low for threats until he rounded the last corner and found Cordero standing with his back to him.

"What's going on?" Travis asked after confirming there were no threats.

"Jesus Christ! Look at this!" Cordero said as he turned toward Travis and sidestepped. Barnhart was slumped over in a chair with something hanging around his neck.

"Somebody killed him, man!" Cordero yelled.

Travis holstered his weapon. He walked up to find a picture hanging around Barnhart's neck. He picked it up. It was Travis's service picture from his time in the Army. With a marker, someone had written JASON TRAVIS, YOU'RE NEXT. YOU CAN TRY TO RUN BUT YOU'LL ONLY DIE TIRED in big block letters.

"They know who we are, man!" Cordero shouted nervously. "Holy shit. We're fucked."

"Settle down," Travis said calmly as he examined Barnhart's lifeless body. He walked behind the chair, finding the dried out blood from where something had been inserted into the back of Barnhart's skull. *A drill? Bullet?* Travis couldn't be sure.

"Someone's been in here. This place is compromised!" Cordero continued.

"Shut the fuck up," Travis ordered.

"C'mon man, look at this!" Cordero protested.

Travis shot Cordero a look of disgust. "Stop."

Travis began looking around the immediate area, searching for clues that someone had been in. There were no footprints on the dusty floor, no signs of entry, and nothing had been disturbed in even the slightest. The alarm had been set and all the doors were locked. Whoever had been in here had been a professional.

"What are we going to do?" Cordero asked. "We can't stay here."

"We're going to continue the mission," Travis said calmly.

"What?" Cordero asked. "There is no mission! They know who we are! *No one* knows about this fucking place! We're fucked!"

Travis instantly closed the distance between himself and Cordero, stopping within inches of Cordero's face like a Marine Drill Sergeant. "I said calm the fuck down," he growled.

Cordero stayed silent, avoiding eye contact as Travis's jaw clenched.

Satisfied that Cordero had calmed down, Travis took a step back. "This was a professional job – CIA. Chapman is trying to scare us," he said calmly.

"Well, it worked," Cordero replied.

"Don't be such a pussy," Travis said. "I bet this means they have Martin too. I'll question Chapman and find out where they've stashed Martin before I kill him. Two birds, one stone. This is good."

"Are you fucking crazy? If this is the CIA, they'll know we're coming!" Cordero said. He tried to withdraw as Travis glared at him threateningly.

"Good," Travis said.

"Good?" Cordero shrieked. "How is that good?"

"They'll put up more of a fight," Travis said with a wicked smile.

"You mean like they did on the roof?" Cordero said, pointing at his right leg. "That kind of fight?"

Cordero threw up his hands and turned to walk away. "Fuck this, man. I didn't sign up for this shit. I'm out."

As Cordero started to walk away, Travis called his name. Cordero turned, coming face to face with the barrel of Travis's handgun.

"I'm sorry, Douglas, but quitters won't be tolerated," Travis said as he squeezed the trigger, hitting Cordero in the right eye with a 9MM round.

CHAPTER FORTY

Washington, D.C.
2235 Local Time

He moved quickly and quietly in the darkness. He approached the luxurious home overlooking the Potomac River with deliberate, smooth movements. His adrenaline surged with every step, anticipating the thrill of the kill.

The security detail that stayed behind when Chapman and his family were out of the house was a skeleton crew at best. Only four agents from the CIA's protective services stayed behind when the Director was out of the house – a modest task for the average trained operative to bypass alone, but Jason Travis considered himself far from average. It would be child's play.

He waited in the foliage as a guard completed his half-hour perimeter checks. Through his contacts, Travis had access to all of Chapman's security protocols. He knew exactly where each guard, camera, motion sensor, and trip wire would be. *Child's play.*

As the lone guard cleared the waterfront area, Travis emerged, walking quickly with his suppressed Glock 21 low and ready. He didn't want to have to take out any of the guards for fear of alerting the others, but if he had to, he was ready to do it quickly and quietly.

Travis pulled out a small box from his pocket as he approached the back door. After ensuring no one was around, he opened the box, revealing a small neodymium rare earth magnet. Knowing exactly where the door sensor was, Travis attached the magnet on the outer wall against it. He then pulled out his lock pick gun and went to work on the deadbolt.

With the door unlocked, Travis slowly opened it and walked in. He saw a guard in the kitchen as he made his way quietly through the living room to the stairs. As he ascended the wooden staircase, Travis made slow and deliberate movements, careful not to cause any creaks.

At the top of the staircase, Travis checked his watch. He had fifteen minutes before the Chapman family was scheduled to return home. *Plenty of time.* He turned right and moved slowly down the hallway with his handgun up and ready. At the end of the hall was the door to the master bedroom – exactly as the floor plan had shown. *Cordero had been a coward. This was too easy,* Travis thought.

Travis moved to the master bedroom door. He reached down with his left hand as he held his gun up with his right. He slowly turned the brass knob, careful not to make any noise as he gently pushed the door open.

The master bedroom was mostly dark, illuminated partially by moonlight through the window. Travis turned left toward the bathroom and closet. All he had left to do was set up and wait for Chapman and family to return. He walked through the attack in his head. He would shoot the wife first and then pin down

Chapman, questioning him about Martin's location before finishing off the wife and making it look like a murder-suicide. With the digital evidence he had to give to the news media, no one would suspect a thing. Johnson would probably give him a raise.

As he moved toward the closet, he heard a low, deep voice in the darkness behind him. "Bad idea, bub."

Startled by the noise, Travis spun around to face the voice with his weapon up. As he did, a crushing blow to the side of his head nearly knocked him to his knees, causing him to drop his gun.

"I'm going to enjoy this," the voice growled in the darkness.

His ears were ringing and his vision blurred as he tried to regain his senses. He stumbled back to gain distance from his foe as he looked for the gun. When he didn't find it, he shook off the blow and squared off against his attacker.

"You're definitely not one of Chapman's men," Travis said as he put his hands up and assumed a fighting stance.

"Good observation," the man said gruffly as he stepped into the dim light. The beard instantly gave him away. *Kruger. He's not dead after all! Finally, a worthy opponent!*

Travis smiled as he wiped the blood from his lip. "This is a pleasant surprise."

"It won't be," Kruger said. "I should have done this in Afghanistan."

Travis laughed maniacally. "You were weak then just like you are now — always wanting to fight fair. You don't have the stomach to do what it takes to win."

Travis unsheathed his tactical knife from his belt and lunged toward Kruger. Kruger deflected the blade with his forearm and sidestepped, causing Travis to overshoot toward the bed in the center of the room. Travis followed up, spinning the blade around in his hand to attempt a slashing attack, but Kruger instantly intercepted the blade, blocking Travis at the wrist.

Travis kicked Kruger away from him, creating separation as he coiled to strike once more. "So it was your people that took Martin from the hospital? I knew one of them looked familiar. Whoever I killed wasn't even paying attention. You should probably train them better."

Kruger stayed silent. Travis laughed before lunging forward. As he did, Kruger parried the attack before drawing his own blade and driving it into Travis's abdomen. Travis stumbled forward and fell to his knees, dropping his knife while clutching the open wound.

As Travis tried to turn and fight, Kruger calmly walked up behind him, grabbing him by the hair with his left hand as he closed in with the knife. "You weren't good enough to hold his jock strap," Kruger said before driving the bloody blade of the knife into Travis's throat and ripping it forward.

As the blood gurgled, Kruger kicked Travis in the back with the heel of his boot, driving him face first into the hardwood floor as he bled out and died.

"Fuck you," Kruger said as he wiped the blade on his pant leg and sheathed it.

Kruger walked out of the room and down the stairs. Waiting in the kitchen were Director Chapman and the head of his security detail, Agent Mark Finch.

"Where is he?" Chapman asked as he saw the blood on Kruger's shirt and pants.

"Dead," Kruger said matter-of-factly. "On your floor."

"Did you really have to kill him?" Chapman asked. "We could have gotten intel from him."

"Yes, I did," Kruger replied angrily.

"Alright then," Chapman said, turning to Finch. "Let's get this scene secure and cleaned up."

"Yes, sir," Finch said before excusing himself.

"I guess I should thank you and your boss," Chapman said. Lyons had made a personal appearance at Langley to warn

Chapman of the plan Barnhart had told them about. The presence of Lyons, despite the rumors of his death, helped lend credibility in addition to Chapman's previous experience.

Lyons had laid out the case for Chapman, showing him the recording of Barnhart's interrogation and the mounting evidence they had against Johnson. Lyons discussed Kruger's plan, and despite a few initial objections, Chapman opted to go along with it, and briefed Finch to follow the leaked security protocols by the number to allow Travis unfettered access. The only thing he couldn't predict was Kruger's thirst for vengeance.

"We still have more work to do," Kruger said.

"If there's anything the agency can do for you, let me know," Chapman offered.

"Pretend like this never happened," Kruger said. "We have some more pieces to put together first, but when we do, you'll be playing a major role."

"I hope you're getting more evidence," Chapman said. "If we're really going to bring down Johnson, you'll need more than an illegal interrogation video."

"We'll be in touch," Kruger said before turning to leave.

CHAPTER FORTY-ONE

He was running, but it felt like he was barely moving. Spectre was wearing the same survival gear he had worn after ejecting over Iraq, but instead of the twenty to thirty pounds that it usually added, it felt like two hundred pounds. He could barely move his legs as he trudged through the sand. It felt like a sand storm was raging around him. Everything was hazy and blurry, but he couldn't hear anything. *Am I dead?*

As he cleared the first dune, he saw his ex-fiancée, Chloe Moss. She was in her flight suit, bright-eyed and beautiful as she had been on the day they had awkwardly met in the squadron. She smiled at him as he tried to approach. But as he got closer, she turned and ran. Spectre tried to keep up, but the weight of his gear was too much to overcome.

Spectre climbed another sand dune on his hands and knees. As he regained his balance, he found himself on an airfield. He could see Chloe in the distance. She called out to him as a man appeared behind her. The shadowy figure put a gun to her head and pulled the trigger. Spectre fell to his knees.

He felt himself being pulled up from the grass. It was his old friends Joe Carpenter and Marcus Anderson. They pulled Spectre to his feet and dusted him off. Marcus said something to Spectre, but he couldn't make out what Marcus was saying. After they checked Spectre over, they turned and walked away. Spectre tried to follow, but he couldn't. They turned back and waved to him just as an explosion hit.

Spectre was thrown into deep water. He could see the surface above. He swam toward it. He felt like he was drowning. Instead of propelling him to the surface, his survival vest seemed to be pulling him down, deeper into the murky water. He tried to shed his gear, but he couldn't disconnect the buckles. His lungs burned.

He felt a hand grab the carry handle on the back of his survival vest and pull him from the water. As he opened his eyes, he saw Kruger and Decker standing over him. She smiled at him as she brushed her beautiful blonde hair out of her face. Spectre hugged her, refusing to let go as Kruger turned to face off against Vice President Johnson.

Johnson shot Kruger in the chest. Spectre knocked the gun away from Johnson, but Johnson pulled out a knife. Spectre tried to strike Johnson, but his punches carried no force. The Vice President laughed before stabbing Spectre in the chest again and again.

Spectre fell to the ground, knowing that he was dying. He tried to roll over and crawl toward Johnson. Johnson turned and approached Decker. Spectre struggled to breathe as he tried to scrabble toward them. He gasped for air. Johnson grabbed Decker by the throat, lifting her up as he turned to make sure Spectre was watching.

Johnson crushed her windpipe and dropped her lifeless body to the ground. Spectre tried to scream, but nothing came out. He could only gasp for air as Johnson approached to finish him off.

Spectre was suddenly jolted awake. He felt like he was choking. His eyes darted around the room, fixating on a nurse standing over him. He felt someone grab his hand. "Cal, it's ok," the soft voice said.

The nurse removed the tube from Spectre's throat. He coughed, making the pain worse as he struggled to breathe. The nurse set aside the tracheal tube and encouraged Spectre to try to breathe normally. He felt panicked. His heart raced. He heard a machine beeping behind him.

"Cal, sweetie, you're ok," the voice said again. The nurse stepped aside as another woman stood over him. *Michelle?* Her hair was up in a bun and her eyes were swollen and bloodshot. *Am I dead? Is this another dream?*

"Try to relax, baby," Decker said as she squeezed his hand and stroked his hair. A tear rolled down her cheek. "It's ok."

"Michelle?" Spectre asked weakly. His voice was hoarse.

"It's me, sweetie," Decker said as she leaned down to kiss his forehead. "I am so glad to finally hear your voice."

"Are we dead?" Spectre asked, still trying to make sense of Decker's presence.

Decker shook her head as she chuckled. Tears were now streaming down her face. "You're alive, baby. Thank God, you're alive."

Spectre grimaced as he tried to sit up in the bed. His chest and abdomen caused extreme pain. "But the paper," he said before coughing again. "It said you died."

"Shhh," Decker said. "Save your strength."

"You and Kruger. Dead in the crash," Spectre said.

"Oh my God," Decker said as she realized what he was talking about. "You found out about that?"

Spectre nodded. "The newspaper. I knew y'all were together."

Decker leaned in and kissed his forehead. "I am so sorry! I didn't think you would find out. Please don't tell me this happened because of that."

"I didn't want to live without you," Spectre said as his eyes watered. He closed his eyes as he looked away.

"I'm so sorry, Cal. I didn't think you'd find out. We were trying to buy some time to deal with Johnson's thug," Decker said as she squeezed his hand. "This is all my fault. I am sorry, baby."

Spectre turned and looked back up at her. "I love you," he said weakly.

"I love you too," Decker replied. "You have no idea how much I love you. I am so sorry for putting you through all of this. You were right. We should've just gone away."

Spectre squeezed Decker's hand. "No. No fault," he said.

"You need to get some rest," Decker said. "We've been pretty worried about you."

"Is Johnson dead?" Spectre asked.

Decker shook her head. "No, but Kruger took out his henchmen and managed to get the Director of the CIA on board. He'll be in jail soon enough," Decker said.

Spectre shook his head vehemently. "Not jail. *Dead.*"

"One step at a time," Decker said. "This is a good start."

"What's a good start?" Kruger asked as he walked in. "Look who finally decided to join the land of the living!"

"Thank you," Spectre said as he coughed.

"For what?" Kruger asked as he walked in and stood next to Decker.

"Saving her," Spectre said softly.

"Nah," Kruger replied. "She had it covered. I just got her a ride out of there."

"I saw the video," Spectre said.

"Really?" Kruger asked. "You know the camera always adds ten pounds."

"Thank you," Spectre repeated.

"I'm glad to see you back with us, but you need to get some rest. I'm sure the boss is ready for you to stop squatting in his hospital," Kruger said.

"Where am I?"

"The private hospital of Jeff Lyons," Decker replied. "Kruger works for him now."

"Will you kill Johnson?" Spectre asked, looking at Kruger.

"Well, that's what I came to talk to your girlfriend about," Kruger said as he turned to Decker. "I need your help with something."

Decker shook her head. "I'm not leaving Cal's side," she said. "I'm done with that."

"Are you sure?" Kruger asked. "We tracked down Senator Wilson's chief of staff. I thought you might be more effective talking to him."

"Go," Spectre said.

"No," Decker said. "Every time we're apart bad things happen, and I almost lost you for good this time. I'm not going anywhere until you're healthy. End of story."

"Need to finish this," Spectre pushed. "The only way."

"Cal—"

"*Kill him*," Spectre said as he closed his eyes.

Decker looked up at Kruger and let out an exhausted sigh. "Ok, but only if you stay here with Cal."

"Me?" Kruger asked with a confused look.

"Yes, *you*," Decker said. "You're the only person I trust here."

Spectre opened his eyes suddenly. "I'll be fine," he mumbled.

"You stay or no deal," Decker said, looking at Kruger.

"Roger that, ma'am," Kruger said submissively before turning to Spectre. "Looks like it's you and me, bub."

CHAPTER FORTY-TWO

Cincinnati, Ohio
1000 Local Time

It was the biggest church in Ohio, but Decker and Tuna barely managed to find standing room in the back of the large Catholic cathedral. They were both dressed in all black. Decker wore a brunette wig, brown contact lenses, and black-framed glasses to help disguise herself, but they both knew that it was unlikely that anyone would recognize her at the crowded funeral. Secret Service, FBI, and local law enforcement were everywhere, keeping a watchful eye on the services for Senator Wilson and his son.

President Clifton was in attendance. She sat in the front pew with her chief of staff next to Wilson and Long's families. Decker spotted Wilson's former chief of staff, Chet Marks, sitting in the pew behind them with his wife. Decker wondered how the man who had at least been a party to his boss's death could sit there so solemnly with a straight face while feigning sadness. She looked forward to watching him fold like the fraud he was.

The cathedral went silent as the priest stood at a podium and said an opening prayer. As he finished, an Air Force Colonel dressed in his service dress blues took the podium.

After thanking the priest and addressing the President, Air Force Generals, families, and distinguished guests, Colonel Taylor gave a heartfelt eulogy for Major Kenny "NotSo" Long. He spoke highly of Long, calling the fallen fighter pilot a hero and gifted aviator. He told several stories of flights they had been on, and then closed with a touching story of Long as a father and husband.

Decker noticed that Taylor made no mention of the circumstances surrounding the crash. The news media had been reporting pilot error, completely discounting claims by ISIS on social media that it had downed the stealth fighter. She wondered if he had been directed to avoid it as a topic or if it were just common practice not to discuss it at memorial services.

Colonel Taylor thanked everyone once again before stepping down from the podium. The priest led the congregation in another series of prayers before Senator Ted Thompson from Tennessee took the podium.

"Art Wilson was a good man," Thompson said. "He and his son had a lot in common. They were both decorated combat-tested fighter pilots who spent their lives in the service of their country.

"I met Art when I was just a junior Senator. He took me under his wing and showed me the ropes. I had been a soldier, and I showed up to the Beltway trying to change the world. But Art showed me how to effectively maneuver the various political minefields of this city. He kept me out of trouble.

"When he told me he was running for President, I told him he was crazy. After a life of service, I couldn't understand why he'd want that heartburn just a few years from retirement. And he told me, 'Ted, it's not about me. This country needs leadership and I think I can help.'

"I told that story at the convention later that year after he was nominated. He was a man of service that had a vision for making the country better. Unfortunately, it wasn't meant to be. The country had made its decision. I was heartbroken for my friend. As President Clifton can attest, the campaign trail can take its toll on a person.

"But it didn't take the toll I would've expected on Art. No, he wasn't devastated. He wasn't even sad. His exact words to me the day after the election were, 'Ted, it just wasn't meant to be. I'm going to respect that decision and continue my work here in Washington.'

"And that's exactly what he did, continuing his work in the Senate in trying to bring new funding to the troops and strengthening our intelligence services. The man was a true patriot until the day that he died.

"I remember talking to him that day. Art was so proud of his son. He was shell-shocked by what had happened. Like any parent, he wanted answers. He wanted closure.

"But unfortunately, that closure would never come. Art Wilson was the victim of a terrible and heinous attack later that evening. The person responsible has been brought to justice, but the devastation for this family cannot be measured. These two great men were taken from us far too soon. Our great country mourns alongside these families. It is a terrible loss.

"To the people that have joined me here today in honoring these two men, I say thank you. Thank you for taking the time to pay your respects to these men that lived a life of service before self. Thank you for supporting and respecting these two families as they go through the grieving process.

"Art, you were a good friend and mentor. May you rest in peace. God bless you and your family. And may God bless

America. Thank you," Thompson said before leaving the podium.

The priest concluded the services with another call to prayer before the pall bearers in military uniform carried the two caskets outside. The attendees were invited to the graveside services where the father and son would be laid to rest next to each other.

Decker and Tuna watched as the President and her security detail exited through a side door. The families and Chet Marks headed out through the front entrance. Decker and Tuna blended into the crowd behind them, trailing the chief of staff as he made his way toward the procession.

Once outside the cathedral, Marks headed for his car that was already prepositioned near the back of the procession. Decker and Tuna followed, careful to keep a safe distance so as not to arouse suspicion.

"You're on, Coolio," Tuna said into his in-ear transmitter as Marks and his wife reached their car.

Marks tried to open the door just as Meeks sent the hacked On Star command to lock the doors. They had left the vehicle running since security stood watch outside, but now the keys were locked inside.

Tuna and Decker coolly kept their distance as they watched the panicked Marks try to open the door. When he realized he was locked out, he frantically searched for one of the agents to help. Tuna put on his sunglasses and nodded at Decker as he walked toward Marks.

Holding up Decker's FBI badge, the freshly-shaven operator approached Marks. "Is everything ok, sir? This line needs to start moving."

"Does it look like I'm ok?" Marks snapped. "My keys are locked in the car!"

"Do you have a spare set, sir?" Tuna asked. Decker kept her distance, chuckling to herself as she watched the scene unfold.

"You must be a goddamned genius. Of course not!" Marks said as his wife tried to calm him down.

"Don't worry, sir, I can help you," Tuna said with a smile.

"I can't miss this!"

"You won't, sir," Tuna said. "In fact, I can hand your car off to another agent and give you a ride myself, if you'd like."

"Let's go," Marks barked.

Tuna nodded at Decker as they passed. He took Marks and his wife via a circuitous route through the crowds to their waiting SUV. Tuna held up the key fob in front of Marks and unlocked the door. "We're in luck," he said as Marks glared at him.

"Mrs. Marks, ma'am, you should take shotgun," Tuna said as he held the front passenger door open for her. She nodded graciously as he helped her into the vehicle. As he closed the door, he hurried around the to the driver's side and slid in behind the wheel.

"Hurry, they're leaving us," Marks ordered from the back seat.

"No problem," Tuna said as he started the engine. An instant later, Decker opened the back door and jumped in next to Marks. Tuna immediately locked the doors and started rolling.

"Who are you?" Marks demanded. Decker noticed he didn't seem scared or startled – just annoyed that another agent was riding with them.

Decker removed her wig and glasses, shaking her head as her blonde hair fell down to her shoulders. She watched as Marks tried to make sense of her presence. "Michelle?" he yelped.

"Surprise," Decker said. Tuna peeled off from the procession and headed toward the airport.

"You're supposed to be…"

"Dead?" Decker asked. "Well, it's nice to see you too."

"Where are you taking us?" Marks's wife demanded from the front seat.

"A little detour," Tuna said as he pushed the accelerator pedal to the floor.

"What is going on here?" Marks asked nervously. Decker could tell he was scared as he tried to put it all together. "Who are you?"

"We need to have a little chat, Chet," Decker said. "What happens next is totally up to you."

"You wouldn't hurt us!" Marks protested.

Decker laughed. "Are you sure? I'm already dead, remember?" she asked with a wink.

Marks turned away from her and tried opening his door to no avail. "Honey?" his wife asked as she watched his fruitless efforts to escape.

"Smooth, man," Tuna said as he watched him in the rear view mirror. "Real slick."

"Don't hurt us!" Marks yelled as he turned back toward Tuna.

"Chet, what in the hell is going on here?" Marks's wife asked.

"Your husband has a bit of explaining to do, Mrs. Marks," Decker said. "We're just going to take a little ride and have a chat."

"What did you do, Chet? What does the FBI want with you?" the angry woman asked.

"They're not FBI, dear," Marks said dejectedly.

"Actually, I am, but that's neither here nor there at this point. Your husband is still in a lot of trouble," Decker said.

"What did you do, Chet?"

"Honey, stay out of this," Marks said. "These people are very dangerous."

"He's right," Tuna added as he winked at Marks's wife. "I've got a monthly kill quota I haven't met yet."

"Chet!" his wife screamed.

"Not now, honey," Marks said as he turned nervously back to Decker. "Leave her out of this."

"Did you know your husband killed Senator Wilson?" Decker asked rhetorically. "Planted the bomb and everything."

"I did not!" Marks yelped.

"Then who did?" Decker asked.

"Your boyfriend!"

Decker grabbed Marks by the tie and pulled him forward as she wrapped it around her hand. "Try again," she said menacingly.

"I'm not afraid of you," Marks said defiantly.

Decker hit Marks with an open palm strike to the nose, shattering it and sending blood everywhere. "You should be," she said as he screamed out in pain and tried to stop the bleeding with both hands.

Marks's wife unbuckled her seatbelt to try to intervene. Tuna pushed her back into her seat as she tried to turn around. "I'd sit this one out if I were you, ma'am," Tuna warned.

"Now, here's what's going to happen," Decker said, still holding Marks by his tie as blood dripped onto her forearm. "We're going to take a flight back to Virginia one way or another. What happens after that is entirely up to you."

"You see, I have a friend that's going to meet us at the plane. He's a ghost just like me. Died in a tragic plane crash, you see. Like me, he has nothing to fear. But unlike me, he's a pretty gruff individual. Used to interrogate terrorists in Afghanistan or something like that, I don't remember. He did a nasty number on your friend Jason Travis though, do you remember him?" Decker asked. Despite his exaggeration of pain, she could see the look of recognition in his face as he heard the name.

"Of course you do," Decker said. "I already know you do. I know a lot about you, Mr. Marks. So, if you're honest, you'll walk away from this. To jail, of course, but at least you'll be able to walk and see Mrs. Marks every once in a while."

"But if you don't," Decker continued, "my friend in Virginia will make sure you never walk again. Understand?"

Marks nodded slowly as he pinched his nose. Decker released his tie, causing him to fall back against the door.

"What do you want to know?" Marks said in a nasal tone.

"Everything," Decker said. "Start from the beginning. We've got plenty of time."

CHAPTER FORTY-THREE

Oval Office
White House
0855 Local Time

"**M**adam President, your nine o'clock appointment is here to see you," Plonski said, peeking his head into the Oval Office as President Clifton reviewed the speech on immigration she had to give later that day.

"Refresh my memory, Todd, who's the nine o'clock?" Clifton asked as she took off her reading glasses and set them aside.

"It's Director Chapman, ma'am," Plonski said as he walked in and closed the door behind him.

"What about?" Clifton asked.

"He said he had an urgent national security threat to advise you on," Plonski replied. "It was a last minute appointment."

"Will the other cabinet members be attending?"

"No, ma'am, he asked for a one on one with you only," Plonski said.

"Any idea what it's about?" Clifton asked with a raised eyebrow.

"I'm sorry, ma'am, but I don't know. I'm just as blindsided as you are," Plonski replied.

"Fine, send him in," Clifton said.

"Two people, ma'am," Plonski said. "He brought one of his advisors."

"Ok, send *them* in," Clifton replied.

Plonski excused himself. Moments later, he returned, ushering in Director Chapman and a brunette female advisor. Plonski offered them seats across from the President's desk before taking his seat near them.

As they sat, the advisor removed her glasses. Clifton watched as the woman carefully removed her brown contacts and set them aside. As the woman took off her wig, Clifton gasped.

"It can't be!" Clifton said as she pushed back into her chair.

"I'm sorry for the deception, Madam President," Decker said.

Clifton stood and walked around her desk, stopping in front of Decker. She examined Decker's face, not sure what to make of it, but convinced she was looking at an apparition. "How? What is going on here, David?"

"For security reasons, I didn't want Ms. Decker's visit here to be public. I used an alias and disguise to get her here," Chapman responded.

"Why?" the shocked President asked as she studied Decker's face. "To what end? Was the plane crash a hoax?"

"Well, ma'am, Mr. Lyons's plane did crash in the Atlantic, but none of us were on it," Decker said.

"*None of you?* Lyons is alive too?" the President asked incredulously.

"Yes, ma'am," Decker said.

The President leaned against her desk and folded her arms. Her shocked facial expression suddenly became very stern. "Someone better get to explaining right now," she demanded.

Chapman looked at Decker and nodded.

"Well, ma'am, do you remember why Cal and I were on Air Force One in Taiwan?" Decker asked.

The President shook her head. "I've tried to block most of that horror out of my head."

"Well, we were there to talk to you about Vice President Johnson, but obviously we were unable to because of the hijacking," Decker explained.

"That's right," Clifton said. "Martin mentioned something about him before we flew off in that fighter jet."

"Yes, ma'am," Decker said. "Well, after the attacks, we were approached by Senator Wilson because he had similar reservations about the Vice President. He asked us to investigate discretely."

"Did you know about this?" Clifton asked, turning to Chapman.

"I knew that Senator Wilson had reservations. During the Midway Crisis, he expressed several doubts to me," Chapman replied.

"What kind of doubts?"

"Doubts about Johnson's intentions. He couldn't quite put his finger on it, but he thought Johnson had some level of insider information on what the hostage takers were doing. He also thought Johnson was intentionally delaying action to ensure he would become President," Chapman said.

Clifton frowned as her face reddened. "Go on," she said, turning back to Decker.

"Well, ma'am, we did what was asked of us, starting with the pilot of Air Force One. We found surveillance video from a nearby house of the night the pilot's family was kidnapped, but we were unable to review it before Senator Wilson's son was shot down," Decker said.

"Shot down? You mean crashed?" Clifton asked. "That was never confirmed."

"Our intelligence assessments of ISIS chatter said otherwise," Chapman interjected. "We also learned of man portable surface to air missiles being smuggled in through Mexico."

"Cal and I spoke to several witnesses that initially said they saw a flash and streak of light in the area of the aircraft before it exploded and crashed," Decker said. "But that narrative was changed before the end of the first day we were there."

"Changed how?" Clifton asked.

"We talked to several witnesses who said they were interviewed by Department of Defense agents. Each person that originally said they saw the flash of light changed their story after speaking to the DOD agents," Decker said. "We had another witness to interview, but the explosion put a halt to that investigation."

"Your boyfriend. He murdered Senator Wilson. Why?" Clifton asked angrily.

"He did not, ma'am," Decker said.

"He confessed!"

"To save me, ma'am," Decker replied. "He was told by one of Johnson's men that if he confessed, I would be set free and not harmed."

"How romantic," Clifton said sarcastically as she rolled her eyes.

"You'd have to know Cal, ma'am, but it's true," Decker said.

"What does this have to do with Johnson?" Clifton asked impatiently. She walked back behind her desk and took her seat, folding her arms as she leaned back in her plush leather chair.

"I was ordered to go back to Jacksonville to meet an administrative review board to determine my fitness for continued duty, but in the process I realized I was being tailed. Instead, I went to Miami to discuss it with my former supervisor," Decker said. She decided to intentionally leave out Simms, deciding that she had dragged him deep enough into it without namedropping him to the President of the United States.

"Who?" Clifton asked.

"Special Agent in Charge Rick Fields. He was responsible for approving the report that cleared Cal from prosecution regarding the Florida bombings," Decker said. "He told me that then U.S. Attorney Larry Engall had him change the report to remove all traces of the Chinese and my captivity in Tampa."

"The Chinese?" Clifton asked with a shudder, remembering how ruthless they'd treated her at Midway.

"Yes, ma'am. They were behind the Florida bombings and took both Cal and me hostage in Tampa," Decker said.

"Well, Larry died at Midway, but I don't see how this ties to the Vice President still," Clifton said. "Where is this Special Agent Fields person now?"

"Dead, ma'am," Decker said solemnly.

"*Dead?*"

"During our meeting, a group of gunmen attacked us. He was shot in the throat and died. That's when I met up with Mr. Lyons's security team," Decker said.

"You're just leaving a trail of bodies everywhere you go, aren't you? Why should I believe anything you say?" the President asked suspiciously.

"Please give her a chance, Madam President. I think her information is solid," Chapman said before nodding at Decker to continue.

"After meeting up with Mr. Lyons, we discovered that his aircraft had been sabotaged by one of the maintenance workers at the field. He confessed to doing the same thing to Tom Jane's aircraft a year earlier," Decker said.

"The oil tycoon?"

"Yes, ma'am. Mr. Jane was a business partner of Mr. Johnson," Decker explained.

"I see," the President said softly.

"The maintenance worker led us to the person that paid him to sabotage both aircraft, a Special Agent with the ATF named Mark Terry out of Fort Lauderdale," Decker said. "He gave us the name of Jason Travis."

"And where is he now? In custody, I presume?" Clifton asked.

Decker shook her head slowly. "No, ma'am, he was on Lyons's jet that went down in the Atlantic."

"So he's dead too?" the President asked.

Decker nodded. "We allowed the narrative of our deaths to go to press because we wanted whoever was behind it to lower their guard. It was the only way to turn the tables and go on the offensive."

"Again, a trail of bodies, Agent Decker," the President said as she looked over at her chief of staff. Plonski shrugged. He was leaning forward with his elbows on both knees, riveted by Decker's story. "Wouldn't you be an advocate of due process?"

"Yes, ma'am, but when people are trying to kill you, there's no time for due process," Decker said.

"So who did you kill next?" Clifton asked dryly.

"We tracked down Jason Travis and his men," Decker said. "Travis served in the Army for a short time and then worked security for Johnson's oil company until Johnson became SECDEF. At that time, he directly appointed Travis to a secret military organization that directly reported to Johnson. He was subsequently removed from that organization and went back to work privately for Johnson. We traced his finances to a shell corporation that Johnson still has access to and we questioned one of his men."

"And what did he say?"

"He told us that Jason Travis took orders directly from Marvin Bradley, the Vice President's Chief of Staff. He also confessed to helping Travis set up the explosives that killed Senator Wilson, as well as attempting to kill Cal in prison," Decker said.

"And where is this person?"

"Dead, ma'am," Decker said.

"*Of course*, why wouldn't he be?" Clifton said with a fake laugh. "Go on."

"Travis was caught attempting to set up an ambush for my family and me at my personal residence, Madam President. He was going to kill us," Chapman said.

"Let me guess – dead?" the President asked.

"He died while resisting apprehension," Chapman said flatly.

"Ah! Convenient!" Clifton said. "Do you have *any* witnesses?"

"Senator Wilson's Chief of Staff Chet Marks," Decker said.

"And where is he?"

"In a secure location in Virginia, ma'am," Decker replied.

"Alive?" the President asked.

"Alive and well, under heavy security," Decker said. "He will testify that under threat of harm to his family, he was coerced into falsely accusing Cal of planting the bomb that killed Senator Wilson."

"Agent Decker, what do you hope to gain out of all of this?" Clifton asked.

Decker was caught off guard by the question. "Excuse me?"

"What is your goal? What would you like to see happen?"

"Well, for starters, I would like to see all charges dropped and Cal's name cleared."

"And?"

"I'm not sure I understand the question, ma'am," Decker replied uneasily.

President Clifton leaned forward, placing both elbows on her desk. "It's a pretty direct question, Agent Decker. You're here for a reason. You obviously have an end goal in mind. What is it?"

"Justice, ma'am," Decker replied. "Justice for Cal. Justice for Cal's friends. Justice for the victims on Midway."

"So you want the Vice President of the United States to go to jail?" President Clifton asked.

Decker tilted her head slightly, trying to read the President. "If convicted, absolutely."

The President turned to her chief of staff. "Call Marvin. I want the Vice President in my office within the hour. Also call the Attorney General," she said.

"Anyone else, ma'am?" Plonski asked.

"That will be all, Todd. In fact, no one else is to know about this meeting, understand?" Clifton directed.

"Yes, ma'am," Plonski said before leaving.

CHAPTER FORTY-FOUR

Number One Observatory Circle
United States Naval Observatory
Washington, D.C.
0930 Local Time

Bradley hung up the phone and scurried into the Vice President's private gym. The President's Chief of Staff had been vague in his reasoning for summoning them, but he conveyed a certain sense of urgency that Bradley didn't like. *They were up to something.*

As he walked in, he found Johnson working out on an elliptical trainer in his blue tracksuit. He shook his head as Bradley walked in, using the towel draped around his neck to wipe the sweat from his brow. "Not now, Marvin. I'm only at a hundred and fifty calories," he said.

"Sorry sir, but it's urgent," Bradley said as he walked over and unplugged the Vice President's iPod from the speaker system, killing AC/DC mid-chorus.

Johnson stopped pedaling and stared at Bradley. "This had better be good," he said as the machine beeped to indicate it had paused his workout.

"We've been directed to report to the President's office within the hour," Bradley said anxiously.

"*Directed?* What kind of bullshit is that?" Johnson asked as he stepped off the machine.

"Plonski sounded serious," Bradley said, handing Johnson a fresh towel from the stack next to him.

"What happened?"

"I don't know, sir. He wouldn't tell me," Bradley replied.

"Who else is going?" Johnson asked as he wiped the sweat off his face.

Bradley shrugged. "He didn't say. But I do know that Chapman had a last minute appointment at nine."

"What?" Johnson barked. "I thought you took care of that problem?"

"I haven't heard from him in a couple of days. He's not answering via the usual methods," Bradley whispered.

"Have you tried going to where he lives?" Johnson asked.

"That was my plan today, sir," Bradley whispered.

"Goddammit! You don't think *that's* what this is about, do you?"

Bradley shook his head. "I doubt it. Besides, there's absolutely no way to tie that to you. You're safe."

"And you?" Johnson asked.

"Circumstantial at best," Bradley replied reassuringly. "I don't think that's what this is about. Relax, sir."

Johnson looked at the clock. "Tell them I'm taking a shower first. We'll be there when we get there."

"Yes, sir," Bradley replied.

Johnson went back to his private residence. His mind worked through the various possible scenarios as the warm water hit his worn out body in the shower. He didn't like Clifton ordering him to do anything. She was weak and had proven herself undeserving of the office. Who was she to order him anywhere at such short notice? *It was insulting.*

It bothered him that Chapman had scheduled a private meeting with her. It wasn't completely uncommon for the nation's top spy to meet privately with the President, but in the wake of all that had been going on and Chapman's recent bravado, it didn't bode well. He was the final loose end to deal with.

Johnson was relieved that the rest of his problems had been neatly taken care of. Wilson, Martin, Decker, Lyons – all muted. He was especially glad that Martin and Decker were names he'd never hear again. Martin was a threat that just wouldn't go away. The creepy handshake during the awards ceremony at the White House in which Martin told him that he'd tear Johnson's castle down brick by brick and bury him in the rubble still haunted Johnson's dreams. He hoped Martin had died a slow and painful death after being raped in prison multiple times. Cal Martin deserved as much, if not more.

Johnson killed the shower, toweled off, and hastily dressed himself. He hated being rushed. He couldn't wait for the worthless affirmative action President to finally call it quits so he could start calling the shots. His twenty-four hours of Presidency had been intoxicating. He had savored every minute of it and longed for the day that everyone would call him *Mr. President* once more.

Bradley greeted Johnson with a mug filled with hot coffee as he stepped out of his private residence. He picked up the Vice President's briefcase as they followed the Secret Service out toward his motorcade.

"Any updates?" Johnson asked as they entered his armored limousine.

"I found out from one of my Secret Service contacts that Director Chapman was not alone," Bradley said as he took his seat across from the Vice President.

"Who was with him?"

"The agent just said it was a Senior Advisor. He said she looked familiar, but didn't recognize the name," Bradley said.

"I don't like this at all, Marvin," Johnson said. The hair on the back of his neck was standing up. He had been to Vietnam and knew the feeling of an ambush. That's what he felt like he was walking into as the motorcade sped toward the White House.

"Well, I also found out that we weren't the only ones directed to the White House," Bradley said with a frown.

"Who else?"

"Attorney General Chase," Bradley said as he winced.

Johnson let out a groan as he made a sour face. "Oh, I hate that bitch! What the fuck is going on, Marvin?"

Attorney General Jennifer Chase had replaced Larry Engall after Engall had died during the attacks on Midway. In his run-ins with her, Johnson had decided she was a cocky know-it-all. And to make matters worse in Johnson's eyes, she was morbidly obese and not even worth looking at. He thought she had zero redeeming qualities and loathed any meetings with the loudmouthed behemoth.

"It may not be a bad thing, sir," Bradley offered, trying to put his typical positive spin on things.

"How do you figure?"

"The Attorney General plus Chapman probably means some new terror threat," Bradley said.

"How is that better?" Johnson snapped. "You know we can't afford any more terror attacks. We barely put the F-35 fiasco to rest."

"It's better than a conspiracy, sir," Bradley said.

"I guess you're right, Marvin," Johnson replied. "But let's hope for neither."

The motorcade stopped in front of the West Wing entrance and a Secret Service agent opened the door for them. Bradley followed Johnson out of the car and into the White House. A staffer offered Johnson and Bradley coffee. They both declined as they headed straight for the Oval Office.

At the office, a Secret Service agent opened the door for Johnson. He walked in and saw Chapman and a blonde haired woman sitting in chairs across from the President with their backs to him.

"Glad you could make it," the President said as she stood to greet him. It was an obvious jab at the fact that he was thirty minutes past their requested arrival time.

"I was working out," Johnson said. "Didn't think you wanted me showing up in my drenched track suit. What's going on?"

The blonde woman stood with Chapman and turned to face Johnson. Johnson's heart nearly stopped as he recognized the woman standing next to the Director of Central Intelligence. *Decker.* His jaw dropped.

"Surprised to see me?" Decker asked, obviously enjoying the shocked look on Johnson's face.

Bradley stepped forward, instinctively trying to protect his boss. "All of the news reports said you died in an airplane crash, Miss Decker. Anyone would be surprised to see you after such tragic news, but we're happy you're alive."

"Are you?" Decker asked facetiously. "Really?"

"Let's all sit, shall we?" Plonski offered, directing everyone to the parallel couches separated by an oak coffee table in the center of the room.

Plonski set up a chair for the President between the couches as Johnson and Bradley took their seats across from Decker and

Chapman. The President sat and crossed her legs, observing Johnson as he studied Decker.

"Are we waiting for the Attorney General?" Bradley asked.

"She had a hearing to attend and had to leave," Plonski replied. "She's aware of the situation now."

Johnson sat in silence, waiting for the President to say something. The tension was palpable. Decker being alive was a major setback. His gut had been correct. *This was an ambush.*

"What exactly is the situation, Madeline?" Johnson asked.

"Well, *Kerry*, it seems Special Agent Decker and Director Chapman have levied some pretty serious accusations against you and Mr. Bradley. I wanted to give you the opportunity to answer for them directly and in a private setting before pursuing them further," President Clifton said calmly.

"Oh really? And what charges are those?" Bradley asked as he looked with raised eyebrows at Decker and Chapman across from him.

Decker smiled as she pulled out her smartphone. She placed it on the coffee table and turned it to face Johnson and Bradley. She waited for Johnson to retrieve his glasses as he leaned forward to view it and then hit play.

"What is this?" Johnson asked impatiently. "Maddie, why are you playing games with me?"

"Just watch," the President replied.

The video began. A man with his back to the camera stepped aside, revealing a larger man restrained to a chair. His hand appeared to be bleeding, but Johnson couldn't tell why due to the phone video quality.

There was silence and then the man in the chair let out a deep breath. "What do you want to know?" he asked finally.

"Who is Travis working for?" the man standing asked.

"His name is Marvin Bradley," the captive said as he looked at his interrogator. "A real slimy little prick. Jason hates him, but he makes sure we're well taken care of."

Johnson turned and gave Bradley a questioning look. Bradley ignored him, fixated on the video as it continued playing.

"Who's *we?*" the interrogator asked.

"Who isn't?" the man in the chair replied. "He has so many people on the payroll; it would be easier to tell you who doesn't work for him."

"Who does he work for?" the interrogator asked.

"Bradley?" the captive asked with a chuckle. "You mean you've never watched the news?"

"Humor me," the interrogator said, he appeared to hold something up, but it was off camera and Johnson couldn't tell what it was.

"Alright, geez," the captive said weakly. "He's the Vice President's Chief of Staff."

"What is the meaning of this?" Johnson demanded as the video continued playing.

"Just watch," Chapman said, pointing to the video.

"And Travis reports directly to him?" the interrogator asked as the video continued.

The man in the chair nodded. "It didn't always used to be that way. Back in the old days, Johnson used to call the shots. But ever since he got into politics, Bradley has been his shit screen. Plausible deniability or some shit."

"Why did he try to kill Jeff Lyons?" the interrogator asked.

"*Try?*" the captive asked with a raised eyebrow.

"Answer the question, bub," the interrogator asked. *Bub.* Johnson instantly recognized the interrogator. It was Fred Mack, the former interrogator from Project Archangel. He had seen Mack's work before.

"Look, man, I don't get into the weeds of the *why*, I just worry about the *how* and the *how much* I'll be pocketing," the man in the chair said. "But I heard it was because that spoiled prick was talking shit about Johnson. Johnson hates that sort of thing."

The video stopped. Decker retrieved the phone and put it back in her pocket with a look of satisfaction.

"What do you have to say for yourself?" President Clifton asked.

Bradley started to talk, but Johnson interrupted him with a hearty laugh. *"This* is what you called us here for? Are you serious?"

"Dead serious, Mr. Vice President," Chapman said as he stared him down. "You know, *dead*, like you wanted me to be?"

"I don't know what you're talking about," Johnson scoffed. "But this," he said, pointing vaguely to where the phone had been on the coffee table. "This is nonsense!"

"How so?" President Clifton asked.

"Who is this person? Who is asking the questions? There is absolutely no context to this video. Anyone could just throw names and accusations around like that," Johnson said. "It doesn't mean anything."

"That man is Steven Barnhart," Decker said.

"So?" Johnson asked. "And that's supposed to mean *what* to me?"

"He worked for Jason Travis," Decker replied. "Who worked for you."

"Lots of people have worked for me, sweetie," Johnson replied. "You can't expect me to remember all of them. I have no idea who either of those names are."

"Travis is still on the payroll of one of your shell companies," Decker said. "He can be traced directly to you and your little lackey here."

"Nonsense!" Johnson said. "I have many investments. Whether someone works for them or not means very little and is circumstantial at best. Besides, what proof do you have that such a person even committed a crime?"

"I have security camera footage of him breaking into my house and attempting to ambush me," Chapman added.

"Sounds like you have a security problem, but that's not *my* problem. Where is he? Has he confessed? Said anything about me or my chief of staff?" Johnson asked.

"He was killed during the break in," President Clifton interjected, having been quiet as she observed the back and forth between the two couches up to that point.

"Of course!" Johnson said incredulously. "So what you're saying is you interrupted my workout to make me watch an illegal interrogation video and try to tie me to a home burglar who conveniently didn't survive to go to trial? Madeline, excuse me, but with all due respect, I am disappointed in you."

Decker pulled out a piece of paper and placed it on the coffee table.

"What's this?" Johnson demanded.

"Before you became Secretary of Defense, you owned forty percent of a company called Cajun Oil and Natural Gas, correct?" Decker asked. Her early years as a prosecutor were starting to come back to her.

"I'm a businessman," Johnson said as he studied the paper.

"I'll take that as a yes. Well, Cajun is pretty pivotal in all of this, actually. That's where you first met Jason Travis, the man you say you don't know. He was on your personal security detail for quite some time for someone you don't know," Decker pressed.

"If you say so," Johnson said as he looked up from the papers. "What's your point?"

"You sold your shares to Hua Xia Holdings, a Chinese oil exploration company, but you didn't sell all of it. No, you put a royalty option with Hua Xia in your contract. They also pumped money into your Vietnam Veterans Non-Profit charity," Decker said.

"That's just business, but get to your point," Johnson said.

"Hua Xia moved into the exploratory drilling off the coast of Cuba, becoming the first international oil driller to do so," Decker continued. "Ironically, years later an F-16 defected into Cuba as part of a Chinese intelligence operation. You personally gave the order to stand down when the idea of a rescue mission was launched."

"That aircraft crashed," Johnson said, feigning ignorance. "There was no evidence to go to Cuba."

Chapman pulled out a file from his attaché marked Top Secret and put it on the table.

"You'll see my name on that debrief because I was there. I was there when Cal tried to convince you to send in a team," Decker continued.

"And as I told him then, there wasn't enough evidence to support sending a team into that country," Johnson said. "But I fail to see how this has anything to do with me."

"Oh, I'm getting there," Decker said with a smile. "You may have coincidentally ordered that stand-down, but the jet was recovered. A year later, as you were thinking about running for Vice President, a Project Archangel mission was compromised in Syria, resulting in the shoot down of Cal Martin."

"Little lady, you shouldn't be speaking of things above your pay grade and security clearance," Johnson said.

"Relax, we're all read in here," Chapman said. "I've cleared it."

"Anyway, a simple trace revealed that the operational plan for that mission came from Mr. Bradley right here and was routed through the Chinese embassy before the Syrians found out and launched fighters to intercept it," Decker said. "Pretty big coincidence, huh?"

"Keep digging, little girl," Johnson warned.

"I think I might," Decker said. "So let me tie it together for you. A Cuban Intelligence Agent named Victor Alvarez was behind the operation to steal the F-16. He was also linked to several murders in South Florida. His hotel room and the farmhouse he was operating out of were both paid for by your buddies at Hua Xia Holdings. I guess that's just another coincidence, huh?

"Don't answer, there's more. We found an oil rig owned by Hua Xia operating in the Gulf of Mexico. They were using it to gather intelligence from the Air Force and Navy jets operating in the training airspace over the gulf. The agent running that operation was Jun Zhang, who also happened to be behind the F-16 espionage mission. Another coincidence, I'm sure.

"But enough of a coincidence that his top lieutenant murdered Charles Steele, the director of Project Archangel, who had gigabytes worth of audio files recording conversations in which you ordered him to work with the Chinese," Decker said.

"I'd sure love to see such evidence, if it exists," Johnson said smugly.

"Save your questions for the end," Decker said. "Because shortly after your inauguration, a series of terror attacks orchestrated by the Chinese resulted in the murder of several innocent cabinet members and gave you the Presidency."

"You're going to blame that on me too?" Johnson said with a forced laugh. "Please."

"Glad you asked," Decker said before pulling her phone back out. She swiped to the next video and hit play as she put it on the table.

It was the same interrogation video as before.

"So, we were worried that the cameras saw us," the man in the chair said. "Or saw Travis."

"Why? What did he do?" the interrogator asked.

Johnson watched as the man tilted his head and shook his head slightly. "That was a nasty one. He was supposed to just take their family and make it look like they were kidnapped so the guy would land Air Force One where we wanted him to, but Travis took it way too far."

"How far?" the interrogator asked.

"He chopped them up. Even the little boy. Said it would be more believable that way. It was gruesome," the captive replied, shaking his head.

"And you went along with it?" the interrogator asked.

"Hey, I ain't perfect. Sometimes you have to look the other way when the money is this good," the man in the chair replied casually. "Job security, ya know?"

The video stopped playing. Decker let it hang in the air for a moment before she continued. "All roads go back to Mr. Travis again, right?"

"And as I mentioned earlier, I don't even know who he is," Johnson said defiantly. "You're spinning your wheels here."

"So your henchmen gave the Chinese the ability to strike Air Force One, giving you the ability to assume the Presidency," Decker said. "You even delayed the rescue efforts to give your Chinese friends more time."

Johnson looked at the President for help. "Maddie, you can't seriously be entertaining this nonsense? This is outrageous!"

The President sat in silence as she nodded for Decker to continue.

"You even killed a sitting U.S. Senator," Decker said.

"That was your boyfriend," Johnson replied.

"I have a witness that will testify otherwise. Ordered to lie to authorities under the threat of physical harm to his family by Mr. Travis," Decker said.

Bradley finally broke his silence as he stood. "Vice President Johnson had nothing to do with any of this," he said as he closed his eyes. "It was all me. He knew nothing about it."

"What are you doing?" Johnson asked.

"I won't let them tarnish your name, sir," Bradley said stoically.

"Enough!" Johnson snapped as he stood with him. "You people have lost your minds."

"And you're a criminal," Decker said angrily, standing up to go toe-to-toe with him.

"No, I'm a survivor, kitten," Johnson said as he walked away from the couches to the center of the room. "You see, you can make all these wild claims and push out all these baseless accusations, but at the end of the day, none of it will stick."

"Your time is over, Kerry," President Clifton said.

"Maybe it is, Maddie, but if I go down, so do you. The world will find out that you bombed China in your little temper tantrum and nearly started World War III. Or the Super PAC donors that bought your beach house in Malibu. You think this is going to end well? You're all idiots!"

"You're going to jail!" Decker yelled.

"No, I'm not, sweetheart," Johnson replied. "Because none of this will ever come to light."

"I want your resignation," Clifton said.

"Fine," Johnson said as he turned to the President. "I'll resign and cite health reasons. Are you going to argue that point?"

"There will be an investigation," Clifton said defiantly.

"Go ahead!" Johnson shouted. "Investigate me. Go down that rabbit hole and see where it gets you. You'll have to burn your Presidency and this entire country down to get me. Are you willing to do that? No American will ever trust this office ever again, because I'll make sure they know every dirty secret all of you have ever had. Is it worth that to you?"

President Clifton stared angrily at the Vice President. Johnson looked around the room with a wicked grin, his wild eyes drunk with adrenaline.

"That's what I thought," Johnson said as he motioned for the stunned Bradley to follow him as he started to walk out. He stopped and turned back toward Decker, and approached to

within a few feet. "People like you and your little boyfriend –
you're losers. You'll always be bottom feeders. Consider yourself
lucky you were able to stand in my presence, because you'll
never get this close to greatness again, sweetie."

"Fuck you," Decker said, resisting the urge to punch him in
the testicles.

Johnson smiled. "Good girl," Johnson said. "Let that anger
build. It's what losers do."

Johnson motioned for Bradley to follow and they walked
out, leaving Decker and company in a stunned silence in the
Oval Office.

CHAPTER FORTY-FIVE

Houston, TX
Three Months Later
2335 Local Time

Johnson turned off the Late Show and retracted the foot of his recliner as he started to stand. It was a routine he had come to enjoy in his retired life. *No more meetings and pretending to like pompous figureheads. No more condescending orders from unqualified women.* He just spent his days working on his two-hundred-acre ranch and enjoying the natural beauty Texas had to offer.

The previous three months had gone better than expected. Clifton had made true on her threat of investigation, but as expected, it had gone nowhere. Like the good man that he was, Bradley had stepped in front of that bullet for Johnson. They had managed to make the transmission of classified information to the Chinese stick, a charge that he pled down to six months in minimum-security federal prison. Johnson intended to reward Bradley's loyalty when he finally got out.

Johnson hadn't decided if he was quite ready to hang up his life of politics and desire for the Presidency just yet. He had resigned under the auspices of medical problems, but had let the rumor slip that he intended to get healthy and consider a later run as Clifton served the remainder of her term. He knew that the investigations and accusations would probably become an issue in the primaries if he did decide to run, but he had overcome much worse and the American people had short memories anyway.

Picking up the plate from his late night snack, Johnson headed to the kitchen. He heard the rumble of thunder in the distance and remembered that a cold front was moving through. They were expecting freezing temperatures for the weekend. He'd have to get more firewood.

As Johnson navigated through the dark ranch home, he suddenly froze just short of the kitchen. A ghost-like figure stood in the darkness, his hands calmly at his side as he watched Johnson approach. Startled, Johnson dropped the plate and the glass he was holding. They shattered into hundreds of pieces as he reached into a nearby drawer for his Colt 1911 handgun.

"Tyler!" Johnson screamed, calling out to the head of his private security detail.

The apparition approached him. Johnson's hands shook as he brought the handgun to bear on the figure. With simple and efficient movements, the figure instantly closed the remaining distance. Before Johnson could react, the handgun was snatched from his hand and he was staring down its barrel.

"Tyler!" Johnson screamed again as he backed up with his hands up.

"They won't help you," the man growled as he stepped into the light. He tossed a bloodied earpiece onto the floor between them. *Cal Martin.* Johnson's stomach turned.

"You!" Johnson cried. "You can't do this!"

Johnson continued to backpedal. Spectre held the gun up, released the magazine, and racked the slide, ejecting the chambered .45 ACP round. Johnson stopped as Spectre tossed the gun aside. It crashed onto the tile floors and skidded away from them. Spectre was wearing black tactical gear with a handgun holstered in a drop-leg holster on his right hip.

"You took everything from me," Spectre snarled.

Johnson stumbled backward as Spectre slowly walked toward him. He frantically looked around the room as he did, searching for a weapon that could be used to bludgeon his attacker to death.

"Work for me!" Johnson pleaded. "I can make you rich!"

"Didn't work so well for Mr. Travis now, did it?" Spectre asked as he continued toward the former Vice President.

"He was weak. You're a survivor. *We* are survivors! We can go far together!"

"This is as far as you go," Spectre said. "I told you I'd bury you in the rubble."

Johnson stopped as he backed into the sectional in his living room. As he leaned back, his hands searched for a weapon, finding a shard from the broken plate.

"You know what the difference between you and me is? I'm a winner. You and your girlfriend will always be losers," Johnson said as he attempted to stab Spectre in the neck with the sharp object.

Spectre effortlessly blocked the attack, stepping in as he blocked with his left hand and brought his right hand up under Johnson's arm to meet it. Spectre twisted, dislocating Johnson's shoulder as he drove him backward and sent his boot into Johnson's right knee. There was a loud cracking sound as Johnson buckled to the floor and dropped his improvised weapon.

Johnson howled in pain as Spectre squatted over him. "You can't do this!" he screamed.

"I already have," Spectre said with a smile. He pulled out a knife and slid it under Johnson's good leg, violently ripping through the tendons as Johnson cried out in pain. Satisfied that Johnson was immobilized, Spectre wiped off the blood and stood as he put the knife back into his vest.

"You'll burn for this! They'll fry you in the chair!" Johnson screamed defiantly.

"You first," Spectre said. He walked back to the kitchen as Johnson tried futilely to crawl with one arm toward him. Reaching the stove, Spectre turned on all six of the gas burners. He blew out the pilot and then pulled a lithium battery out of his cargo pants pocket. He put it in the microwave above the gas stove and set the microwave cook time for five minutes.

Johnson screamed at Spectre as he jogged out the door. As he cleared the ranch home, Spectre turned back. Seconds later, the house was suddenly engulfed in flames. A secondary explosion caused Spectre to shield his eyes as he watched the house collapse on itself.

"Burn in hell, you piece of shit," Spectre said before turning to jog toward the helicopter waiting for him in the adjacent field.

CHAPTER FORTY-SIX

Morgantown Federal Correctional Institute
Morgantown, WV
0615 Local Time

B radley rolled out of his bed as the wakeup call was announced on the public address system. After stretching, Bradley slipped on his sneakers and headed out of his dorm room, greeting the unit correctional officer as he passed.

Prison had been good to him, if the minimum-security prison facility they had sent him to could even be called that. It was actually a bit of a vacation to Bradley. Although the food sucked, he enjoyed the minimal responsibilities, lack of stress, and basic structure the facility provided.

He was halfway into his six-month sentence, but Bradley thought he could easily survive a full year if he had to. Sure, the mandatory education classes were remedial, and his prison job was secretarial, but there was something to be said for the security the federal government afforded him.

Bradley made his way into the cafeteria and devoured the runny eggs they were serving. He topped it off with dry wheat toast before heading to the morning physical activities. He had lost ten pounds since showing up and felt years younger. It was nice not having to deal with the stresses of Beltway politics. Overall prison had been good for him.

As physical training concluded, Bradley went back to his room and showered. He went to the business office where he found a newspaper rolled up on his desk. Bradley's jaw dropped as he opened it and saw the front-page headline. FORMER VICE PRESIDENT DIES IN DEADLY HOUSEFIRE.

Bradley's stomach turned as he read through the article. Johnson and his private security detail had been killed when a gas leak ignited. There were no further details, but foul play wasn't suspected. His hands started shaking as he turned to the next page. The article recapped the Vice President's resignation and Bradley's conviction. Someone had circled Bradley's name and individual letters in words following.

Confused, Bradley pulled out a piece of paper and scribbled down the letters.

URNEXT

* * *

Kruger moved slowly and methodically through the woods as he headed for the tree line. He checked his watch as he saw the clearing past the trees. Right on time. Tuna followed close behind as they made their way to the edge of the trees.

"He's in the business office, boss," Meeks said over their tactical frequency. He had hacked into the inmate tracking system and was using Bradley's ankle bracelet to track him through the facility.

"Copy that, we're moving into position," Kruger said.

"Just say the word, boss," Meeks said.

Kruger stopped ten meters short of the edge of the trees. He took off his pack and went to work setting up his platform. Tuna unpacked a spotting scope and range finder from his pack and took his spot next to him.

"Do it," Kruger ordered over the tactical frequency.

"Signal sent," Meeks said. A minute later, Kruger heard the fire alarms of the minimum-security prison sounding and an announcement to evacuate was made. Kruger screwed the suppressor into the end of his Remington 700 rifle and took a good shooting position.

"Starting to evacuate," Tuna said as he watched people emerge from the main office through his spotter's scope.

Kruger heard sirens in the distance responding to the fire alarm. He watched inmates and staff exit the building as he looked for his target.

"Vader is on the move to the northwest corner of the building," Meeks said over the tactical frequency, using the code word they had come up with for Bradley as Johnson's evil second in command.

"Contact," Tuna said. He watched Bradley nervously exit the building. His head appeared to be on a swivel as he looked out into the distance looking for threats. "Three hundred and fifty meters. Cakewalk, buddy."

"Searching," Kruger said as he scanned through the crowd looking for his target.

"He's headed for the parking lot with the others," Tuna advised.

"Got him," Kruger said as he found the sniveling little man standing at the edge of the crowd, nervously looking around.

"Wind is calm. Cleared to engage," Tuna said.

Kruger lined up the crosshairs as he adjusted the windage on his scope. He took a deep breath as he applied pressure to the trigger. With a smooth pull, he squeezed. The rifle recoiled as the round was sent downrange. Kruger cycled the bolt as he watched the round hit Bradley in the temple, sending bone fragments and pieces of bone matter splattering onto bystanders as Bradley dropped to the ground.

"Good hit, Vader is down," Tuna reported calmly.

"That was for Ironman and Axe," Kruger whispered as he broke down his rifle and packed up.

"Eagle confirms, Vader has been neutralized," Meeks said, using the code word for the Micro-UAV he was piloting high above that had watched the hit unfold.

"We're moving to exfil," Kruger said coolly over the radio as they picked up and disappeared into the woods.

CHAPTER FORTY-SEVEN

Glynn, LA
1908 Local Time

The GMC 2500 HD pickup towing a cargo trailer kicked up a cloud of dust as it made its way down the dark and narrow dirt road. The former military working dog riding in the back seat perked up and shook, jingling his collar as he realized where he was.

Spectre pulled his truck up to the metal gate as he crossed the cattle guard. The familiar camera and call box were like a welcome home for him. Decker grabbed his free hand and squeezed it as she gave him a warm smile.

"We're home," she said softly.

Spectre nodded. As he went to lower the window, the gate opened. His childhood mentor, Bear, had beaten him to the punch as always. Spectre pulled through the gate and continued down the road before stopping in a clearing with a large cabin.

Bear appeared with his pack of rescue dogs in tow. The small statured man with sandy white hair winced against the headlights of Spectre's big truck. Spectre killed the engine as Zeus barked. He opened the door for the veteran pup and Zeus sprinted to him, nearly knocking Bear over as he whined and growled with happiness.

"I think he missed you," Spectre said as he walked up and gave Bear a handshake that turned into a hug. Bear had been like a second father to Spectre growing up after his parents had been killed.

"You're late," Bear said, pointing at his wristwatch.

"It's a long drive," Decker said.

"I'll bet you're both hungry," Bear said. "Come on in. I made sausage gumbo."

Spectre and Decker followed him in, preparing bowls of gumbo for themselves as Bear served them in the kitchen. Spectre unpacked Zeus's food and bowl and made him dinner. Bear tossed in a few pieces of sausage to spoil his "granddog" as he called Zeus.

Bear sat across from Spectre and Decker. "So you two have been busy."

"A little," Spectre said as he inhaled his first bowl of gumbo.

"I know what the media narrative is," Bear said. "Why don't you tell me what *really* happened."

Spectre and Decker took turns recounting their story since they had last seen Bear before moving to Washington, D.C. They stopped only to refill their bowls and drinks as Bear hung on every word.

"I knew that son of a bitch didn't resign for health reasons," Bear said as Decker finished telling him about her encounter with Johnson in the Oval Office.

"Believe me, we wanted him to go to jail, but President Clifton thought that the country wouldn't be able to stomach a crisis of that magnitude after what happened at Midway, especially if they found out he was involved," Decker said.

"What did he say before you offed him?" Bear asked, looking directly at Spectre.

"What makes you think I did anything?" Spectre asked with a sly grin.

"I know you," Bear said. "Do I need to say more in front of your fiancée?"

Spectre laughed. "Valid," he said as Decker kissed his cheek. "Well, he tried to pay me off and get me to work for him. And when that didn't work, he tried to fight."

"Why didn't you just walk in and put a bullet in his head and walk off?" Bear asked.

Spectre shrugged. "After everything he put us through? I wanted to watch him bleed."

"What did they get his assistant on?" Bear asked.

"Unauthorized disclosure of secrets," Spectre said. "It's supposed to be ten years and ten thousand dollars per event, but he made a plea bargain to get it down to six months and five thousand dollars."

"You popped him too? I read on the internet that he was assassinated," Bear said.

"Friends of ours," Spectre said. "They had a score to settle."

"So what's next for you two love birds?" Bear asked. "I feel like you've been engaged forever."

Decker smirked at Spectre. "Well, that's priority one," she said. "We're going to get married and get a house."

"Where?" Bear asked.

"New Orleans area," Spectre said. "I'm coming back home."

"You mean I'll have to put up with you more than once or twice a year?" Bear asked jokingly.

"I'm afraid so," Spectre said.

"Who else is going to babysit for us?" Decker asked.

"The dog? I'm going to have to start charging," Bear said dryly.

"Or Cal Martin part two," Decker said with a wink.

"Wait, what?" Bear asked with wide eyes. "You mean—"

"We're having a baby," Spectre announced proudly.

"Well, *you're* not. You've already done your part. She's doing all the work," Bear corrected him.

"Fair point," Spectre said with a chuckle. "Ok, she's having a baby and I'm going to be her cheerleader."

"Holy shit! Congrats!" Bear said jubilantly.

"It's a new beginning for us," Spectre said with a big smile.

"Is the FBI going to be ok with that?" Bear asked.

"I'm sure they would be," Decker said. "If I was still working for them."

"You quit?"

"I like to think of it as moving on," Decker said. "That life isn't for me anymore. I'm going to take the bar exam here in Louisiana and open my own private practice."

"Another lawyer in this state. *Great*," Bear said with an exaggerated eye roll. He turned to Spectre while laughing. "And what about you? Are you going to sit on her couch and be a stay at home mom?"

"So about that," Spectre said as he exchanged a knowing look with Decker.

"About what?" Bear asked.

"I'm going to fly Hawgs," Spectre said, using the nickname for Air Force A-10Cs.

"What? How?" Bear asked. "Didn't you just say you lost a kidney in all of this?"

"Well, technically you only need one, but they're giving me a medical waiver," Spectre said.

"Where? How'd you pull that off?"

"My old buddy Foxworthy told me about it. They're moving a squadron of A-10s back to NAS JRB New Orleans. So, we called in a favor and—"

"We?" Bear asked.

"I did," Decker said with a grin. "I talked him into it. It's what he's always wanted to do. President Clifton said she owed me one, so I made the phone call."

"Who was I to argue?" Spectre asked. "Anyway, they needed senior guys and I just happened to want to move back to New Orleans, so after I do a transition course in Tucson, I'll be flying the Hawg as a full-timer."

"Wait, didn't you get out as a Captain?" Bear asked. "How's the promotion thing going to work?"

"Field promotion to Major and I'll be on track for Lieutenant Colonel in a few years. It should work out. They're going to count the last couple of years as time in service," Spectre explained.

"Well, you definitely were serving," Bear said. "That's great. I'm glad you guys are finally turning the corner. It'll be great to have you home."

"I'm just ready to live a normal life," Spectre confessed. "These last few years felt like they aged me ten years."

"Ha! You think that was bad? Just wait until little Cal Junior becomes a teenager. If he's anything like his dad was, you'll age another twenty!" Bear said with a hearty laugh.

EPILOGUE

New Orleans International Airport
1555 Local Time
Two Weeks Later

The Air Force C-17 Globemaster cargo aircraft touched down gently and taxied to an isolated corner of the New Orleans International Airport. As the aircraft came to a stop on the open ramp, it was greeted by six plain white tour buses with their hazard lights flashing.

Kamal Hamid Salman and his brother Ali Husain Salman grabbed their backpacks and exited the cramped seats. They were ushered by the loadmaster down the cargo ramp and into a line for the busses.

They were shuttled to a staging area outside the airport with fences topped with barbed wire. They were then processed under white tents. The Americans checked their papers and identification and sent them on their way to a holding area.

Kamal knew that the challenging part of their journey to America was over, but he could not rest easy. It was not in his nature.

Kamal and his brother had enlisted in the Syrian Army together as young men, serving together until the Syrian Civil War began to rip the country apart. They joined the Free Syrian Army, a group of officers and soldiers that had split from the government with the goal of bringing down the ruthless regime of Bashar al-Assad, a ruthless man who had no reservations when it came to killing his own people.

They were given weapons and training by American intelligence operatives. The Americans taught them how to wage guerilla warfare and defend themselves against an army with superior numbers.

But as they fought against the oppressive Assad regime, they fought alongside Al Nusra and Islamic State fighters. Kamal, in particular, had taken to these men. Theirs was a righteous endeavor, for they fought in the name of Allah to reunite the Middle East and restore the caliphate.

Kamal and Ali fought alongside the Islamic State in Syria and Iraq, taking large portions of both countries in glorious battle. Ali didn't much care for the ruthlessness against some of the Christian civilians, but Kamal assured him that it was a necessary measure to destroy the will of the non-believers.

With their training and battle experience, they were recruited by high-level Islamic State commanders to take the fight to the Westerners. The Americans and their partners had begun more targeted strikes in Syria, taking out oil pipelines that ISIS used to fund their operations. The Islamic State would not be able to continue its fight if they didn't step up their actions.

Refugees fled from Syria in droves. Some fled by sea to Europe. Others by foot to Israel and Turkey. But when Kamal learned that the Americans were flying refugees directly out of Iraq, he knew he had found his way into the belly of the beast.

Using their extensive network of computer experts, Kamal's commanders were able to forge documents for him and his brother. They were poor farmers, driven off their land after it had been bombed by coalition fighters. They were fleeing to escape the death and destruction, they told the aid workers.

The cover story had worked. They mixed in with the flood of other refugees fleeing the war zone. The Westerners were overwhelmed and couldn't begin to process them all. Kamal noticed that they had done little more than a cursory inspection of their papers at each station. More could easily follow behind.

After processing in the tents, they were bussed once again to another secure facility. This one had trailers for them to sleep in. They were told that these were their temporary shelters until they could be properly placed in neighboring cities. They were allowed to leave the compound but were told to be back by an eleven o'clock curfew. Kamal couldn't believe how complacent the Americans had become.

On their third night in the camp, Kamal and Ali walked out of the camp. A vehicle flashed its lights three times across the street. Kamal nodded to his brother and jogged toward the vehicle. Kamal took the front seat as Ali slid into the back.

"My brother, it is good to see you," Siddiqui Ghalib said to Kamal. The two had served together in Iraq. "Assalamu 'alaykum"

"Wa 'alaykum as salaam," Kamal replied. "I am surprised to see you so soon."

"Plans have changed, old friend," Siddiqui said as he put the car in gear. Kamal knew that Siddiqui's path into America had been much more difficult, as he had snuck in through Mexico with the drug cartels a year earlier.

"Where is Tariq?" Ali asked from the back seat.

Siddiqui shook his head solemnly. "He has gone to paradise as a martyr," he said in a low voice. "Allahu Akbar."

"Allahu Akbar," Ali and Kamal repeated out of respect.

"I am sure he died with glory," Kamal said.

Siddiqui nodded. "We had gone out on a scouting mission. When we returned the next evening, he and several more of our brothers had been ruthlessly murdered. We were forced to move our operation."

"Is the plan the same?" Kamal asked.

"We will make it a hundred times worse than anything they can imagine," Siddiqui said proudly. "We will make them pay for the brutal death of our brothers."

"But he was successful before that?" Kamal asked with great curiosity. Little had been reported on the downing of the American fighter jet.

"The Americans are liars. They told their people that the fighter jet had mechanical problems. They believed it like sheep. Tariq planned an attack that will make it impossible for the infidels to deny," Siddiqui said.

"When do we strike?" Kamal asked with a wide smile.

"Patience, brother," Siddiqui said as he pulled onto the interstate. "We must train and hide for the time being. We do not know what information the Americans learned from their raid on our base. We must wait until their guard is down."

"How long will that be?" Ali asked impatiently.

"The Americans have a short memory. They are easily distracted by other threats. Let our brothers to the east continue to fight this holy war so that the Americans forget about us. When the time is right, we will strike like a cobra and show the Americans that they are not safe even away from their major cities," Siddiqui said.

"Good," Kamal replied. "Let them know the constant state of fear that they subject our people to on a daily basis."

Kamal smiled as they headed east on I-10. The afternoon sun glared off the rooftop of the symbol of the Great Satan's greed and excess, the Super Dome. Kamal smiled. He would strike the infidel Americans with a crippling blow. "There are no innocents in this country," he said to himself.

Thanks for reading!

If you enjoyed this book, please leave a review!

VISIT WWW.CWLEMOINE.COM FOR MORE INFORMATION ON NEW BOOK RELEASE DATES, BOOK SIGNINGS, AND EXCLUSIVE SPECIAL OFFERS.

ACKNOWLEDGMENTS

First and foremost, I'd like to thank you, the reader, for taking the time to join me in the story of Cal "Spectre" Martin. I hope you've enjoyed reading this story as much as I enjoyed writing it. If you get a moment, please leave a review.

To **Mrs. Beverly Foster** and **Mr. Sam Hill** – *you guys rock*! I cannot thank you enough for stepping up and helping with the Herculean effort of polishing this series. Thank you. I am forever grateful.

To **Dr. Doug Narby,** thank you for continuing to be my best sounding board. Your suggestions, comments, and edits are always welcomed. I appreciate your mentorship.

Pat Byrnes, you have become a fixture for the writing process. I enjoy your handwritten notes, following along with each plot twist as you try to guess the ending. I am thankful to have you as a reader.

To my family and friends, I couldn't do this without your support. Writing is hard. Editing is harder. Thank you for understanding when I get caught up in the creative process.

I hope you've all enjoyed this series. No, it's not over. I'm working on spin-off, and Spectre might even make a return down the road. I appreciate all the feedback (positive and negative) from all of my readers. Thank you.

Thanks for reading!

C.W. Lemoine is the author of ***SPECTRE RISING***, ***AVOID. NEGOTIATE. KILL.***, ***ARCHANGEL FALLEN***, ***EXECUTIVE REACTION,*** and ***BRICK BY BRICK*** He graduated from the A.B. Freeman School of Business at Tulane University in 2005 and Air Force Officer Training School in 2006. He is a military pilot that has flown the F-16 and F/A-18. He is also a certified Survival Krav Maga Instructor and sheriff's deputy.

www.cwlemoine.com

Facebook
http://www.facebook.com/cwlemoine/
Twitter:
@CWLemoine

CPSIA information can be obtained
at www.ICGtesting.com
Printed in the USA
LVHW091326280720
661023LV00006BA/25/J